The Girl in the Garden

The Girl in the Garden

Kamala Nair

GRAND CENTRAL
PUBLISHING

NEW YORK   BOSTON

Grand Central Publishing
Hachette Book Group
237 Park Avenue
New York, NY 10017

www.HachetteBookGroup.com

Printed in the United States of America

First Edition: June 2011
10 9 8 7 6 5 4 3 2 1

Grand Central Publishing is a division of Hachette Book Group, Inc. The Grand Central Publishing name and logo is a trademark of Hachette Book Group, Inc.

Library of Congress Cataloging-in-Publication Data
    Nair, Kamala.
The girl in the garden / by Kamala Nair.—1st ed.
        p. cm.
    ISBN 978-0-446-57268-2
    1. East Indian American women—Fiction. 2. East Indian Americans—India—Fiction. 3. Mothers and daughters—Fiction. 4. Villages—India—Fiction. 5. Gardens—Fiction. 6. Family secrets—Fiction. 7. Domestic fiction. 8. Psychological fiction. I. Title.
    PS3614.A565G57 2011
    813'.6—dc22

                    2010016492

For my parents, Sreekumaran and Lathika Nair

Acknowledgments

I am deeply grateful to:

My wonderful editor, Karen Kosztolnyik, and everyone at Grand Central Publishing, for believing in this book and bringing it out into the world.

Marly Rusoff, my brilliant agent, for her warmth, faith, encouragement, and perseverance. Thank you also to Michael (Mihai) Radulescu and Julie Mosow.

My professors and fellow students at Trinity College Dublin, for their invaluable comments during the early stages of writing, especially Brendan Kennelly, Patrick Finnegan, and Roisin Boyd.

Elena Morin and Maya Frank-Levine, my New York writing group, for always wanting to know what would happen next.

All of my friends for their support and enthusiasm. With special thanks to the following for reading drafts and offering insightful feedback: Shil Goswami, Ariana Hellerman, Alexis Lawrence, Sarika Mehta, Alison Schary, Elana Shneyer, and Nora Singley.

My dear friend Danielle Town for never failing to cheer me on.

Seemi Syed—faithful friend and beautiful writer—for

poring over draft after draft with a patience and intelligence that awe me.

Kavitha Nair Bindra, my incredible sister, for all her love and wisdom.

And finally, my parents, Sreekumaran and Lathika Nair...for everything.

The Varma Family Tree

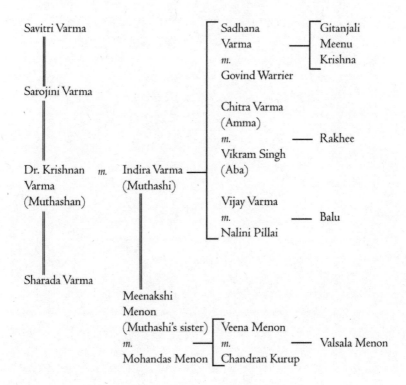

Savitri Varma

Sarojini Varma

Dr. Krishnan Varma (Muthashan) *m.* Indira Varma (Muthashi)

Sharada Varma

Sadhana Varma *m.* Govind Warrier — Gitanjali, Meenu, Krishna

Chitra Varma (Amma) *m.* Vikram Singh (Aba) — Rakhee

Vijay Varma *m.* Nalini Pillai — Balu

Meenakshi Menon (Muthashi's sister) *m.* Mohandas Menon — Veena Menon *m.* Chandran Kurup — Valsala Menon

Unbreakable, O Lord,
Is the love
That binds me to You:
Like a diamond,
It breaks the hammer that strikes it.

My heart goes into You
As the polish goes into the gold.
As the lotus lives in its water,
I live in You.

Like the bird
That gazes all night
At the passing moon,
I have lost myself dwelling in You.

O my Beloved—
Return.

—Mirabai
Translated by Jane Hirshfield

Chapter 1

By the time you read this I will be flying over the Atlantic on my way to India. You will have woken up alone and found the diamond ring I left on the bedside table and beneath it, this stack of papers that you now hold.

But for the moment, you are sleeping peacefully. Even when I lean down, touch my face to yours, and inhale your scent, you do not stir.

Watching you sleep, my heart aches. I have done a terrible thing.

I would like to say it began with the letter I received two days ago, but it goes back much further than that. It goes back to the summer I turned eleven, when Amma took me to India and everything changed. Anyone who knows the full truth about my past, and there are not many who do, might say I have emerged unscathed from the events of that summer—in a few weeks I will graduate with a master's from Yale School of Architecture and begin a promising career at a design firm in New York City; I have a good relationship with most of my family; a wonderful man has just proposed marriage to me—but I haven't overcome any demons, really. I may have wrestled and bound them beneath my bed, but they have clawed their way free, as I should have known they eventually would, and I cannot marry you until I've banished them.

This is why I am leaving behind the diamond ring you gave me, which I never should have accepted in the first place, not when there are still these secrets between us. Until I have gone back to the place where it all started, and told you everything, I cannot wear your ring or call myself your wife.

You know the basic facts, but I have never filled in the details. I haven't even told you about Plainfield. You still think I grew up in Minneapolis, and when you ask why I never take you home I tell you Minnesota has nothing to do with who I am now. I left when I was eighteen, built a new life for myself, and have never looked back. For a long time I convinced myself this was the case. Aba has kept quiet as well, even though my father has met you on numerous occasions. He doesn't think it's his place to say anything, but I know he disapproves of my reticence. I remind him of her.

Once while searching through my desk drawer for a pen, you found the old family portrait I keep. Amma is wearing a blue silk sari and her hair is loose and long. You told me my mother was beautiful and that I look like her. I took the photo from your hands and tucked it back into the drawer under a pile of papers. *No I don't*, I said, and went back to my sketching, even though I felt a swell of pride and longing at your words.

It is no secret that I have been writing back and forth to India for years, though whenever you asked whom I was corresponding with, I lied and said it was a lonely relative I felt sorry for, nobody significant. When I called on the phone I made sure you were not around to hear the conversation. If I had told you the truth, then the whole story would have had to come out.

But once you asked about my mother. *Do you ever write to her or call her?* When I answered no, that was not a lie.

This letter that I received the other day was from a person in India whom I have not seen or heard from since that long-ago summer. But I immediately recognized the handwriting on the old-fashioned aerogram stamped Par Avion, and I had to sit down on the bench in the lobby. The doorman asked if I wanted a glass of water.

I drank the water, went upstairs, and locked myself in my little art studio with its paint-splattered walls. I sat on the floor and read the letter. I read it over and over again.

That night I dreamed I was in a garden surrounded by shriveled, coal-black flowers. The only hint of color was in the branches of a giant tree studded with red blossoms. An Ashoka tree. My mother was sitting underneath it dressed in the white cotton of a widow.

Amma, I called out, and she stood up and began moving toward me. Her face seemed not to have aged—she could not have been much older than I am now—but her body had shrunk to skin and bone. As she came closer, I stretched out my arms, but she glided past me as if I were invisible. I turned to find her leaning over the edge of an old stone well sheathed in moss. It took me a moment to realize what was about to happen, but when I opened my mouth to scream *No!* it was already too late. She had dived off the edge and, in a fluttering arc of white, disappeared into the well. I ran over and looked down into the hole, hoping to catch another glimpse, but she was gone, swallowed up by the dark water.

I woke up and booked a flight to India right then and there. I met you for dinner later that night, but I of course kept my trip and my dream a secret, like so many other things.

It has been this way between us since the beginning. Not long after we met in drawing class our first year, you told me about your parents' divorce and of your conflicted relationship with your father, who left when you were a child, and how you had vowed never to be like him. I listened and nodded, and my heart pulsed with the first stirrings of love, even though I hardly knew you then. Still, I could not share my own story. As much as I wanted to tell you everything, I was paralyzed. Keeping secrets had become second nature, an inheritance passed down from mother to daughter like an heirloom. But one night, the night of our big fight, you refused to let the subject of Amma drop. You kept asking questions.

What was she like?

Where does she live?

Why don't you speak?

Is she even alive?

I got that panicked feeling that used to plague me as a young girl during piano recitals, sitting on the hard bench with my foot trembling on the pedal and my fingers forgetting their hours of practice. I gave a few vague, stumbling answers about how she had gone back to India when I was young and she was no longer in my life and that was that, but you were not satisfied.

Look, obviously this is something that still bothers you a lot. Why won't you talk to me? Maybe I can help.

You placed a hand on my shoulder and something inside me closed up.

There's nothing to talk about, I said, and changed the subject. We made stilted conversation over dinner, then I excused myself and left early.

After that night I avoided you for a week, turning off my phone and ignoring the doorbell. I skipped all my classes and stayed alone in my apartment. The first two days I lay in bed, unable to move. The third day I got up and showered, then went into my studio with a pot of coffee and began to paint. I think I might have gone temporarily crazy in those days, painting in a frenzy. I don't even remember if I slept or if I ate. All I remember is painting and the feeling of relief it gave me, like taking a drug, and also the feeling of not wanting to lose you. Finally I stopped. I packed up all the paintings, threw on my coat, and ran outside into the winter night. I ran all the way to your house, clutching the portfolio.

You looked shocked when you opened the door and found me standing there, out of breath and contrite. I can only imagine how wild I must have appeared, and you had every right to hate me after the way I behaved, but in spite of everything you let me in. You let me in.

I went over to the kitchen table, set down the portfolio, and began pulling out my paintings, one by one.

This is Amma's magenta parka that I still keep in my closet.

This is the daffodil cake she baked for my third birthday.

This is the canopy bed she convinced Aba to buy for me when I was seven.

This is her orange pill bottle.

This is the oil lamp she lit in the hall closet when she was praying.

This is a rose from her prizewinning garden.

This is her hair covered in snowflakes.

This is the scar on her right shoulder from a snakebite.

You looked at each painting and listened. When I got to the final one I hesitated. It was of a magnificent white bird against a bright green background.

And what about this one? you asked.

I looked up at you.

I'll tell you about this one another time, I promise.

For then, it was enough. But I knew it would not be forever.

So I began to write it all down, partly for myself, and partly for you.

For months I wrote feverishly, late at night while you slept, and though I felt immense relief when the story was complete, I still locked it up in a drawer.

I am finally ready to share it.

I hope that when you are finished reading, you will understand why I have left like this with no warning, no explanation, no good-bye; only this story, the ring, and an address in India where you can find me.

Most of all, I hope I am not too late.

Chapter 2

For the first ten years of my life I lived with my parents in a big, airy house on a hill in Plainfield, Minnesota. Our neighborhood was known as Pill Hill because all the doctors resided there in fancy brick houses built on neat green lawns, high above the rest of the town and surrounded by rippling cornfields. Aba was a cardiologist at the Plainfield Clinic, where he conducted experiments on laboratory mice. Amma had a part-time job in a department store at the Chippewa Mall, but she spent most of her time at home, gardening, cooking, and caring for me.

I would be giving the wrong impression if I said our domestic life was idyllic, but it was at the very least comfortable. I took my parents' relationship for granted, content in the belief that if I loved them and they loved me, they must love each other.

School was another story. I was shy about my dark skin, unruly hair, and thick glasses, which separated me from most of the other kids at Plainfield Elementary with their blue eyes, hardy frames, and Lutheran church, whose vaulted ceiling soared above their golden heads every Sunday morning.

But at home I felt safe. As long as nothing disturbed our routine—Aba worked in his study or tended to his mice at the lab, Amma cooked or crouched over bulbs in her garden, coaxing them to sprout, and I read, sketched, or played with my dog Merlin—I was secure.

Looking back, I see that things were far from okay; the disturbances in our household were obvious, even before those months leading up to India. But like most children, I believed the world revolved around me, and I was oblivious to the signs that indicated otherwise.

One icy winter afternoon when I was in fifth grade, Amma received a letter.

That day my heart felt particularly heavy. Lindsay Longren was having a birthday party and she had invited every girl in our class but me. Lindsay had made a big show of handing out invitations on the ride home, calling out names, one by one, and making each lucky recipient stand up and walk down the aisle to collect her pristine pink envelope. This enraged our bus driver and added an even more dramatic flavor to the ceremony. When Lindsay had reached the bottom of the pile she looked at me with her pale blue eyes and said, "Oh, Rakhee, I think I have an invitation here for you," and a surge of hope filled my chest. A few seconds later, she handed out the last envelope. "Never mind, I guess not," she said with a light shrug, and my face felt as if it had burst into flames. I took my tattered copy of *Arabian Nights* out of my backpack and buried my nose in it for the rest of the ride, anything to hide the tears that had begun to sting my eyes.

When I finally got off the bus, I rubbed my mittens across my damp cheeks before picking up the mail from the box at the top of our driveway as I always did. A letter on top of the stack immediately caught my attention. It looked different from what we usually received—bills, catalogues, flyers, magazines, an occasional greeting card. It was a simple blue envelope with the words *Par Avion* stamped across it in red ink and Amma's name and address written in fine black cursive—Chitra Varma, 7 Pill Hill, Plainfield, Minnesota. I knew that Amma's last name before she got married had been Varma, but no one ever called her that. I found it odd that it didn't read "Chitra Singh," which was her full name now, like Aba's, Vikram Singh, and like mine, Rakhee Singh. Just seeing Amma's name written like that, Chitra Varma, the name she held before either Aba or I came into her life, unsettled me. The flowery cursive handwriting was so unlike my fifth-grade teacher's blocky print, or Aba's illegible doctor's scrawl.

Carrying the mail inside, I set it down on the table in our front hallway, and pulled off my wet snow boots. My dog Merlin bounded up, his backside wriggling, and almost knocked me off my feet in his excitement. The sharp, delicious scent of spicy vadas sizzling in oil wafted from the kitchen. Amma was singing along to a tape of romantic film songs in her native Malayalam language, the music punctuated by the sound of spluttering oil and the steady beat of her knife hitting the wooden cutting board.

I grabbed the stack of mail and walked into the kitchen, dropping it on the table. She had three different pans going and was chopping magenta onions. Even with tears sliding down her cheeks, she looked lovely.

I used to think Amma was the most beautiful woman in Plainfield, maybe even the world. She was young then, only thirty-one, with pitch-black hair that fell below her waist, skin the color of milky tea, and wide, dreamy eyes, deep and dark as a clear midnight sky. Even though she usually dressed in jeans and sweatshirts, just as the other mothers at my school did, when she walked among them she was like an exquisite rose surrounded by drooping daisies.

Her good looks made me proud and also gave me hope. At night I peered into the mirror and prayed with all my might that I wouldn't always have to wear my big glasses, that my teeth would straighten out, and that my skinny, plain-featured, knobby-kneed self would one day erupt into a beauty as glorious as Amma's. I would think about this for a while until a wave of embarrassment swept over me, and I would look away, blushing.

"How was school, molay?" Amma asked. *Molay* is an affectionate term for "daughter" in Malayalam, and Amma often called me that.

I sat down on a stool at the kitchen counter, in front of a cheese sandwich and a glass of chocolate milk. "Fine."

"What did you do?"

"Nothing."

Amma glanced up. "You can't have done nothing all day. Don't be silly, Rakhee."

"A letter came for you Amma. It's addressed to Chitra Varma," I said, trying to distract her.

It worked. She stopped chopping and moved to the sink where she began washing her hands. Amma's hands were very small and shapely but covered in scratches from the many hours she spent gardening in the spring and summer. They always gave off a fresh, lemony scent. She wiped them dry with a dish towel, dabbed at her eyes, and went over to the pile of mail.

Amma picked up the letter and stared at it. A red flush began to burn across her face. She dropped it, gripped the sides of the table, and closed her eyes for a long time. Finally, she opened them and took up the letter again.

"Amma, what is it?"

"It's nothing, just a letter from back home, from India, that is all," she said, but her voice had changed. It was subdued and slightly haughty, as if I were a stranger who had made a nosy inquiry.

India. *India.* My curiosity was aroused, but Amma did not say another word; instead, she tucked the letter into her apron pocket and went back to cooking and humming.

After a quiet dinner, we sat together in the family room waiting for Aba to come home from the lab. Amma had left a covered plate of food for him in the microwave. I was doing my homework and Amma was reading a novel. At one point I glanced up to find her crying. It wasn't the chopping-onions kind of crying. Her chest heaved, her hands shook, and tears coursed down her cheeks.

I hadn't seen Amma cry in years, and the vision made my heart freeze. It made me remember a time when I was little and I would wake up to hear shrieks and shattering glass coming from my parents' bedroom, or would walk into the bathroom to find Amma doubled over the toilet sobbing and retching. One day Veena Aunty, Amma's cousin who lived down the street, came to look after me, and Aba took Amma away in the car. He returned alone.

Veena Aunty stayed in our guest room for a month, and when the month was over, Amma came back clutching a bottle of pills. She was a new Amma, a serene, sedate Amma who never screamed or cried. I remember when she walked in the door for the first time, I ran away, and she followed me, caught me, and hugged me close to her breast, whispering, "I'll never leave you again."

As I watched her crying on the sofa now, these memories came back to me in searing flashes. I willed myself to speak. "Amma, what's wrong?"

She glanced up, and at first it was as if she didn't recognize me. Her eyes focused and she cleared her throat, but didn't bother wiping away the tears, which flowed freely. "I'm just reading a sad book, molay, nothing to worry about."

But I was worried. When I walked behind her, pretending I needed a glass of water from the kitchen, I saw something blue lying flat against the pages of her book.

~

By the time Aba came home, it was late and both Amma and I had gone to bed. I stared up at the yellow frill of my canopy and listened to my father's light, quick steps, still so full of energy, coming up the stairs. Merlin, who was curled up at my feet, lifted his head, and the tags on his collar jingled. Throwing off my quilt, I got out of bed, opened the door, and squeezed through a thin crack, leaving Merlin, who gave a breathy whine, behind.

Aba did not see me at first, and I watched him. He was thirteen years older than Amma. His hair had begun to turn gray in patches around his ears, and there were lines around the corners of his mouth and eyes, but I still thought he was a handsome man. Distinguished. Tall and thin, with black, deep-set eyes behind wire-rimmed spectacles, thick, dark eyebrows, and a clean-shaven face. He was carrying a sheaf of papers under his arm.

"Rakhee, what are you doing awake?" Aba did not sound angry, only distracted.

"I couldn't sleep."

"Why not? Is something the matter?"

I paused, uncertain of what I would say, or why I had even come out in the first place. "Um, no."

"Well then, you'd better go back to bed. You don't want to be sleepy in school tomorrow and let the others get ahead." Aba patted my hair before he turned and disappeared into his study.

I went back into my room and climbed into bed. Merlin came to sit beside me and placed a heavy paw on my arm. The moon was huge and gold; it winked at me through the curtains. I didn't want to go back to school tomorrow. I didn't care if the others got ahead, like Aba said. I wished I could just stay there forever with Merlin and my books and my art supplies, and never leave.

I lay awake like that, stroking Merlin's paw for a long time, and finally I heard Aba moving into the room he shared with Amma. Not long after that, the drone of his snores reverberated through the wall. The numbers on the face of my digital clock cast a green glow across the room and I stared at it. The numbers kept changing and changing until they began to blur and fade, and at last I fell asleep.

~

After that day our lives began to unravel quickly. A steady stream of blue envelopes addressed to "Chitra Varma" in that same flowery cursive began flowing into our mailbox. I never picked up the mail anymore because Amma always beat me to it, but all the same I knew they were coming. I found the blue shreds in the trash or ashes in the fireplace, which we hardly ever used; and Amma grew increasingly unpredictable.

Some days she behaved as she always had, but at other

times she would float around the house singing Malayalam songs and smiling at nothing in particular, or she
would lock herself in the bathroom and sob. Some mornings she would be up early running around the house
cleaning and preparing a huge breakfast for me and Aba,
and other mornings she would stay in bed with the curtains drawn, and she would still be there when I came
home in the afternoon. Even when she was in a happy
mood I was afraid. She had this new faraway expression
on her face, and I felt that she had retreated into a part of
her heart where neither Aba nor I would ever belong.

Aba was so preoccupied with work that I don't think he
noticed anything at first. But one evening I heard them ar-
guing. He had invited a few of his most important colleagues
from the Clinic to our house for dinner, and Amma had left
a steel knife encrusted with lemon rind inside the elaborate
cake she baked for dessert. The day before that, she had
dropped me off at the dentist's office and never picked me
up. I ended up shamefacedly accepting a ride home from
the sympathetic dentist, who later informed Aba.

"Chitra, what is wrong with you?" Aba's voice boomed
into my bedroom. "I depend on you for certain things—to
take care of our child and this house—I depend on you to
do these things in order for me to focus on my work, and
to provide you with all this."

"I don't care about *all this*," said Amma in a harsh voice
I didn't recognize. "It means nothing to me."

Aba was quiet and when he spoke next his tone was
concerned, gentle. "Then what do you want? How can
I help you? Has something happened that I don't know
about?"

"All I want right now is for you to go away," Amma said
in that same harsh voice. "Can you please do that for me?"

There was a long pause, and then I heard Aba leave the room, closing the door behind him. A week later he moved into the guest bedroom.

One day in the spring, I came home to find Amma fast asleep on the sofa. A letter was lying on her chest, which rose and fell in shallow breaths, like a wounded deer I once found in the ravine in the woods behind our house. Gingerly, I took up the thin blue paper and read it. It was short, only two sentences, and it had not been signed:

Remember the flock of green parrots that used to sit on the Ashoka tree outside your bedroom window? They were so perfectly green that you thought they were leaves, until a gust of wind would send them flying off into the dawn sky.

I placed the letter back on Amma's breast, thinking what a strange thing it was to send all the way from India.

The week before summer vacation tension lived with us like a stubborn houseguest. Aba and Amma barely spoke anymore, and Aba would stay at the lab until long after my bedtime. But what scared me most was that Amma grew peaceful. The crying, the singing, the forgetfulness, all stopped. She was calm and balanced, as if she had come to some kind of important decision.

Even Merlin sensed something was wrong; he was normally well-behaved, but he became anxious and restless. One night I awoke to a high-pitched moan. I did not feel his familiar warm weight against my feet. A latch of fear pinched my spine.

"Merlin?" I climbed out of bed, put on my glasses, and tiptoed across the room.

I found Merlin cowering inside my closet, his long snout pointed toward the ceiling, his mouth opened into the shape of a small triangle. The rack of clothes muffled his sonorous howl and his legs quivered above a wet patch on the carpet where he had urinated.

Amma came running into my room in her nightgown, her hair loose and rumpled. Two violet half-moons ringed the undersides of her eyes. "Rakhee, what is it? What is going on?" She switched on the light and I squinted. Merlin bowed his head.

Amma instructed me to fetch a sponge and a bucket from under the bathroom sink, and to fill the bucket with soapy water. I expected her to scold Merlin, but instead she just got down on her hands and knees inside my closet and scrubbed. "We'll take him to the vet tomorrow and have him checked out," she said.

The next night I was shaken awake. I sat up, alarmed by the rattling bed frame. Merlin was lying at the edge of my bed caught in the midst of what seemed to be an especially vivid dream. He was moving his paws back and forth in a frantic motion, as if he was chasing something, or perhaps running away. I reached across, placing the palm of my hand on his belly, and he grew still. One shiny black eye opened and he raised his head to look at me. He whined softly, then went back to sleep.

~

On the last day of school Amma picked me up in the car, instead of making me take the bus. When we got home, she asked me to sit down on a stool in the kitchen.

"Rakhee," she said, "I must speak with you."

My neck stiffened and I felt a pinprick of panic in my chest.

"It has been a long time since I went back home to

India. I've been thinking about how much I would like to spend time with my family, especially my mother—she's getting old now, you know. Since you have vacation, this may be a good time for us to visit India together."

I stared at her. She glanced back at me, trying to gauge my reaction before continuing in a tone that sounded artificial. "I think it's important for you to learn about where you came from and to meet your extended family. Think about it, molay, it could be fun. You'll have cousins around your age to play with, and it will certainly be more exciting than sitting around here all summer."

"But what about Aba? What will he do about work?"

"Aba won't be joining us." Amma bit her bottom lip. "It will be just the two of us, a girls' adventure." She gave me a forced smile.

"Are you and Aba getting a divorce?" I don't know what made me say it, but as soon as the word slipped out it did not seem implausible. It made me choke, that word. *Divorce.*

Some of the kids at school had parents who were divorced, and I thought it must be the worst thing in the world. I had a vision of Aba living all by himself in a sloppy apartment, having nothing to eat, and no company, and my having to live alone with Amma and her stupid letters.

"Rakhee, don't talk like that." Amma's face blanched and she began rubbing her finger against an invisible stain on the kitchen counter. "We're just going for the summer, and I really think you'll have a nice time."

"But why can't I stay here with Aba? What if I don't want to go to India with you?"

Amma's jaw went rigid. "Rakhee, Aba is at work all day. He won't have time to look after you, you know that. Why do you have to make this so difficult?"

I had no choice. It had already been planned and decided and no one had bothered to consult me. In that moment I hated Amma. I scowled. "So, when are we leaving?"

"In a week."

With the force of a few words, my entire world was smashed, and I was furious.

"I don't want to go to India!" I shouted before leaping off the stool and stalking up the stairs and into my bedroom. Glancing around, my eyes fixed upon a small green plant in a clay pot resting on the windowsill. I stormed over to the plant and seized it in my hands.

Back in April, everyone in my class had been given a plant to care for. Within a month most of the plants had shriveled up. By the end of the school year only mine continued to flourish. The day before I had carried home the clay pot and Amma had praised the glossy green leaves. Just that morning I had watered it faithfully.

With one motion I sent it crashing to the ground. Streaks of dirt tumbled out of the pot. I lifted my bare foot and stomped over the leaves, flattening them and grinding the mess deeper into the carpet, savoring the feel of the crumbling soil under the arch of my foot. Then I burst into tears and flung myself facedown on the bed. Amma came in later that day and cleaned up, without saying a word to me.

Chapter 3

I had never left the country before and knew little about Indian culture. Amma sometimes told me stories about her village in Kerala—Malanad, it was called—of how they could pluck ripe mangoes and eat them straight from the tree, and of frogs so plump that when they leaped out of the river they looked like green bowling balls. She read me a Hindu epic called the *Ramayana* at bedtime, and once a year on Vishu, the Kerala New Year, she woke me up at dawn, before even Aba had risen, with the cool touch of her fingers over my eyes. She would lead me, blinded, down the stairs and into the living room. When she removed her hands the first thing I saw was a fantastically decorated table draped in a gold brocade shawl. A framed picture of the goddess Saraswati ("the Goddess of Knowledge," she told me, "so you do well in your studies") sat propped at the center, surrounded by a flickering lamp, roses, carnations, oranges, apples, bananas, and gold coins.

Aba had been raised as a Sikh but now was an atheist who disapproved of any organized religion. Amma kept a windowless prayer room in our house—a closet, actually—at the end of our upstairs hall. Every morning she went in carrying a lamp, a bottle of oil, and a wick, and soon I would see a strip of light shining from the crack below the door. About ten minutes later the light would go off and Amma would emerge with a secretive smile on her face. I never joined her, and she never asked me to because she knew Aba wouldn't like it.

The room confused and scared me, but there was also something alluring about it. Every now and then I crept in on my own and would be greeted by the sharp musk of incense along with dozens of sets of staring eyes. The walls were hung with pictures of different gods and goddesses—a big-bellied half man/half elephant, a fierce-eyed woman with many arms, a blue man with a snake wrapped around his neck. The fear would return and I would run out, closing the door behind me. Later they would pay me visits in my dreams—the woman would dance at the edge of my bed, waving her arms around with a taunting smile, or the blue man would press his face against the window and his snake's tongue would dart in and out, in and out. I always woke up in a sweat.

Neither Aba nor Amma was very forthcoming about the lives they had left behind in India. I knew that Aba was an only child who came from a wealthy Punjabi family in Delhi and that his parents had died suddenly in a car crash when he was a college student. Fueled by sorrow and ambition, he chopped off his hair, folded away his turban, cut ties with his extended family, and moved to the United States, armed only with his inheritance, to pursue his medical studies. Eventually the Plainfield Clinic heard of his research and offered to shower it with money. He accepted, tempted by the idea of a simple existence in a small town that would never remind him of what he left behind.

Whenever I asked him about India he told me stories about its history—about Gandhi and the struggle for independence, about the old Mughal emperors, famous Indian mathematicians, and the Indus Valley Civilization. If I ever asked him about his own life there, he would brush me off: "There's no point in dwelling on that, Rakhee. People who live in the past never get ahead, just remember that. We're here now and we're Americans."

Amma grew up in Malanad, a rural village in Kerala, a sliver of a state at the southernmost tip of India. She came to Plainfield when she was only eighteen to live with her cousin Veena, who had gotten married and left the village a few years before. She attended classes at Plainfield Community College during the day and helped Veena Aunty around the house at night. Amma told me she left Kerala because she needed a change of scene and because Veena Aunty was lonely. I did not question this explanation at the time, but it should have struck me as odd. Veena Aunty was a vibrant, sociable woman who blended into the Plainfield community almost seamlessly, heading committees, power walking through the Hill with the other housewives in the mornings, swapping recipes, and grilling on the deck in the summers. But even after thirteen years in Plainfield, Veena Aunty was Amma's only friend.

Veena Aunty's husband, Chandran, worked with Aba at the Clinic. Aba was a bachelor at the time, living in cramped hospital quarters, eating frozen dinners, and working so hard he rarely went out and socialized. Because he was the only other Indian in Plainfield, Veena Aunty and her husband felt a kinship and began inviting him over for weekly dinners. This was how Aba met Amma and eventually married her.

Sometimes I wonder why he did it. She was a young, uneducated country girl with whom he shared nothing, except a common desire to avoid the past. Aba was a kind man, but he had a distant, professional demeanor, even with me, and he disliked showy displays of emotion. When I wanted something, I had to appeal to his logic; my tears only hardened his heart. But with Amma, he was different. She had a funny effect on him.

When we all sat together in the family room, he would look up suddenly from the newspaper, take her hand in his and stroke it, delicately, as if he were holding a dying bird. If she got up and walked away, he would watch her go with an expression of deep longing in his eyes. There was something otherworldly about Amma that we both sensed; it was as if she was not a flesh-and-blood woman but a dream conjured into existence by Aba's and my love. Aba gave her whatever she asked for, which was never anything much. Not long after she came home from the hospital following her long absence, I heard him ask:

"Chitra, tell me what I can give you that will make you happy."

Amma told him what she wanted more than anything else was a garden.

The next day Aba hired men to tear up the fortress of bushes at the front of our house to make room for a flower bed and a vegetable patch. That weekend, armed with a shovel, he lovingly turned up the earth himself.

Even when they were fighting, I saw the love burning behind his sad gaze.

I know they must have been happy once. Old photographs reveal to me two young souls with faces radiating love and hope: A windy beach shot of a rakish Aba with his arm wrapped around a beaming Amma's shoulder.

Amma pregnant and red-cheeked, bundled in a winter coat, laughing in the snow. Aba holding me as a newborn at the hospital, awkward but full of proud joy. I wish I could remember it.

~

When I thought about India I felt a sense of dread. I had always dreamed of traveling, of leaving behind plodding Plainfield for some distant land. Aba kept a set of picturesque travel books, a gift from a grateful patient, in a neat row on one of the shelves in his study. Sometimes I went in when he wasn't around and paged through them, imagining myself into the colorful photographs, drifting down the Amazon or on a safari in the Tanzanian jungle. It was what made school endurable, those pictures and the dream of escape that was both sweet and punishing. Sweet because it meant the end of my suffering at school, and punishing because it would take me away from Aba and Amma.

Maybe it would be different if the three of us went together to the Taj Mahal or to a tiger-infested forest or even to the ocean, which I had never seen. But staying on a farm in a rural Indian village with Amma, far away from Aba, did not hold the same allure in my imagination as any of the places I yearned after in the travel books.

I had never been away from home for such a long time. I was used to whiling away the dry summer days exploring Pill Hill on my roller skates, letting Merlin pull me along on his leash. Or I would run through the woods to the ravine, where I always found interesting objects: decades-old soda cans, stubbed-out cigarettes, the occasional woodland creature. I could perch there and watch the sun sink low beneath the cornfields, and then I would go home and sit on my bed surrounded by pillows, reading or drawing to my heart's content without having to worry about homework or being teased or ignored by my classmates the next day.

Some afternoons I helped Amma in her garden, the garden which pleased her more than anything else Aba ever gave her. She spent many hours shoveling soil, planting seeds, and watering flowers. One summer her garden was featured in the Home section of the *Plainfield Chronicle*; Aba framed the article and hung it in his study (now it sits under a pile of sweaters in my dresser drawer). I loved gardening with Amma because that was when she seemed happiest, kneeling among the roses and the anemones, a wide-brimmed hat shading her face, humming a soft tune. I would kneel beside her, obediently pulling out weeds and watching worms wiggle through the soil. There was a lulling rhythm to our work that comforted me. It drew us closer together, gardening side by side, Amma and me. At the end of the day we would gather vegetables that were ripe and ready to be plucked, and carry them inside in a basket, where Amma would pour them out onto the kitchen counter and gaze at our mini harvest with triumphant eyes. The vision of us returning home after the long summer to a stubble of dead stalks and stems flitted through my mind.

We would return from India just in time for the leaves to crumble from the branches, leaving them bare and ready to be weighed down by icicles. Plainfield winters were brutal, and we rarely went outside. The cold stabbed through my skin to the bone. Even the snow was altered so that I couldn't shape it into a round snowball; it just hardened in my mittened fist, a cluster of sharp, blue-tinged diamonds.

In the winters, when the garden was frozen over, Amma went into hibernation. She wandered around the house, restless and fidgety, and more often than not with a lost expression on her face. But she always came to life at night when we read fairy tales together, my bedtime ritual. I treasured that sacred hour when witches, princesses, sprites, and all manner of magical beings whirled around my room, and Amma's eyes glowed. Even when I got too old for those stories, I still begged her to read them, and she always obliged.

But when the letters started coming, she stopped reading to me.

"I'm too tired," she would say at first when I asked, and by spring, "You're too old for bedtime stories."

So I began to pore over books by myself at night, but not the stories I had read with Amma; I couldn't bring myself to touch those. Instead I went to the library and checked out new ones—*Frankenstein, Wuthering Heights, The Scarlet Letter, Heart of Darkness*—books that made the librarian give me a perplexed smile, books that I didn't fully understand, books that frightened me and flooded my nights with dark visions, but that also gave me a secret, uncontainable thrill.

~

Over the next few days, Amma and Aba did not speak to each other at all. I was their emissary, still furious at Amma, but somehow unable to leave her side.

"Rakhee, go bring your father his dinner in the study," Amma would say.

"Why can't you take it yourself?"

"Do as I say," she would snap.

The thought of leaving Aba behind for an entire summer and the prospect of a divorce were unbearable. Even under the same roof our family was fractured—how could it survive being separated by an ocean?

Aba spent most of his time at the lab, and when he came home, he would retreat to his study, where he would work all night. He stopped shaving, and his eyes sank deeper into their sockets. "Thanks," he would say, his voice cracking, when I carried his dinner in on a tray. He would hold my chin for a moment and force a smile before waving me away, even though all I wanted was to stay in there with him forever.

School was over and I had nothing to do—my heart wasn't in my usual activities. So I followed Amma around as she packed and cooked. She prepared curry after curry, then sealed them in Tupperware containers, labeled them with a heavy black marker, and slid them into the freezer. "For Aba," she informed me briskly. I did not understand why Amma cared enough to cook for Aba but not to talk to him.

One day as I was walking down the upstairs hall, I heard a noise in the bathroom. The door was ajar, so I peeked in and saw Amma standing over the toilet holding a clear orange bottle—her pills. She was turning it around and around in her hands, stroking the label with her fingers, a thoughtful expression on her face. She had taken off her clothes, which lay in a heap on the floor, and was wearing only a pale slip that revealed the pink crescent-shaped scar that ran across the length of her upper arm.

That scar was a reminder of how Veena Aunty had once saved her life, Amma had told me the first time I ran my fingers up and down across its strange silkiness. I was very young then, but somehow I can still hear her voice telling the story:

"We always used to go running recklessly around the jungle in the village together, Veena Aunty and I. One day, we were sitting in the forest, when a snake came and bit me. We were far away from home and I immediately felt my strength draining from my body. Veena Aunty carried me on her back all the way to the hospital so my father could give me medicine. If it weren't for her quick thinking, I would have died and you would never have been born."

The story was fantastic and frightening, and I believed every word. A few days after she told it to me she went away to the hospital.

Amma, unaware of my presence, shook the bottle like a rattle, and in one rapid motion, opened the lid and dumped the pills into the toilet. They fell in a white cascade. Amma laughed and hugged herself.

On Saturday morning, the day before we left, Aba woke me up early and told me we were going to spend the day together, just the two of us.

I dressed hastily. When I got downstairs Aba was pacing around the kitchen table, the way he did when he got excited. Amma was standing at the counter, ignoring him.

"Rakhee, I'm going to take you to my lab today. How would you like that?"

I grinned, pleased that Aba deemed me important enough to take to his lab.

Amma glanced up at us. "Do you think that's a good idea, Vikram? She's too young."

Aba looked back at Amma. "It's never too early to experience the thrill of digging for the truth and finding it."

When we arrived at the lab, Aba outfitted me in a loose white coat and a pair of oversized goggles. He had to tighten the strap so they wouldn't fall off my face. A black-barred cage was on the counter, and inside it sat a white mouse. Although I was not sure what exactly was about to happen at the time, I felt chilled by the sight.

"Rakhee, we're going to dissect this mouse," Aba announced in a matter-of-fact tone. "You can see the inner workings of the body. I still remember the first time I saw real-life organs—the heart, the stomach, the lungs—right before my very eyes. It was truly remarkable."

Aba went to fetch the necessary instruments and I tried to avoid looking at the mouse, who was wriggling his pink nose through the bars at me. For one mad moment I considered opening the cage and setting it free, but I repressed the urge. I didn't want to disappoint Aba and make him think I was a coward or, even worse, a bore who could not see the thrill of science.

When Aba had returned he opened the cage and in one deft motion caught the mouse, encircling its head between his gloved thumb and forefinger, and holding its squirming hind limbs with his other hand.

He released the mouse inside a large bowl that had a clear plastic cover fitted with a nozzle. The mouse began to run around in circles inside the bowl. Aba attached a small glass vial to the nozzle.

"Now we wait," he said. Its movements grew lethargic. Finally, it settled down in one corner, a sluggish white lump. Next, Aba took the mouse out of the container and filled a syringe with another clear liquid, which he injected into its limp bottom. The mouse stiffened, but I could still see its chest continuing to rise and fall in slow, methodical breaths.

"We're ready to begin." Aba stretched the rigid creature out onto a metal tray and used strings to tie its limbs down; it looked so helpless lying there like that with its soft white belly exposed. A blade of nausea rose at the back of my throat. Aba picked up an instrument that I thought was a small butter knife until he ran it along the length of the mouse's body, and I saw the thin thread of blood that welled up. He drew back the white flaps of outer flesh and revealed the inside of the mouse.

"Can he feel anything?"

"No, no, don't worry, it can't feel a thing," said Aba. "This way you can see how the organs actually work in life."

I stood up on my stool and peered down, deep inside the mouse's body—at its pulsing, purplish innards, at the droplets of blood that had dribbled down onto the tray and coated Aba's cream-colored latex gloves, at its live, beating heart. I couldn't hold it in anymore—I stumbled off my perch and landed on my knees, where I proceeded to vomit all over the floor.

Aba rubbed my back, took me into the bathroom to wash my face, and let me sit in his office while he cleaned up the mess in the lab. As I waited for him in his leather chair, shame consumed me. Aba had been kind about it, but I felt that in some fundamental way I had let him down.

Before we went home, he took me to Dairy Queen, but I couldn't eat a thing. "It's my fault," he said sadly. "Your mother was right. Maybe you are too young."

~

The morning of our flight to India, I rose early to make sure that I had packed my most important belongings.

When I had confirmed that my sketchpad and colored pencils were safely tucked away in my backpack, I crept downstairs in my nightgown. Amma was talking on the phone in the kitchen. I knew that it must be Veena Aunty on the other end of the line because of the casual way she cradled the receiver under her ear, the thickening of her accent, and the Malayalam words and phrases that peppered the conversation.

"I just don't know what else to do," I heard Amma say, as I lingered unnoticed in the doorway. "This is killing me, but I can't tell Vikram, I can't, I *won't* ask him for help."

That is all I heard or understood because Amma then saw the edge of my pink nightgown peeking out from behind the door frame.

"Ah, you're up. Go upstairs and get ready. We have to leave soon."

She told Veena Aunty that she had to go then, so I did as I was told and went upstairs, my limbs heavy.

What was Amma talking about?

I resolved then to bring my parents back together. I would use the summer in India to find whatever was tearing them apart and fix it. If I did not want to end up like the mouse, alone and doomed in his cage, I had to figure out a way to save our family. At that moment, I believed it could be that simple.

Chapter 4

Istumbled as I stepped off the plane in Bombay, and Amma caught my moist hand in hers. The sun was white and blinding, and the wall of heat that greeted us was unlike anything I had ever felt before. The lenses of my glasses fogged, and a scarf of sweat spread across the bridge of my nose. Amma was hurrying across the steaming black runway toward a row of glass doors, and pulling me along behind her.

I stayed close to her side as we wove through the sweaty throng to identify our baggage so it could be transported to our connecting flight. Children darted by swift as multicolored arrows. Unsuppressed body odor invaded my nostrils. All around us, barefoot women dressed in identical saris swept the dusty floors, stooping over their long bristled brooms like agile, purple-winged insects.

Mirrors flashed through puffs of smog and bold silks swished. Gold ornaments dangled from necks, ears, and arms. The people seemed much smaller than they did back in Minnesota, and livelier, too. There was a grace combined with unrelenting energy that propelled each muscle and tendon into motion.

Two young boys who looked to be around my age

came running up to us chanting "Madam, madam, please madam" in reedy voices, and tried to take our suitcases and place them on top of their heads. Amma shooed them away with one hand like flies.

I tugged at the dampening cotton of the sundress I had changed into in the airplane bathroom. Moisture prickled my skin and I felt unsteady on my feet.

A cluster of men in khaki uniforms passed by and I noticed their eyes scanning Amma's jeans-and-T-shirt-clad figure, up and down, up and down, a dirty look that made me clutch the crook of her arm and press closer against her side.

A full day had passed since Aba had dropped us off at the Minneapolis airport and unloaded our suitcases onto the sidewalk. He had bent down low and taken me in his arms, holding me close. He seemed exhausted and resigned. I longed to tell him how much I loved him, that he should trust me and I would make everything right again. But I knew if I said that I would start to cry, and I wanted Aba to think I was brave.

"Promise you'll take care of Merlin," I said instead.

"I will," swore Aba with a smile. I had elicited a similar promise from Merlin as I embraced him earlier that morning, curling my fingers in his black fur, and he had given my palm a dignified lick in response.

"I've heard that the phone lines where you're going are not very reliable, so we won't be able to speak much, but we can write letters," said Aba. "Take this anyway, in case of an emergency." He handed me a folded-up piece of paper. Inside, he had written down the code that I would need to punch in before our phone number in order to call home from India. I placed the paper in my pocket and resolved to memorize it as soon as I got on the plane. "And Rakhee," said Aba, standing up, "Look after your mother for me, all right?" He was gone before I could respond, just like that. Amma didn't even say goodbye to him.

"Come, Rakhee, don't dawdle." Amma tugged at my hand.

We had to board a second plane, smaller and bumpier than the last, which carried us south, along the western coast of the country. My heartbeat quickened as I peered out the window, down through the clouds at the blue waves tossing and turning below us. My first glimpse of the ocean.

"Your grandmother will be so pleased to see you, Rakhee. Do you remember her—your Muthashi?" Amma asked over the whir of the engine.

I did remember Muthashi, my grandmother. She had come to stay with us in Minnesota when I was around three or four. I could not recall the exact details of her face, but I had a vague mental picture of a slight woman draped in white who used to sit me on her knee and sing a song in Malayalam about ants.

I used to run out onto the driveway humming the ant song, and guide a string of the black insects into my palm. Weaving my fingers together and making a delicate cup with my hands, I would transport them into the house, giggling as the ants tickled inside their little cage. Muthashi would always act so pleased when I proudly deposited the squirming ants into her outstretched hand, although I'm sure she would let them out the back door as soon as I wasn't looking.

"Rakhee," continued Amma. "I haven't told you much about our family, have I?"

I shook my head.

"Well, the Varmas are the most prominent, respected family in the village. My father was a doctor, and he started a hospital across the street from our home. He died a long time ago, so now my younger brother, Vijay, is in charge. You'll also meet my big sister, Sadhana, and her three daughters. One of them is about your age. And Vijay's wife, Nalini, who I have never met, recently had a baby boy. Everybody lives together at Ashoka—that's the name of the house where I grew up. You see, in India families stick together under one roof. It's not the same as it is in America."

"Welcome to God's Own Country." The voice of the smooth-skinned stewardess over the intercom interrupted Amma, as the plane glided to a halt at Cochin Airport. "Enjoy your stay."

This airport was not as crowded or chaotic as the one in Bombay, and the people seemed neater and more subdued. In the bathroom Amma changed into a buttercup-yellow sari and painted a red raindrop on her forehead with a bottle that she produced from her purse. "I can't show up at home dressed like an American," she explained.

I loved seeing that transformation, from my regular mother who took the trash out every morning with a bulky coat flung over her nightgown to this wondrous creature. From the moment she put on the sari and released her hair from its bun so that it streamed down her back in a lustrous river, she appeared younger and somehow more natural.

"How do I look?" she asked, as she ran a comb through her hair.

"You look beautiful, Amma," I told her honestly.

A compact man with a bushy mustache and a symmetrical crescent of sweat under each arm met us outside the airport, holding a sign with "Mrs. Chitra Varma Singh and daughter" printed across it in block letters. He led us through the thick heat toward a white car and loaded all our suitcases into the trunk. Amma and I both slid into the backseat. My legs stuck to the synthetic leather.

"Are you hungry, molay?" Amma asked me. "We'll be home soon." But she sounded absent, as if my hunger was hardly her main concern.

I stared out the window as we drove. Unlike the gray, arrow-straight highways I was accustomed to, here the roads were red and twisty. In the distance I could see groves of coconut trees, their green fronds waving against the sky like pinwheels. We passed forests of rubber trees and stretches of lime-green grassland that Amma told me were rice paddy fields. Wiry, mustachioed men with protruding rib cages spiraling down their torsos and white cloths knotted around their waists ("Those cloths are called *mundus*," explained Amma) were scattered here and there in the treetops, tapping the trunks and collecting sap in metal buckets.

At one point the driver stopped the car abruptly. I leaned over the seat and was shocked to see a cow blinking her long black lashes at me. The driver honked the horn and she took her sweet time ambling out of the way.

Soon after, I heard a dull thud and a hulking elephant rounded the corner, heading toward us, the tough black ripples of its trunk swaying to and fro.

"Amma!" I cried.

But Amma only laughed. "It's normal for elephants to walk around on the street here, don't worry."

A man wearing a faded blue turban and carrying a gnarled stick was riding atop the great animal. I waited for either the turbaned man to steer his charge out of the way or for the car to slow down, but neither thing happened. The driver pushed forward with alarming speed, straight toward the elephant. I gasped, but at the last second he swerved, and both he and the man nodded politely to one another, as if this were perfectly normal. The elephant lumbered past the car window so close that I could have reached out and brushed my fingers against its sagging hide.

It was nearing sunset by the time we reached Malanad. My stomach lurched as we passed over the bumpy roads. The scenery had grown increasingly hilly and even more rural; through the scrim of trees I could see houses, like miniature boxes painted in weathered peach and white. Barefoot children loitered in yards and saris fluttered on clotheslines. The village square consisted of a row of thatched stalls where shopkeepers sold fruits, vegetables, and oily sweets. People craned their necks to steal glimpses inside the car as we drove past. Amma kept her eyes focused on an unseen target straight ahead, her body stiff.

The Varma house was massive compared to the other houses in the village; it stretched across a sandy lawn, long and narrow, like a tunnel aboveground, and was bordered on three sides by a jungle of overgrown greenery. Columns of tall, slender trees with red flowers blooming upon their leafy branches fringed the broad stone, petal-strewn steps that led up to the house. "Those are called Ashoka trees," Amma said as we climbed. The light of the setting sun bathed the sloping roof of the house, and it seemed to glow with the radiance of a lantern. Etched into the wrought-iron entrance gate at the top of the steps was a sign that read: "Ashoka."

"My father named the house Ashoka—in Sanskrit, this means 'without grief,'" Amma explained. "It's an uncommon name for a house in Kerala, but my father loved the meaning. He hoped the house would keep sorrow out of our lives."

As Amma unlatched the gate and pushed it open, a flash of black writhing against the sand caught my eye and made me jump back. A shirtless workman darted forth with the quickness of a cat and slammed a stick down three times hard upon the sand. He lifted the stick, and I saw the crumpled black form of a snake dangling from the wood. I later learned that the man, whose name was Hari, had thought it was a cobra, and only after he had crushed its skull and examined the carcass did he realize that it was a harmless rat snake. He flung the stick into the bushes, shrugged, and grinned at us, his teeth startlingly large and white in his dark, bony face.

I held back, too horrified to go any further, but Amma tightened her grip on my hand and guided me forward with a determined breath. She steered me across the front lawn toward my grandmother, who was waiting on the verandah, seated in an old rocking chair. She was wearing a white cotton sari, the same one from my memory, and a beige shawl wrapped around her frail shoulders in spite of the heat. Amma had explained to me that older widows in Kerala traditionally did not wear colors. My grandfather had been dead for thirteen years.

Amma knelt to touch her feet, and then Muthashi turned her face toward me. I shrank away. There was a vacant expression in her eyes that was new. I did not remember that.

I shifted my weight from one foot to the other and flexed my toes inside my sandals. Muthashi was smiling, her face crinkled with childlike tenderness. Her quivering arms reached out, ready to gather me in.

"Say hello to your grandmother," said Amma, gripping my shoulder and propelling me forward into her embrace. Pressing her nose against my cheek Muthashi inhaled, taking in my scent. Her skin was crisp and dry as a moth's wing.

"She has grown taller," Muthashi said, in Malayalam, as if she had expected me to still be the size of a three-year-old.

Because at home Amma sometimes spoke to me in Malayalam when Aba wasn't around, I had a decent grasp of the language.

In the corner of the verandah two young girls giggled. I turned to look and they immediately grew solemn, but the moment I turned away they once again exploded into laughter.

My face burned.

"Those are your cousins," said Amma, placing a reassuring hand on my arm.

A thin woman dressed in a forest-green sari appeared on the verandah. She was barefoot and a threadbare towel was draped across one shoulder. Her thick gold bangles jingled as she moved her fingers through her hair, smoothing the feathery black strands, which were streaked with white, away from her temples.

For an uncomfortable length of time the woman and Amma stood staring at one another. Amma seemed hesitant. I looked at the woman's hard, austere expression and for a moment pictured a hawk wheeling through the sky with a baby bird in its beak.

The woman finally spoke. "Chitra," she said simply, and moving forward, she wrapped her arms around Amma.

They hugged for a long time with their eyes closed, and the smile on Amma's face appeared to be one of relief. Muthashi watched them, her features glazed into a peaceful expression.

The girls laughed and whispered back and forth. I tugged at the corner of Amma's sari.

"Oh, Rakhee," she said, finally breaking away from the woman, "This is my older sister, Sadhana. Your aunty."

"Hello, Rakhee," Sadhana Aunty said, and in one crisp motion she yanked the towel from its perch on her shoulder and crumpled it up in her fist.

I examined Amma's sister with fascination. In spite of her shabby garb, she appeared to me as majestic as a queen. Her face resembled Amma's, only it was older and less attractive. The features, which on Amma were sharp and arresting, were harsher and more dignified on Sadhana Aunty's lined face; and where Amma's figure was soft and curvy, Sadhana Aunty's was straight and angular, like the Ashoka tree. But what struck me most was the air of weariness that hung about her, as if she had lived an altogether more difficult life than Amma.

"Come, eat." Sadhana Aunty led us into the dining room. The knotty wood table was long and surrounded by men in crisp cotton shirts and mundus that hung down around their ankles like white skirts.

"Chitra Chechi!" A rotund man with full, creamy cheeks and a thick mustache came around the table and patted Amma heartily on the back. Like Sadhana Aunty, though to a lesser extent, the man seemed tired. In spite of his overall jovial appearance, there were pouches under his eyes.

"Vijay!" said Amma, laughing.

"Chitra Chechi, you never told me I had such a pretty

niece!" said the man, turning to me and widening his eyes in mock admiration. He was chewing something, which Amma later told me was tobacco wrapped in a betel leaf, and when he grinned, I saw that his teeth were crooked and stained a vivid orange.

"Rakhee, this is my little brother—your Vijay Uncle."

"Put out your hand, I have a surprise for you," said my uncle.

He rummaged through his shirt pocket and pulled out a hard yellow candy. Amma nudged me so I stuck my hand out and he placed it in the center of my palm. "A little something sweet for someone sweet," he said.

I stared at the unwrapped candy coated in a thin film of dust.

"What do you say, Rakhee?" urged Amma.

"Thank you," I said, and slipped it into my dress pocket.

I sat down on the wooden bench next to Amma, and Sadhana Aunty placed a banana leaf in front of me. On the wall over the dining table hung a giant black-and-white portrait of a regal, unsmiling man. He had a broad, high forehead, deep-set eyes, and a prominent, commanding nose. Pinned in a cluster beneath the polished black frame was a garland of fresh white jasmine flowers; their sickly sweet scent sifted down and lingered in a fog over the table.

I nudged Amma's arm. "Who's that?"

"That is my father, Dr. Krishnan Varma. Your Muthashan, which is how we say 'grandfather' in Malayalam. He was an impressive man. The entire village looked up to him." Amma's tone struck me as insincere, but everyone at the table fell into a respectful silence.

"Our father was the most revered man in the village,"

continued Sadhana Aunty, "and not only because of our family's noble lineage, but because he was a truly principled man. He was a great healer who saved many lives in this village and beyond."

Servant women in colorful saris began to emerge from the kitchen, each carrying a bowl containing a different curry. They moved around the table in an efficient circle, ladling generous spoonfuls onto each banana leaf. By the time the assembly line had finished, my leaf was heaped with piles of multicolored foods.

I stared at the leaf, uncertain of what to do next. We ate Indian food at home, but always, at Aba's insistence, with a knife and fork.

"You have to eat with your hands," Amma whispered into my ear. She took a crisp round wafer shimmering with oil from her own leaf and cracked it between her hands. It made an appealing crunch.

I brushed my fingertips across the food. Feeling brave, I stuck my hand into a golden dal, swirled it around with a ball of rice and a dab of spicy pickle, and scooped it into my mouth. As I ate, thick curries dripped down my chin and along the front of my dress. My tongue burned and my nose began to run. I could feel the various textures—smooth, lumpy, liquid—squelching between my fingers, and the sting of spices pinching my skin. I found the sensation both intimidating and satisfying, like finger painting or skimming one hand quickly through a flame.

Even though Amma cooked many of the same dishes at home, it tasted different, somehow blander, when served on a white porcelain plate and scooped up with a fork.

After dinner we moved into the sitting room, where I was formally introduced to Sadhana Aunty's daughters, my cousins. The room, which appeared to have once been

grand, was furnished with intricately carved wooden tables and chairs. But the material that covered the sofas
was frayed and patched at the edges, which were tucked
beneath the cushions, and the tabletops were scuffed and
dusty. The floor was cool, smooth, and hard as slate.

Gitanjali was the oldest daughter—a diminutive girl
of seventeen with wavy black hair, fair skin, and moody,
long-lashed eyes. Next was Meenu, a snub-nosed, sharp-
tongued thirteen-year-old who terrified me—she had
been one of the giggling girls. The other, her little sister
Krishna, was the same age as me, but I was taller. She was
barefoot and her scrawny brown legs stuck out from under a faded party dress, which to my surprise I recognized.
The dress had once been mine, and Amma had taken
it from my closet along with a number of other items I
had outgrown and had told me she was donating them to
Goodwill. Krishna was precariously balancing a squirming
toddler on her outstretched hip. She had a sweet, open
face that I couldn't help but like.

"This is Balu," she told me in practiced, deliberate
English.

Balu's boneless features crumpled into a gummy smile.
His mother, Nalini, Vijay Uncle's plump young wife, came
over and took the child in her arms. "Time for sleep," she
said, and whisked him away.

A gush of rain slammed into the shingled roof and it
began to thunder. The fluorescent tube lights that illuminated the house crackled and went out, leaving the room
in darkness.

"Do not worry, this happens all the time," Krishna said
to me. I heard the swish of Sadhana Aunty's sari and the
jingle of keys on a ring. Within seconds the room was lit
by the warm orange glow of candles.

Amma yawned and looked at me. "Maybe that's a sign it's time we went to bed, what do you think? You look tired. It's been a long journey."

"Yes, it is best we all get some rest," said Sadhana Aunty. "I will have your bags brought to your rooms."

Amma got my toothbrush and lit a candle for me in the bathroom. "I'll be right back," she said.

The floor was damp, the walls were dingy, and the air had a musty scent. My face in the cloudy mirror was the only familiar thing in that place. I swallowed and turned on the tap, which emitted a weak stream of lukewarm water. A trail of fire-red ants filed in a methodical line through the open window. The low hum of the ant song played in my head and I was suddenly compelled to reach out and touch one with my finger. I felt a terrible sting.

"Ready for bed?" Amma had reappeared in the doorway barefoot, with her hair in a braid and the silhouette of her body apparent through the flimsy white material of her tunic. She looked lovely and unfamiliar in the weird light of the candle.

Sucking on my sore finger I followed Amma, who was cupping the candle in both hands, from the bathroom across the darkened verandah and through the hallway. For the first time I noticed the vastness of the house, the twisting alley of corners and rooms haphazardly tacked on like afterthoughts.

"This house used to be full of people," said Amma, "back when my father was alive—he liked the house to be lively. There were always cousins, aunts and uncles, and friends around. Muthashi used to love cooking huge feasts for everyone when she was still—well, you know, young." Amma smiled, but it was a sad smile.

We reached the end of the hallway, which curved into

a little alcove with two doors. Amma led me into a corner room with a low-beamed ceiling. Another portrait of my grandfather, Muthashan, hung on the wall of this room. I could feel his eyes boring into me.

"Can't I sleep with you?" I asked, as Amma set the candle down on a side table and drew back the sheet so I could climb into the narrow bed.

"I thought you would want to sleep in here. This was my old room. Rakhee, you have to be brave," said Amma, kissing my forehead and blowing out the candle, "If you need me, I'm just in the next room."

Long after she left I lay frozen. The night was moonless and the room pitch-black. Silence had replaced the sound of beating rain, save for the bushes rustling outside the window.

I shifted in the bed, which felt like a table covered in a sheet. The pillow was heavy and hard as a rock.

I sat up and looked out the barred open window. In the sky, the moon was a gray sliver so thin its light faded before it even hit the treetops. They lay veiled in darkness. I thought of Aba wandering alone in our lonely house, and of Merlin bewildered by my empty bed, howling up at the sky.

Through the thick dark trees, far away, I thought I saw the brief twinkle of a light, but then I blinked and it disappeared. Exhaustion swept over my limbs and rushed me to sleep.

Chapter 5

I awoke to the sound of whispers. A shaft of morning light coaxed my eyes open and the blur of a small, brown face hovered above me. Startled, I fumbled for my glasses on the bedside table, knocking over the half-melted candle stub in the process.

"Good morning." It was my cousin Krishna. Her short hair was wet and neatly combed behind her ears, and she was wearing the same faded party dress from the previous night. She smelled of soap and Nivea cream. Behind her I could see Meenu, also dressed, her well-oiled hair twisted into two thick braids. They were both grinning broadly. I had the feeling they had been standing there waiting for a long time. I was not used to this lack of privacy—even Amma always knocked before she came into my room back home.

"Come," said Krishna, taking my hand, and yanking me out of bed and toward the open door.

"Wait," I said, slipping on my sandals and trying to smooth my hair. Krishna pulled me into the dining room where I paused in the doorway. Amma, Sadhana Aunty, Nalini Aunty, Gitanjali, and Muthashi were all seated around the table already, sipping tea and eating miniature golden bananas from a silver dish. Balu was crawling on the floor batting a half-deflated red balloon around like a kitten. They all looked fresh and fully dressed, as if they had been awake for hours.

"Oh, you're up!" said Amma, who was wearing a cheerful pink sari. "Come sit, have breakfast." Her accent sounded more Indian than usual. It surprised me how quickly Amma seemed to have settled in.

"Oh, see how tall she has grown," said Muthashi in a flat voice, repeating her sentiment of the day before and gazing at me with pride.

Krishna smothered a giggle with both hands, and Gitanjali shot her a disapproving glance.

I felt suddenly angry at Amma. "Why didn't you wake me up?" I hissed into one ear.

"I wanted to let you sleep—here, try one of these," Amma handed me one of the little bananas.

"Janaki!" called Sadhana Aunty, and a small, harried-looking woman with a gold stud in her nose and droopy earlobes came running out. "Breakfast for Rakhee, please."

"Ah," said the woman, shaking her head from side to side, and hurrying back into the kitchen.

The idea of having servants made me uncomfortable, but Amma told me that all the good families were expected to employ servants and that they needed us just as much as we needed them; this was the way the society here worked.

Janaki bustled into the room carrying a round metal plate and a glass of milk, the sight of which alerted me to the hungry groan of my stomach. I ate two soft white rice cakes called idlis, with a minty green chutney. The milk was thick and soupy, and left a sour film on my tongue.

"Chitra Chechi, she looks just like your husband," said

Nalini Aunty, watching me eat, "She really has that Sardarji look, no?"

I didn't know what the word *Sardarji* meant, but I knew that it had something to do with Aba, and I didn't like the sound of it.

"Oh, I don't know," said Amma, glancing down at her hands.

"Well, she must have gotten her bad eyes from him at least. Nobody in the Varma family has ever needed specs before old age." Nalini Aunty peeled a banana and chewed it with her mouth open. I could see a lump of pale, doughy flesh creased with stretch marks jutting out from the space between her blouse and the waist of her sari.

"I'm going to go heat some water for Rakhee's bath," said Amma, pushing her chair back and leaving the room.

It annoyed me that Amma would just walk away like that without defending me.

I finished eating and went into the bathroom, where Amma was standing over a plastic bucket with her skirt hitched up around her calves.

"Where's the shower?" I asked.

"There isn't one," said Amma. "You must use this bucket and a cup to bathe."

Amma offered to stay and help me, but I rejected this idea, and found myself alone in the bathroom once again, struggling with the bucket and the cup, and keeping my petrified eyes upon a palm-sized spider basking on the wall near the window.

When I finally emerged, unsure of how clean I actually was, Krishna came up to me and said: "Would you like to play now?"

"Sure."

Both my cousins' English was shaky, as was my Malay-alam, so we developed a system early on in our acquaintance where they spoke to me in Malayalam and I replied in English.

The sun was already burning the sand in the yard outside, so we sat under the shade of the verandah, on the swinging bench that hung by a rusty chain from the ceiling. I could hear the impatient grunts of cows and goats mixed with the rustle of wild creatures in the tangled greenery that boiled over the dilapidated stone wall encircling the house. The air seemed thicker here, more palpable somehow, swirling in and out of the drum of my ear like the ocean churning inside a shell.

I brought out my colored pencils and a sheaf of paper. I decided to draw Hari, the workman, who was pulling a cow by a frayed rope out of its pen. Amma told me that Hari had been with the family since he was a little boy; she said his mind was "not all there," so he had never gone far in school. Instead, he had devoted himself to working for my grandfather. His black chest was slick with sweat, and his muscles strained and flexed against the stubborn cow. Krishna peeked over my shoulder.

"That is very good," she said, and I beamed.

Amma came out to check on us, carrying two glasses of cold lime juice. She set the glasses down on a side table and handed Krishna a bottle of red nail polish. "Just a little something from America. Have fun, girls, I'm going in for a nap," she said. Amma had spent a harried day at the mall just before our trip and had packed an entire suitcase full of gifts, ranging from expensive electronics to scented lotions to candy, which she parceled out to various members of the household.

We put down our drawings and began painting each other's nails.

"Everybody is always just sleeping around here. It's so boring. I'm very happy you are here," Krishna told me.

"What about your sisters, and—your father?"

"My father is dead. He died when I was just a baby. And my sisters are not very good company. Meenu Chechi just bosses me around all the time, and Gitanjali Chechi thinks she's too old to play with me."

"Chechi?" I asked.

"Oh, that is the word for older sister," responded Krishna. "Anyway, Vijay Uncle talks to me from time to time."

"Doesn't he work at the hospital?"

"He's supposed to but he never does. He just sits around and chews paan all day and daydreams. Nalini Aunty calls him lazy. So now Dev practically runs the hospital."

"Who's Dev?"

Krishna stuck out her bottom lip, "He is just a man from the village. Do not tell anybody, but I don't like him."

I was curious, but something about the way she knitted her brow at the mention of his name prevented me from pursuing the subject of Dev right then.

Meenu sauntered out onto the verandah and interrupted our conversation, her face stretched into a languid yawn.

"What are the two of you doing?" she asked, nudging Krishna to make room on the swing.

"Look at what Rakhee drew, it is very good, isn't it?" said Krishna, handing Meenu my drawing. I liked the lilting way in which she pronounced my name, effortlessly rolling the r, emphasizing the h. Not like the kids at school, who called me "Rocky."

Meenu glanced at the picture and sniffed: "It's all right, I suppose. For a little girl. Come, let's do something—you want to walk around and see the place?"

I nodded. We got up off the swing and skipped down the steps.

"First, the cows," said Meenu, leading us across the lawn toward a wide, wooden pen. Hibiscus curled in a neon pink tangle above the roof, and the odor of fresh dung hung in the air. "This is where we get our milk from every day," she said, motioning to the stoic brown and white spotted creatures.

Beside the cows were a mother goat and her kid, both kept together in a small cage made of splintered wooden planks. The mother goat fixed her wide-set, disoriented eyes upon me and gave a loud bleat, which made me leap. Krishna and Meenu laughed hysterically.

Around the back of the house steam billowed out from the kitchen and women crouched over earthen vessels, peeling vegetables with large, curving blades and chatting amongst themselves, their voices blending with the birdcalls issuing from the trees. A few chickens clucked and paced back and forth across the yard, bobbing their heads. The women grew silent as we approached. One of their group was sitting apart from the others, muttering to herself and shaking her head back and forth. The deep lines in her face hinted at a hard life spent under the scorching sun, but her hair was snow white and surprisingly luxuriant. Her eyes were milky and unfocused.

"Who's that?" I asked, nodding in the woman's direction.

"Oh, that's Hema—she's the servant Hari's sister. She works for our neighbors, but sometimes she hangs about here too. She's—" Meenu whirled her finger around the side of her head and crossed her eyes. "She's been there for a long time, though, so they keep her around even though she's useless. I think she used to work at Ashoka, but then our grandfather loaned her to the neighbors because they needed someone, and she just kind of stayed after that. She likes to come over here a lot, though."

"What does she keep saying?"

"Nobody knows. All I know is that she's always muttering about something or other. Anyway, who cares about crazy old Hema?"

Meenu sauntered off toward a nearby tree brimming with round green fruit. She plucked one off a low-hanging branch. "These are the best guavas in Kerala," she said, rubbing the dusty skin against her skirt.

"Let's go in and ask someone to cut it for us," said Krishna.

"Wait, what's back there, beyond that stone wall?" I asked, squinting out into the trees behind the house, the same trees I could see from my bedroom window.

"Oh, we never go into the forest," said Krishna, shivering.

"Our mother forbids us to go beyond the stone barrier. She says a Rakshasi lives there, and that she'll eat us if we invade her territory," Meenu said.

"A Rakshasi?" The word sounded familiar—I remembered hearing it in the *Ramayana*, the Hindu epic that Amma used to read to me at bedtime.

"A hideous she-demon who feeds off the flesh of children," said Meenu, widening her eyes for dramatic effect. I wanted to laugh, but I could see that she was genuinely scared. "Only adults are allowed to go back there. Our mother brings the Rakshasi offerings so that she doesn't come out of the forest and eat us in our sleep."

I laughed. "Come on, there's no such thing!" How

could they really believe a flesh-eating she-demon lived in the forest behind their house?

Meenu and Krishna shrugged.

"Don't you even want to go and find out what's really there?" I continued, incredulous.

They both shook their heads emphatically. "If the Rakshasi doesn't kill us, then our mother certainly will. Come, let's go play cricket—we'll teach you," said Meenu, tucking the fruit into her dress pockets and tossing her plump braids.

I didn't believe them. I couldn't. I was too old to believe in witches and monsters. But still, when I looked over my shoulder as we went back toward the front of the house, I remembered the light I had seen through the trees the night before, and felt a chill, like a strand of cold silk, rustle up and down my spine.

~

Dev was not a tall man; in fact, he was slight of stature. But somehow when he entered the room he seemed to control, to possess, everything inside—the furniture, the walls, the inhabitants. He came to the house for dinner that night, and when I stumbled in with Krishna and Meenu, our hands and feet dirty from playing cricket in the front yard, I instantly knew it was the man whom Krishna disliked.

"Ah Ch-Ch-Ch-Chitra, so this is your daughter. H-h-h-how are you, molay?" He spoke with a stutter and his voice, though gentle, still made all the fine hairs on my arms and the back of my neck stand at attention.

I didn't answer, just frowned up into his face, and he chuckled: "She's a g-g-g-grumpy girl, eh?" He came around the table toward me, and I felt Krishna and Meenu shrink away, leaving me standing alone, framed by the doorway. Bending down, he patted my head with his hand. A sparse mustache prickled his upper lip, and his plentiful hair, parted on one side, looked wet, even though I knew it was dry.

"Rakhee, say hello to Dev Uncle," Vijay Uncle said. I looked at Amma, but her eyes were cast downward, and she was knotting her fingers together. I turned to my cousins, but they, too, had their heads bowed.

"Hello," I mumbled, and went to wash my soiled hands.

Sadhana Aunty had let the servant women go early after they had finished preparing an elaborate meal. That night she, Amma, Nalini Aunty, and Gitanjali served the food. I noticed that Sadhana Aunty was extremely attentive to Dev, always giving him the largest portions before everyone else. He even sat at the head of the table, although Vijay Uncle was technically the head of the household. I watched Dev eat, shoveling the food into his mouth, then running his flat palm across the leaf, and licking off the remaining curry. Dev reminded me of a raccoon that used to steal food from our backyard bird feeder, with his rummaging paws, his long, pink tongue darting in and out, and his face expressionless. He ordered the women around in a sleepy yet demanding voice: "M-m-m-more yogurt," "M-m-more dal," "Another pap-pap-pap-papa-d-dam," he would say, and Sadhana Aunty would immediately fetch it for him, though her mouth was compressed into a lipless line. When he had eaten three helpings and polished off the banana leaf so that it gleamed, he folded it over and belched. I eyed him in shock and disgust, but no one else seemed to react.

We ate in two rounds; first the men, children, and Muthashi, while the women stood around supervising the distribution of food; then the women ate, while the men retired into the sitting room, closing the door behind them.

Tired out from the day's activities, I slept well that night, and the next morning Krishna and Meenu showed me all around the village, from the marketplace, where we used our pocket money to buy chocolates from the sweets stall, to the river, which was swollen from the torrential monsoon rains. When we walked down the main road, people came out of their stores to stare at me, whispering amongst themselves, and grinning. "It's because you're from America," said Meenu. "And because you are a Varma. We are the most important family in this village." Normally this kind of attention would have made me self-conscious, but the presence of my cousins on my either side, who seemed to accept me without any question, gave me strength.

"What's going on with Dev?" I asked them at one point. "Why does everyone treat him like a king?"

Krishna was silent, but Meenu screwed her face up into a ball of resentment.

"I don't know," she said. "But I can't stand him. And I hate the way the grown-ups are always fawning over him. It makes no sense, but if I ever say anything I get smacked."

In the afternoon we sat on the verandah listening to the thrum of bees in the banana leaves. Muthashi rocked back and forth in her chair, watching us. She still had that vacant look that made me afraid to go near her. I felt ashamed because my cousins would dutifully hug and kiss her, and when they did, I would see a flash of joy in her eyes, but somehow I could not bring myself to do the same. That look and the way she kept repeating her sentences filled me with dread.

Meenu came over to me. "Want me to show you something I learned from a girl at school?"

Taking my hands, she folded them together, lining up each of my fingers. Then she opened them up and examined my palms. "Do you see how these two lines connect? That means you are going to have a love marriage."

Krishna squealed. "My turn! My turn!"

Meenu did the same thing to Krishna's hands. "You're going to have a love marriage, too!"

We all erupted into delighted, embarrassed laughter.

"Chechi, let me see your hands," said Meenu, going over to Gitanjali, who was sitting on the rail with a book in her lap. But she wasn't reading, she was just staring off into space.

Meenu looked at her older sister's hands and pronounced solemnly, "Chechi, your lines don't connect—you are going to have an arranged marriage."

Krishna and Meenu danced around Gitanjali in a wild circle, giggling and pointing their fingers at her. Gitanjali rolled her eyes, swung her legs off the rail, and went into her room. I watched my laughing cousins and felt warm inside, as if for the first time I was part of something.

During that first week I loved Amma's village. I wanted to stay in Malanad forever. I loved having friends to play and explore with, and I was surprised to realize I did not want summer to end. But I knew that I could never stay there forever. I knew it when I lay in my narrow bed at night under my grandfather's stern gaze and ached for home. I missed my cozy bed, hot showers, movies, ice cream, Merlin with his floppy ears. But most of all, I missed Aba. Even when I barely saw him at home, when he spent hours and hours at the lab or in his study, just knowing he was nearby gave me a feeling of warmth and security. In India he was so far away and it felt as if a piece of myself was missing. The longer we remained apart, the more broken our family would become.

I wanted to hear his voice, to know that he was all right. I remembered Amma had told me that Minnesota was about twelve hours behind India. That meant it was a Sunday morning, so Aba would surely be at home, and maybe I could call him. It wasn't an emergency, but surely missing him was a good enough excuse. I took from the bedside table the little keychain flashlight Amma had given me so that I could find my way to the bathroom in the middle of the night. I switched it on, crept barefoot into the hallway, and knocked on Amma's door. There was no answer.

"Amma," I said in a loud whisper.

Still no answer.

I opened the door and went inside, but Amma was not there. Her bed was still made up.

I went back into my own room, climbed into bed, turned off the flashlight, and stared up at the ceiling. Where could she be? I knew no one was still awake, since all the lights in the house were turned off. A mosquito whined in my ear; I slapped at it and settled back into the silence.

That's when I heard it—the snap of a twig under soft footsteps, and the sound of a whisper. I sat up in bed and peeked out the window, my heart drumming against my chest. I saw two figures moving across the yard and climbing over the stone wall behind the house. I just made out the blue and pink saris of Sadhana Aunty and Amma before the shapes receded and disappeared into the forest.

Chapter 6

It was late afternoon and Amma was lying in bed with the curtains drawn.

"Please, I can't deal with this right now," she said to me. "My head is splitting."

"But Amma, why can't you tell me what's back there?" I pleaded. "Meenu and Krishna say a Rakshasi lives there, and that she eats children for breakfast."

"Listen to me." Amma heaved herself up with a sigh and her hair fell over one side of her face, shielding it. "It's nothing that you need to worry about, all right? This isn't like back home. It's dangerous to wander too far. Please, just leave it be —this is not the time or place to let curiosity get the better of you. If you love me, promise you'll obey me and stay out of it."

"Fine."

"Promise me, Rakhee." She cupped my shoulders with her hands and gave me a slight shake. "This is very important to me. If you love me."

"I promise," I said.

"Okay, I'm trusting you. Now you need to trust me." Amma gave me a firm look before she lay down again and let her head loll back onto the pillow. "Close the door behind you, please."

I wandered out onto the verandah, bored. Meenu and Krishna were having their weekly music lesson. I could hear their voices—Krishna's high-pitched and a bit sharp, and Meenu's surprisingly melodious—rising up the scale in time with the jarring rhythm of the harmonium. *Sa-re-ga-ma-pa-tha-nee-saaa*, I heard them sing, up and down, up and down. I stretched my body out on the swing, rubbing my hand over the dull throb low down in my belly. The ache had followed me around since breakfast. It must be all the new foods I was eating, I thought.

I could not get my mind off Amma's nocturnal journey. Was there really something living in the forest behind the house, and if so, was Amma helping Sadhana Aunty bring it offerings?

I was never superstitious; Aba always scoffed at any explanation that eluded logic. Once I saved up my allowance and bought a Chinese yin-yang necklace from a trinket store at the mall—all the girls at school were wearing them, and I did not want to be left out. When I came home Amma ordered me to take it off and throw it away. "Where I come from, that symbol is bad luck," she said. Aba intervened when he returned from work and found me sulking. He told Amma she was being silly, that it was only a harmless trinket; he dug it out of the trash for me and refastened it around my neck. The next day I fell on the driveway and skinned my knee. The day after that, Amma was driving to the grocery store when she skidded on the ice in the middle of a busy intersection, and the car spun around and around like a compass needle until it finally smacked into a telephone pole, leaving a dime-sized bump on her forehead. "It's that necklace," she said later that night, sitting in bed propped up by pillows. "No, Chitra.

Sometimes people just have bad days. It's part of life," said Aba, as he stroked her forehead with a wet cloth.

~

"Penny for your thoughts." Vijay Uncle had appeared, smiling, from inside the house and sat down across from me. I jumped up and smoothed my dress over my knees.

"Oh, it's nothing," I said, "Actually, I was thinking about trying to call my father."

"I think we can arrange that later," said Vijay Uncle. "There is a phone in the office at the hospital."

"You mean you don't have a phone here?"

"No, Rakhee, this is Malanad, not America," Vijay Uncle chuckled. "So, you are a very talented artist, I see. Krishna showed me the picture you drew of Hari the other day. It's very good, very lifelike—you must have inherited your artistic talent from me. You know, I used to be something of an artist. I once aspired to study art in Paris." He pronounced it "Par*ee*," in the French way. "I haven't painted in years, though— not since my father died. I had responsibilities here. I couldn't just leave."

As if on cue, Balu wobbled out on two very chubby, unstable legs and fell over, landing with a soft thud on his little hands and knees. He looked from Vijay Uncle to me, his eyes wide with surprise, and began to cry—loud, tearless wails. Nalini Aunty came running out after him, huffing and puffing, mopping up the sweat from her red forehead with the edge of her sari.

"Oh, this child! I have to watch him every second!" she said, and scooped him up in her arms. "Vijay, why are you out here just sitting, doing nothing? Why don't you go down to the hospital and do some work like other husbands?"

Vijay Uncle let out a sigh and looked at me. His whole body seemed to have deflated with that one sigh. "Rakhee, would you like to come with me and see the hospital? It is a very important part of our family."

"As a matter of fact," said Nalini Aunty, wiping her free hand on her sari, "I will go along with you both. Valsala has just given birth to her first child and I have been meaning to pay her a visit." Vijay Uncle stood up and looked at me.

"Shall we go, then?"

I hated being alone with unfamiliar adults—it made me nervous—but I couldn't think of a way to get out of it, so I found myself following my aunt and uncle down the front steps and across the road.

The hospital was a long, rectangular building, similar in design to Ashoka but coated in a peeling pale blue paint. A dirty white cat lurked in the front yard distracting Balu, who ran toward it in glee. Nalini Aunty waved us in with one hand while simultaneously chasing after him. I followed Vijay Uncle past a long line of patients and he cast a guilty glance in their direction. Dev was seated at a desk in the interior office examining a young man's tongue.

"Ah, hello, Vijay," he said, standing up when he saw us. "G-g-great of you to come by—and you brought a little f-f-f-friend along." He chucked me under the chin with a curved finger. I felt his nail scrape against the tender skin.

Floor-to-ceiling shelves lined the walls of the office, all crammed with small glass jars containing various liquids, creams, and powders in striking colors—magenta and turmeric orange—just how I imagined the lair of an old-fashioned apothecary might look. I knew then that this was not an ordinary hospital. It was nothing like the Plainfield Clinic.

"I wanted to give Rakhee a tour," said Vijay Uncle.

"Of course, of course, p-p-please, go ah-h-h-head."

I wondered why Vijay Uncle needed to ask Dev for permission, even though the hospital belonged to our family, not his, but before I could say anything Vijay Uncle steered me out of the office and into a hallway. A door, the only one in the entire hallway, caught my eye. It stood slightly ajar. Vijay Uncle had strolled ahead, so I paused and pushed it open. The room was as small as a closet, with weak light from the narrow window revealing a disheveled single bed, a scuffed wardrobe, and a floor caked with dust. It reeked of sweat.

"No, no, no," came Vijay Uncle's chiding voice, "That is Dev's room. He won't like you poking around."

I wrinkled my nose. "Dev lives here?"

"Yes," said Vijay Uncle, in a voice that was uncharacteristically clipped. He placed a hand on my shoulder. "Now come along."

He led me into another room with a heavy medicinal smell that momentarily left me breathless. The room resembled a shed, with wooden planks serving as makeshift walls. Pale sunlight streamed in through the cracks, mingling with the wisps of smoke that swirled around in curlicues. Shirtless men were standing over giant vats and poised above stacks of burning logs, stirring the contents of the vats with oarlike poles.

"This room is where we make all the medicine," Vijay Uncle explained. Then, as if he had read my thoughts, he added, "This is an Ayurvedic hospital, Rakhee. Do you know what Ayurveda is?"

I shook my head and he took a deep breath, shifting into the formal tone of a schoolteacher.

"Ayurveda is an ancient medical practice that originated in India over two thousand years ago and relies on herbal treatments. Unlike modern medicine, where the immediate cure for a headache is to have a pill, Ayurveda approaches it differently. We believe in prevention more than in the cure."

I nodded and wondered what Aba would think about Ayurveda.

Vijay Uncle showed me all over the hospital—from the assembly line where women in saris and white coats bottled the medicines, to the little thatch-roofed huts behind the main building where special massages and steam baths were administered.

"Ah, there you are," said Nalini Aunty, poking her head in. "Rakhee, why don't you come with me to see Valsala and her baby—they are our neighbors. Valsala is Veena Aunty's younger sister."

"Good. I must actually talk to Dev about some business, now that I think of it," said Vijay Uncle.

Nalini Aunty, Balu, and I entered a long dark hallway lined on either side with closed doors.

The birthing room was dim and stuffy. and the stifling odor of blood and sweat wafted through the air. Veena Aunty's sister was wearing a housedress with frills around the neck. She was lying on her side atop a low cot, covered in a blanket, with a little bundle nestled into the curve of her body.

"Hello," she said in a weak voice.

"Valsala, so a girl, eh? Some of us are not so lucky in these matters, but cheer up, perhaps God will bless you with a son the next time," said Nalini Aunty, making herself comfortable in a chair in the corner of the room. "And how are you feeling?"

Valsala, who seemed impervious to Nalini Aunty's cutting remark, responded in Malayalam, and they spoke back and forth rapidly. Her face looked wan and her hair puffed out in a dry halo around her head. The bundle at her side remained still. I began to feel nauseous.

"I almost forgot," said Nalini Aunty after a while, recalling my presence, "This is my husband's niece Rakhee—Chitra's daughter." She said my mother's name as if she was describing an especially unpleasant insect.

"Oh, Chitra's daughter," Valsala said, eyeing me with interest. "Pleased to meet you."

Balu began to bawl.

Nalini Aunty grunted. "Let me take him outside so he does not disturb the baby. I'll be back in a moment—wait here," she instructed me.

I stood near the doorway, uncertain. My knees felt shaky, as if I might collapse like Balu onto the floor, but there would be nobody around to pick me up.

"Would you like to see the baby, Rakhee?" Valsala was saying. She sat up in bed, gathered up the bundle, and held it out toward me. The baby made a noise, not unlike the sound the baby goats made in the mornings while their mothers were being milked. I stumbled forward through the hot musk toward the bed. "It's a girl—her name is Parvathi."

I peered down into Parvathi's face—it was wrinkled and red, like a miniature ape's. The skin was shiny and plastic, as if the top layer had been peeled off, exposing the rawness beneath. The hair was plentiful, and rose from her lumpy head in black spikes.

I was going to be sick.

"I have to go." I turned and ran out the door, out of the hospital, past Vijay Uncle and Nalini Aunty, past Dev, past the line of staring patients, across the road, and back up the stairs to the safety of Ashoka where I gulped in the clean air of freedom.

I wanted to find Amma; she was no longer in her bedroom. I went toward the sitting room. The door was closed and I could hear the muffled voices of a man and a woman on the other side.

"I've missed you so much," I heard Amma say.

It was Aba she was talking to. It had to be. He had come for us. A senseless joy possessed me, leaving me dizzy. They were not going to get a divorce after all, and we were all going to spend the summer in Malanad together, happily.

"Aba! Aba!" I burst into the room, almost choking on my words I was so excited. Aba was here and everything was going to be okay now.

But it was not Aba. It was a stranger—a slender man wearing loose trousers and a white button-down shirt, with the sleeves rolled up over his elbows.

Amma looked at me in shock. "Rakhee, your father is not here, you know that."

"Hello, Rakhee. I'm Prem, an old friend of your mum's." The man stepped in. His voice was very soft, very gentle.

"Prem is an old friend of the family—we all used to play together when we were children." Amma was speaking too fast.

"I've heard so much about you, Rakhee. I'm happy to finally meet you." The man was smiling at me. His eyes were a light brown color, like maple syrup.

Anger welled up inside me, anger at Amma for ruining

everything and looking at this man, this Prem, in a way I had never seen her look at Aba.

"Why don't you say something, molay? Don't just stand there, it's not polite," Amma was saying, but they both seemed very far away, as if I was watching them through water.

"I'm going to my room," I heard myself say. "I want to be alone."

"Okay, if that's what you want." Amma's brow was creased. "Please join us for dinner, though."

I turned and walked out. I was not going to my room. I wanted Amma to feel pain. I wanted to run away, to escape from Ashoka, from Malanad, from everything in it, even for one day, for one afternoon.

I don't know where everyone was, but the house was quiet, and when I walked purposefully out the front door, around the side of the house, and into the backyard, nobody was around to stop me. The cows and goats watched me go with dark, disapproving eyes.

Rough weeds rose from the earth and encircled my bare ankles as I tumbled over the wall and landed on the other side. I brushed the dirt from my knees and got to my feet. It was not so scary now, in broad daylight. The trees and bushes shone an electric green. I glanced up. The branches of the tallest trees bowed under the weight of their leaves, forming an arched ceiling above the forest floor, and I felt as if I had entered a church. Through the intricate, screenlike pattern of leaves I could see patches of bold blue sky with not a cloud in sight.

A couple of mynah birds were singing; Amma once told me that mynah birds were symbols of undying love because they paired and mated for life. The clear notes of their song floated down to me, comforted me, and compelled me forward with a rare courage. Separating the chaos of snarled vegetation was a narrow pathway, like a neat surgical incision. On either side of the path were explosions of cobwebbed greenery that seemed to be sweating in the humidity. The air had the sharp smell of grass, moist soil, and flowers. I followed the dirt path, using my hands to brush away low, sweeping branches that stretched out protectively before me.

I could hear Amma's voice in my head. *If you love me, promise you'll obey me and stay out of it.* Well, I didn't love her just then, I hated her. I wanted her to hurt the way I hurt—I imagined her grief when she discovered that she had driven me straight into the Rakshasi's oven. Or maybe a cobra would bite me, and I would limp home and swoon on the verandah steps, fang marks ringing my leg.

Hate, anger, determination, thrust me forward, farther and farther down the winding path, deeper into the teeming forest, in spite of my fear at what I might find. The farther I went, the more I wondered if my cousins could be right—what if something dangerous really did live in the forest?

Every so often a bulbous toad or a sleek frog would shoot out from underfoot with a croak. Needlelike mosquitoes hummed in my ears, and enormous black flies took refuge on my arms. I must have walked at least a mile—I had no idea that the property extended so far back.

The sun was preparing to descend for the night. Tinges of primrose and fuchsia began to bleed into the white gold glare of daylight.

I was just about to give up and turn back, when something stopped me. A glass-winged dragonfly hovered just in front of my nose, then glided ahead, buoyed by a soft breeze. A silver thread was wrapped around the tip of the dragonfly's tail, and from the end of the string fluttered the tiniest, most perfectly formed red rose I had ever seen. The strange dragonfly seemed to want me to go after it, so I did. Entranced, I followed it through the forest until we arrived at a clearing and a circular stone wall at least four times my height. The stone was covered in green vines that were punctuated here and there with pink conical flowers, from which bumblebees sucked. The rose-wielding dragonfly, having accomplished its mission, zigzagged back into the forest, and as it did the silver thread unraveled and the rose floated to the ground. For a moment I reeled back. *Wait for me*, I wanted to call after the dragonfly. Perspiration trickled down both of my cheeks. Now that I was about to come face-to-face with the reality of whatever it was that lived in the forest, my anger-fueled courage faltered. What would I find behind that wall? A crazed criminal? A demonic woman? A bloodthirsty monster?

The twitter of birds had intensified into a full chorus, flooding the air from every direction. In the grass, a shrill orchestra of cicadas took up their bows in accompaniment. I could not turn back now.

Slowly I moved toward the wall with my arm outstretched until my fingertips touched its vine-smothered surface. I waited for something drastic to happen when my skin made contact with the stone, but when neither I nor the wall burst into flames or evaporated into thin air, I continued dragging my hand along the wall, emboldened, until my palm felt the roughness of vines give way to a smooth, hard wood.

A door.

The door had an old-fashioned brass knob, which I pushed and twisted to no avail.

"Hello?" I called. My voice sounded hollow and out of place.

Bending down, I pressed my glasses against the keyhole. An amber-throated hummingbird the size of my thumb thrummed in my line of vision, blocking my view.

"Shoo, shoo," I whispered.

The bird's wings were vibrating so rapidly I started to get dizzy until at last it buzzed off. The swimming sensation in my head came to a halt and my mouth fell open.

A Rakshasi did not live here.

A princess did.

I was staring into the most dazzling garden I had ever seen. Cobblestone pathways meandered between rows of salmon-hued hibiscus, regal hollyhock, delicate impatiens, wild orchids, thorny rosebushes, and manicured shrubs starred with jasmine. Bunches of bougainvillea cascaded down the sides of the wall, draped across the stone like extravagant shawls. Magnolia trees, cotton-candy pink, were interspersed with coconut trees, which let in streaks of purplish light through their fanlike leaves. A rock-rimmed pond glistened in a corner of the garden, and lotus blossoms sprouting from green discs skimmed its surface. A snow white bird that looked like a peacock wove in and out through a grove of pomegranate trees, which were set aflame by clusters of deep orange blossoms. I had seen blue peacocks before, but never a white one.

An Ashoka tree stood at one edge of the garden, as if on guard, near the door. A brief wind sent a cluster of red petals drifting down from its branches and settling on the ground at my feet. A flock of pale blue butterflies emerged from a bed of golden trumpet flowers and sailed up into the sky. In the center of this scene was a peach stucco cottage with green shutters and a thatched roof, quaint and idyllic as a dollhouse. A heavenly perfume drifted over the wall, intoxicating me—I wanted nothing more than to enter.

Then I was no longer looking into the garden, but into an eye—brown and inquisitive, like mine, pressing against the other side of the keyhole. I fell backward, then looked again, wondering if in my excited state I was imagining things. The eye had vanished, and the garden sat still and beautiful again.

"Hello? Anybody there?"

I must have imagined it, I told myself, when nobody answered.

But just as I was about to calm down, without any warning, the eye came back, then receded, revealing a face, a terrible face, illuminated by the bleeding sunset light. I did not register the shape of the face, or what hair, if any, framed it. All I saw was a large splotchy pink mark, like a bruise, spreading across the surface of pale skin, and a jagged mouth that had a triangular gash cutting into the upper lip. The open mouth merged with the nose, revealing a set of yellowish teeth.

I screamed, a harsh sound that wrenched my gut, and amplified the screams that sounded from the other side of the door. I leaped to my feet and sprinted back through the trees, numb to the sting of branches and thorns needling my arms and legs, scathing, as if to say *I told you so, I told you so.* I could hear the sound of blood beating, like wings flapping, in my ears, and my heart thundered. My stomach was heavy, full of stones, dragging me down. I ran and ran until I reached the wall at Ashoka, and flung myself over it, back into the safety of the yard.

Everything was still and dark, except for Ashoka, which

was lit up and inviting, oblivious to the horrors that lurked so near. Something warm and wet was trickling down my leg and pooling in my sandals. Stopping to catch my breath, I stuck my hand under my dress and saw that it was covered in blood.

"Amma! Amma!" I ran toward the front of the house.

Amma was standing by herself on the verandah, her features contorted in anger. "Oh my God, Rakhee—where have you been? I checked your room and you were gone. No one knew where you were. I was worried sick—"

"Amma, I'm dying, I'm dying!"

The anger melted from her face, and the last thing I remember before I fell into the darkness was Amma's arms cradling me.

Chapter 7

Rain was falling and red shadows smoked across the face of the moon. Lying on Amma's bed, I felt scrubbed and clean, dressed in an unfamiliar floral gown that covered my feet. Amma was sitting next to me, thumbing through a slim, tattered book—I looked at the title; it was called *The Poems of Mirabai.* I rubbed my eyes with my fists. Waves of memory ebbed in and out, blurred photographs at the edges of my mind.

Amma washing me as if I were a wounded cub. I heard her crying, "My baby, my baby."

My body wrenched with nausea, and the sound of vomit splashing into a metal pan.

Sadhana Aunty spooning a bittersweet syrup down my throat.

The fever clinging to my skin.

The stone wall, birdsong, the enchanted garden, running faster than I had ever run before, my hand covered in blood.

The face. That awful face.

I shuddered. Amma put down her book and laid a cool hand across my forehead. *You're safe now. It was all a dream,* I said to myself. *Just a dream.* I repeated it over and over again, and as my chest rose and fell, I willed myself to believe it.

When I could finally sit up in bed, Amma brought me a plate of warm brown rice swimming in watery yogurt, and we had a long talk. She asked me where I had run off to, and I lied, telling her I had gone to the market to buy chocolates and had lost my way. I pushed everything I had really seen and done into the back of my mind and tried to lock it away. She did not ask any questions. She trusted me.

Amma cleared her throat, grew misty-eyed, and told me in a proud voice that I was a woman now. I sobbed with shame and begged her not to tell anyone. How could this be happening to me? In the spring, the school nurse had come into our classroom to talk to the girls about menstruation. I had doodled in my notebook while she spoke, thinking that what she was saying could not possibly apply to me, not for a long time at least. I hadn't even turned eleven yet. It was all so unfair. Amma tried to reassure me, but I felt miserable. On the outside I looked the same, but on the inside this secret thing bloomed, dirty and unwanted.

"*Chee*, she looks terrible, Chitra. So pale," said Nalini Aunty the next morning, drawing each of my eyelids up, one by one, with her index finger, and clicking her tongue in disapproval.

I glanced at Amma, my stomach turning over. Did Nalini Aunty know? Had Amma told her? Did they all know?

"I am glad you are feeling better, Rakhee," said Krishna, squeezing my hand, and giving me an understanding smile. The sweetness of Krishna's smile relaxed me, and for a moment I wanted to take her aside and confess everything. I knew now it was not a dream, that the creature in the forest was all too real. I kept seeing its monstrous face in my mind. The harder I tried to forget it, the more it plagued me. What on earth was it and what was it doing in that garden? It couldn't be human.

At first I had tried to convince myself it was just a gardener I had seen and the light had been playing tricks with my eyes, but deep down I knew this was not the case. If there was nothing wrong with the garden, if it was simply tended to by a regular human gardener, why would the door be locked, and why would Amma and Sadhana Aunty be hiding it? Perhaps the creature that haunted the garden was magical. I never would have believed it before, but in Malanad anything was possible. It was not like Plainfield, where life was dull but at least made sense. I wanted to unload this burden onto someone else, I wanted to get Krishna's opinion, but if I told her, how would she react? She might think I was crazy and not want to be friends anymore. Or she might tell someone I had disobeyed the rules, and then I would be in huge trouble. How did I know that I could *really* trust Krishna? I couldn't risk it. I had to keep my discovery to myself.

It was Muthashi's birthday, so we were all going to the temple for a pooja. At first Amma thought we should stay at home while the others went ahead. "Why don't you rest today?" she said.

But I insisted that we go. My ordeal had left me flushed with an unusual energy, and I hated the thought of being left out because of my new womanly status. I was determined that nothing would change. I wouldn't let it.

Muthashi paced around the front yard in a circle, a light wind agitating her sari and causing the delicate white fabric to tremble. She loved going to the temple.

We wound our way through the village—Amma and

Sadhana Aunty on either side of Muthashi, holding on to her arms to keep her steady, with Nalini Aunty, Balu, and Gitanjali following closely behind. I ran up ahead with Krishna and Meenu. We had to cut through a paddy field, still soggy from the previous night's rain, and I could feel my sandals sinking into the earth, and a muddy paste coating my toes. Frothy clouds of mosquitoes, drawn out by the wetness, swarmed around us, and Krishna, Meenu, and I waved our hands around to drive them away from our freshly shampooed hair. All around us, the quenched vegetation swelled and brightened with renewed vigor. A ruddy cow was grazing in the field, and it lifted its head to watch us pass, stone-faced. An old brown dog with a weathered muzzle strained against his rope and barked into the morning's stillness. As we passed, he raised his lip to snarl, revealing sparsely toothed black gums.

A dirt road shaded by stiff trees led us to the wrought-iron temple gates. Sandals were heaped at the entrance. Everyone took off their shoes and tossed them onto the pile. I glanced at Amma and she nodded, so I slipped mine off as well, and stepped into the temple courtyard, feeling vulnerable. The stones beneath my feet were sharp and I cringed. No one else seemed to be bothered, so I put on a brave face and began to follow Krishna and Meenu in toward the altar, which housed the goddess's shrine. Amma seized my hand and held me back.

"No, Rakhee, you can't go inside. We are going to wait out here."

"Why can't I go in?"

Amma looked at me. "Because women with their periods are not allowed inside the temple. It's considered unclean."

I jerked away. My chest tightened, and I could feel my cheeks growing hot. Amma took my hand again, this time gently. Her eyes were sympathetic, as if we now shared some unpleasant bond.

"I'm sorry, molay, I know it seems unfair, but it's the tradition and we must obey it, right? We'll come back to the temple again soon, I promise. Come, let's walk around the courtyard." She guided me away. I wondered if my cousins would notice I was gone and figure out the reason. My face burned at the thought.

"This temple was built over four hundred years ago, by our ancestors—can you believe it?" Amma's voice was bright.

"Really?" I was interested in spite of myself.

Amma told me about our ancestors—two young princesses from Rajasthan, a state in the north of India, who had fled their kingdom amid a brutal war and made a pilgrimage south, eventually settling in Malanad. "Our family has been around here for centuries," she said.

"So, that makes us sort of princesses?"

"Yes," said Amma, and we both giggled. "I suppose it does."

We stepped around the particularly rough stones, and Amma pointed out a tree whose leafy, scarlet-tinged branches grew over the temple wall.

"Do you remember what this tree is called?"

"An Ashoka tree."

"Yes, very good. It's a special tree, Rakhee. It's dedicated to Kama Deva, the God of Love. Legend says that it has the power to grant wishes."

As we moved closer to the tree, an exquisite scent enveloped us.

"I used to believe that as long as you could smell the fragrance of its flowers, you would forget all your sorrows." Amma's eyes shone, and I felt for a fleeting second that she was only standing there in body, but her spirit had galloped off.

Jealously, I pulled her back to me. "Is it a magic tree, then?"

Amma shivered. "In a sense. Remember when I read you the *Ramayana*, the story of Rama and Sita?"

I nodded.

"Well, Rama and Sita were bound together by a great love, and even though they had been banished to live as exiles in the forest, they were happy. But Ravana, the evil demon king, was envious of their love, so he plotted to kidnap Sita. He sent his henchman, Maricha, into the forest. Maricha transformed into a beautiful golden deer. When Sita saw the deer, she begged Rama to go after it and bring it back to her. Leaving her under the protection of his brother Lakshmana, Rama left to pursue the golden deer. After leading Rama deep into the forest, the deer, who was actually Maricha in disguise, began to cry out in a human voice so that Sita would hear and think her husband was in trouble. Sita pleaded with Lakshmana to go into the forest to save Rama. He agreed only under the condition that Sita stay inside a magical circle of protection he drew around her. As long as Sita stayed within this circle, nothing could touch her and she would be safe. As soon as Lakshmana was gone, though, Ravana, the demon king, approached Sita disguised as a thirsty beggar, and he asked her to serve him some water. She took pity on him and stepped out of the circle. Ravana turned back into his demon self and dragged her across the sea into Lanka. He kept her imprisoned inside a heavenly garden, guarded by Rakshasis, and she sat there under the Ashoka tree for months and months, dreaming about Rama, waiting for him to rescue her."

"And did he?"

But Amma wasn't paying attention to me anymore. She was staring at a plant rising out of a waist-high earthen pot with intricate pictures carved into the sides. The plant had fine, green leaves shaped like teardrops, branching out in several directions from a single central stalk.

"Amma, what is it?"

She drew in a long breath and said, "It is the tulasi plant, Rakhee. The most holy plant in Hinduism. It can heal both the body and the mind."

We lingered in front of the tulasi plant. Birds sang pleasantly in the trees. I could hear a woman's deep, discordant voice chanting and a bell ringing. The fog of incense curled out and tickled the tip of my nose.

"Rakhee, you know that man who you met the other day—Prem?" Amma said suddenly.

I kept my eyes glued to the plant and did not say anything.

"Well, I would really like it if you could be nice to him and get to know him. He's a very good childhood friend, just like Veena Aunty back in Plainfield."

Without warning, homesickness struck—a giant lump that rose at the back of my throat, making it hard to swallow. I wanted my dog, my house, my father. I wanted us to all be together again. I turned to the Ashoka tree and prayed to the red flowers that if they could make that one wish come true, I promised to be happy and not ever complain.

~

Putting on a play was Meenu's idea. It seemed like a good plan at the time. We were bored and groggy, piled on top of the bed in front of the television, our stomachs full from Muthashi's birthday dinner, watching some melodramatic Malayalam movie.

Even though the sun had set, the heat was unbearable, and we fought for the spot directly under the ceiling fan. I didn't like the nights much, when mosquitoes infiltrated the house and moths singed themselves against the wincing blue tube lights.

"All we need is a story," said Meenu, who had predictably won the struggle for best spot on the bed, and lay between me and Krishna, the wisps of hair that gathered around her forehead quivering in the wind like insect legs.

It seemed only natural to me that we should act out the story Amma had told me earlier that day. The scene had all the elements of a great play—love, fear, war, suspense. And I knew which part I wanted. Sita—beautiful, tragic Sita, with her flowing black hair, waiting under the Ashoka tree for her love.

"Well, I'll be Rama, since I'm the biggest, strongest, and bravest," said Meenu, immediately taking charge.

"Can I be Sita?" I heard myself say, unsure of from where I had drawn such courage.

"You can't be Sita, Rakhee," Meenu said bluntly.

"Why not?"

"Sita doesn't wear glasses, and—besides, how can *you* be an Indian princess? You're not even fully Indian. Can you imagine Sita with an American accent?" She let out a scornful laugh. Blood rushed to my face. For the first time it struck me that even to my cousins, whom I had grown to love, I would always be different. I would never be one of them. "It's settled, then," Meenu said. "Sita will be played by Krishna, and Rakhee, you will play Ravana, the evil demon king."

Krishna glanced at me and shrugged.

Sadhana Aunty stuck her head in the doorway and ordered everyone to bed, the stern lines of her face warning us against any attempts at protesting.

"Rehearsals will start tomorrow," said Meenu. "You are all dismissed."

I could not sleep. I kept thinking about everything that was happening, feeling more alone than I ever had before. I was afraid, with only a thin sheet and a stretch of trees separating me from the thing in the forest. Those eyes and that face kept blazing across the backs of my eyelids every time I tried to close them. I wanted to ask Amma about it, to confess my fears, but she seemed very far away from me, altered somehow, as if this place had possessed her and left behind only a pearly husk.

Amma knew about the creature in the forest. Amma had visited the creature in the forest, but she was not doing anything about it. And she wanted me to ignore it.

I lay on my back, listening to a June bug clicking its wings on the sill. Moonlight streamed in through the window bars. On the ceiling directly above my head, a lizard spread its fat green thumbs across the crumbling plaster.

Something wasn't right. I began to wonder, deliriously, if whatever I had seen really *was* a Rakshasi, and the Rakshasi was guarding an imprisoned princess, like Sita.

My mind raced back to that moment, the moment when I had screamed and fled from the garden door. I had been so preoccupied with my own fear, I had not even considered what I heard coming from the other side of the door—screams, just like mine. Not evil, but scared. Someone on the other side of the door had been just as frightened as me.

My throat was parched as sandpaper. Water, I needed water.

I climbed out of bed, put on my glasses, and, gripping

my flashlight, tiptoed out of the room and down the hall. Light was coming from under the sitting room door, and I heard voices on the other side. As I got closer, I saw that the door was ajar, so I turned off my flashlight and flattened myself against the wall to listen.

"There is simply no more money," Vijay Uncle was saying. "We have no choice but to sell."

"Never," said Sadhana Aunty. "The hospital will never be in anybody's name but ours."

"Well, what do you suggest we do, then?" Vijay Uncle sounded frustrated. "Tell everyone the truth?"

"Vijay, don't talk like that, don't be ridiculous. If our father could only hear you now. Think of what he sacrificed for the sake of that hospital, to fulfill his duty to his people, to this village. We made a promise to him, and we can't let him down. Nothing is more important than honoring his wishes and upholding the Varma name. Nothing. Long after we are all dead and gone, people will still revere and respect our name. I'll die before I see it dirtied."

"Time is running out—Dev is breathing down my neck," said Vijay Uncle.

"We'll have to figure something out," Sadhana Aunty said. "We need just a little more time to think."

"This is all my fault." Amma's voice was shaky.

Sadhana Aunty sighed, either with sympathy or impatience, I couldn't tell. "Don't cry now, Chitra. Tears will not help the situation. Let me get you some water."

I sprinted back down the hall and leaped into bed before anyone saw me. I lay on my side, panting for air, marveling at my luck at not having been caught.

I had become alarmingly good at secrecy.

Chapter 8

Meenu spent the next morning writing out a script for our play in a battered old composition book. After lunch she assembled Krishna and me, both stuck indoors by the steady afternoon downpour, on the verandah to rehearse. We were like puppets, flimsy and bendable to her will, woodenly reading out our lines and moving wherever she pointed her finger.

Amma had one of her headaches and was resting in her bedroom. I desperately hoped that the separation from Aba was taking its toll, and that soon she would forget this Prem person and realize this had all been a big mistake.

"What's the matter with you, Rakhee? Pay attention!" said Meenu.

As the rehearsal wore on, my ability to concentrate waned. I had trouble focusing on anything but the conversation I had overheard the night before. I had spent all night awake, thinking. What had Amma done to cause the family the trouble it was in? And where did Dev fit into all of this? Perhaps it had something to do with whatever Amma was hiding from Aba.

"Rakhee, this is the part where you show up as the

thirsty beggar," Meenu said. "If you are not going to be serious about this play, then perhaps we should find another Ravana." She placed her hands on her hips and fixed me with a petulant stare.

A volt of irritation shot through me. "Fine, then, maybe you should!" I stormed off to my room, sat on my bed, and folded my arms across my chest. An ugly black crow was perched on the windowsill, his feathers slick as an oil puddle. We glared at each other for a moment before he cawed and took off into the rain, beating his wings and disappearing into the forest.

A surge of regret dulled the sharp edges of my anger. What had I done? I considered going back out and apologizing to my cousins, but pride still tinged my remorse and I couldn't bring myself to move.

Instead, I curled up on the bed and closed my eyes. My head sank deeper and deeper into the pillow, my glasses fell askew, and soon, lulled by the rhythms of the rain, I drifted into sleep.

I began to dream. I was standing outside the door that led into the garden with my hand on the knob. Just as I had in real life, I fiddled with the knob and pressed my weight against the door but it would not open. The vines that covered the wall began to unlatch from the cold gray stone and slither down onto the ground, where they coiled at my feet. Soon they were creeping along my body like green snakes, winding around my ankles, my legs, and finally my throat, binding my mouth, hissing. Their forked tongues flickered at the insides of my ears. "Trust us, Rakhee, trust us."

I was airborne. The snakes were carrying me, lifting me like a feather high above the garden wall, and I was floating across the tops of the magnolia trees, then dropping down,

down, down. The snakes were loosening their grip. In a panic, I flapped my arms in the air, but my descent continued in that same slow manner. The softness of the leaves brushed against my skin, the sweet smell of roses relaxed me, and I succumbed to the fall. The flowers enveloped me in their silky embrace and I lay among them, safe as an embryo. A feeling of supreme belonging settled over me.

The Ashoka flowers above shone like rubies, radiating warm rays down upon my face. I stared up at them in a daze until, gradually, my sense of calm turned to horror. Those were not flowers or rubies in the Ashoka tree—they were eyes. Dozens of sets of eyes burning red as blood against the branches. I opened my mouth to scream, but only a pitiful noise emerged, and when I tried to stand, I couldn't budge. The red eyes throbbed and glared at me, and with a terrifying certainty I knew I would never leave, that I was fated to remain within the walls of that horrible garden forever.

"Amma!" The sound of my choking sob jerked me back into consciousness. My palms were sweaty, my face hot. The rain pattered on the sand outside my window.

I stood upon my weak legs and stumbled into the bathroom. The floor was still wet from the last person who had bathed, and the fusty water against my bare feet brought me back to reality.

The dream was a warning sign. Whatever was in that garden, I did not want to see it. I had to squash my curiosity and stay away. I looked at my pale face for a long time in the mirror and concentrated. *You have to forget, you have to forget, you have to forget.*

I went out into the hall, determined to make up with my cousins. Only Gitanjali was on the verandah, swinging on the bench with her eyes closed.

I started to turn around, but she said, "Rakhee."

My oldest cousin rarely addressed me, or even Meenu and Krishna, her own sisters, so although she had clearly said my name, I looked around for someone else.

"Rakhee, I heard about this play you and my sisters are doing," she said. "Did your mother ever tell you how the story really ends? It is not as happy as you think."

"What do you mean?"

"After Rama saves Sita, he publicly rejects her because he is humiliated by rumors that she may not have stayed loyal to him throughout her captivity. In order to prove her innocence, Sita pledges to walk through fire. 'If I emerge unscathed, then you will know I am telling the truth,' she says. But even after she successfully performs this act, Rama sends her away, and she ends up pregnant with his twin sons and abandoned, living out the rest of her days in exile in the jungle. Eventually, she asks Mother Earth to open up and take her back into her womb. Mother Earth takes pity on her and swallows her up, finally putting an end to her suffering."

Gitanjali gave me a hard look. "I just thought you should know," she said casually before closing her eyes again and resting her head against the swing's chain.

Trying to shake off the uneasy feeling, I resumed my search for Meenu and Krishna. I found them sitting in the dining room eating fruitcake and sipping milk from steel tumblers. Sadhana Aunty was at the head of the table, going over some papers covered in handwritten numbers.

She looked up from her papers when I entered the room. "Rakhee, I do not know what you usually do when you are at home, but Meenu and Krishna study for two hours every day during the summer holidays. I've been lenient since you just arrived, but it's time for them to start again. It's important to keep young minds sharp and not waste the entire day in play."

Meenu and Krishna both had miserable expressions on their faces and drank the milk as if their cups were filled with poison.

"Once you are finished eating, I want you both to fetch your books and sit here for two hours. I shall be back by that time." Sadhana Aunty stood and put her papers inside a folder.

"Where are you going?" I asked.

"I have some business to take care of. You girls needn't concern yourselves with it."

After Sadhana Aunty had left the room, I turned to my cousins.

"I came to say . . . I'm sorry. Can I still be in the play?"

"Of course," said Krishna, grinning with her mouth full of crumbling cake.

Meenu pouted for a few minutes but eventually agreed to let me back in. "We're on the verge of finding someone else, but I suppose you can come back. We'll get back to rehearsals tomorrow morning."

While my cousins were studying, I wandered out onto the verandah and sat on the swing, watching the rain cascade from the roof.

Closing my eyes, I inhaled the fresh scent. I always hated the way it smelled when it rained in Minnesota—like worms and wet grass. Here there was something pure and cleansing about a heavy rain, washing away the filth of everything that had preceded its arrival, leaving behind only pinpricks in the sand, like fairy footprints.

"I'm tired of studying. I hate mathematics." Krishna emerged from inside the house after about half an hour and sat beside me on the swing.

"Won't your mother be angry if she finds out you didn't finish studying?"

"She won't find out. . . . If Meenu tells on me, then I'll tell about how she tried to put Cutex on the cat and *that's* how she got that scratch on her arm. It's the summer holidays, I can't believe—" Krishna stopped talking and I realized Nalini Aunty had joined us on the verandah, bouncing Balu on her plentiful hip.

"Balu, don't you have any pity for your poor mother? Can't you ever sleep?" she was muttering.

She placed Balu on the ground and eased herself into Muthashi's rocking chair. Balu joyfully crawled over to Krishna, who scooped him up and began cooing into his ear. I watched them play, self-consciously aware of Nalini Aunty's eyes trained on me.

"Rakhee, what are those spots on your face?"

"What?" My fingers moved to my face.

"You know, those spots—all over your nose and cheeks."

"Oh, freckles?" I said. My face had become peppered with them since arriving in India, due to the long hours I spent under the hot sun.

"Is that what they are called? It must be another thing you inherited from your Sardarji father." She curled up her nose. "You know, I'm sure Dev could find some sort of remedy for that—you would be a much better-looking girl with a clear complexion. No one will ever marry you covered in those spots, not to mention those thick specs."

I picked up a pebble that was lying on the floor and pretended to examine it, hoping that she would not notice the tears that had sprung to my eyes.

Nalini Aunty, having successfully plunged in her sword, rose almost as quickly as she had sat down. "Well, what am I doing here chatting with little girls? This is what my life has come to," she chuckled to herself. "Let me see what those useless servants are getting up to in the kitchen." She collected Balu from Krishna's arms and plodded away.

Once she left, unable to control myself, I hurled the pebble into the rain. "Why does she have to be so mean all the time? I hate her."

Krishna didn't say anything; she just stared down at her toes. After a few moments of silence, embarrassment about my outburst crept in. Maybe Krishna thought I was being disrespectful of my elders. But then she turned to look at me and said in a conspiratorial whisper:

"Come with me, I want to show you something." She took my hand in hers; it felt hot and moist, and she seemed unusually excited.

"Where are we going?"

"Ssshhh, just come." Krishna pulled me down the hallway and into a bedroom I had never seen before—the door was always closed and I had never dared open it. The walls were painted an uncompromising yellow. The bed was neatly made with a dark green spread, and matching curtains that looked as if they were made from burlap covered the window.

"This is my mother's room," Krishna said.

"Won't we get in trouble?"

Krishna shrugged. "She won't be back for some time now—not until the rain stops, at least." My mind immediately went to the walled garden, and for a second I allowed myself to indulge in a vision of the drenched flowers enclosed within, before I pushed the image away.

Krishna went over to the closet and opened it. A row of monochromatic shawls and kurthas hung in a tidy row on one side, and a modest stack of saris sat piled on the shelf beside it. Crouching on the floor, Krishna stuck her arms into the closet and began feeling around.

"Ah, here it is," she said, and with some effort pulled out a dusty cardboard box.

"What's in there?" I was intrigued and impressed.

"Family photos—old albums. My mother hid them in here, but I found them one day," Krishna lowered her gaze. "Sometimes I come in here when no one is looking and open her closet. I like the smell of her things."

I kneeled down beside Krishna; she glanced up and smiled. "Anyway, you will never believe this." She picked up the top album, placed it in her lap, and began flipping through. When she found what she had been looking for, she pushed it over to my lap and pointed to a formal black-and-white portrait of an attractive young woman who seemed familiar. Her petite frame was wrapped in a silk embroidered sari, and she wore a hopeful smile on her delicately rounded face.

"Who is that?"

"Guess," said Krishna with a cheeky smile.

"I have no idea. She seems so familiar, but I can't figure out who it is."

"It's Nalini Aunty."

I turned to face my cousin and laughed. "I can't believe it, look how pretty she is, she's so...so...skinny." But it was true—when you factored in a double chin and sour expression, the face was undoubtedly Nalini Aunty's.

"I think this was taken just before she was married to Vijay Uncle. This is the picture her family sent to our family when the marriage was being arranged. She still looked like this when she first came to Ashoka, I remember. And she was even kind of nice back then, too."

"So what happened?"

Krishna closed the album. "Living here has changed her."

I leaned forward. "What do you mean?"

"I don't know, but it's a feeling. There's something not quite right about this place." Tears filled her eyes, and she wiped them away with an efficient gesture that reminded me of Sadhana Aunty. "It's a hard life here, Rakhee, and you don't know, you're only here for one summer. Then you get to leave. You'll forget all about us."

"No, I won't. I may have to leave, but I'll never forget. I can come back, too, and you can come visit us in Minnesota. Have you ever been on a plane before?" Krishna looked so sad that I wanted to cheer her up by changing the subject.

She sniffled and gave me a halfhearted smile. "Do you want to see some more?" She rummaged through the box and pulled out another album. Passing her palm across the cover, she cleaned off the layer of dust that had collected upon it.

"This is our grandparents' wedding photo." The picture was printed on a thick cardboardlike material that had faded over the years of heat and neglect, but I could still make out Muthashan's high forehead, the aquiline nose, the deep-set eyes that I knew so well. Muthashi looked incredibly young—she couldn't have been much older than Gitanjali—with a face still soft with baby fat and eyes full of acceptance.

"But why would Sadhana Aunty hide these photos? Why aren't they kept out where everyone can see them? Why are there so few pictures hanging on the walls?"

"My mother doesn't believe in remembering the past. Anytime I bring it up or ask questions, she gets angry. She says we should just focus on what God has set before us in the present, and take care of what happens in the future."

"Who's this?" I pointed to a picture of a lanky young man with curly black hair. He was sitting cross-legged on what appeared to be the verandah of Ashoka, smoking a cigarette.

"My father," Krishna said in a soft voice. "Sometimes I wonder if that is the reason why my mother never wants to look back...because she misses him. I don't remember anything about him, but from his pictures I can tell that he was a nice man. My mother says he was always sick and that he just sat around reading all day, but I don't believe her."

She began flipping through the pages again. "You'll like this one," she said, stopping finally, and passing the album back to me. "See, our mothers are still young here."

In the photo, a band of children stood in a haphazard cluster before a backdrop of trees. I examined the picture and determined that the children were in fact Sadhana Aunty, Veena Aunty, Amma, and Prem, and they were standing in front of the forest that grew behind Ashoka. The stone barrier had not yet been erected. My two aunts posed primly in their half-saris; Amma and Prem, who looked to be about my age, appeared decidedly more disheveled. Prem was smiling and poking Amma's arm, and Amma, with a patch of mud on her skirt, was beaming from ear to ear. Judging from the picture they looked as if they had been the best of friends.

"Let's keep going," said Krishna, flipping the page. "Here's a family portrait."

Muthashan, Muthashi, Sadhana Aunty, Amma, and Vijay Uncle were all assembled on the sepia-colored front lawn of Ashoka. In the background everything appeared unchanged—the Ashoka trees lining the stairs, the cow-shed, the goat pen.

Muthashan sat in a chair beside Muthashi in the center of the lawn, and the children looked older than they had in the previous picture. Sadhana Aunty, who must have been about sixteen at the time, posed in a long skirt and blouse behind her father. Although she still wore the same serious expression, she seemed somehow lighter, softer than she did now. A roly-poly young Vijay Uncle, looking very much the same as his present incarnation, grinned complacently at Muthashi's knee. Amma stood a bit away from the rest with her arms folded across her chest. Her chin was tilted toward the ground, but there was a flicker of defiance in the eyes that glanced up to meet the camera lens.

I scrutinized the picture for a long time, searching Amma's young, unmarred face for any resemblance to my own. As I stared, a spot at the edge of the photograph caught my eye and I brought it closer to my face. The spot, I realized, was actually the unfocused profile of a young woman captured unwittingly by the photographer. I ran my finger lightly across her face, mesmerized.

I pointed out the woman to Krishna. "Who is that?"

The woman's features, though not quite beautiful, were arresting. But her eyes were what gripped me—huge, dark, and glowering. She seemed to be watching the scene with unfiltered hatred.

"I never noticed her before," Krishna said, taking the album and squinting into the photograph. She examined it for some time before dropping the album with a start. "Rakhee, it's Hema."

"Who?"

"Hema, you know, crazy Hema, the servant woman."

We looked at each other, unsure of what to make of our discovery. Meenu's footsteps came thumping dramatically down the hallway.

"Where *is* everyone?" came her impatient call.

"Quickly, we must put this away," said Krishna.

I nodded and helped her push the cardboard box back into the closet, understanding that as much as we loved Meenu, some things should be kept just between us.

~

That night after dinner we all gathered around the television to watch the latest installment of a popular Malayalam serial. Amma seemed distracted and kept fidgeting and glancing at her wristwatch throughout the first half of the show. Eventually she got up and slipped out of the room, unnoticed by anyone but me. I hesitated at first—maybe she was just going to the bathroom or to get some water—but curiosity got the better of me when Amma did not return after a few minutes, so I, too, slipped out of the room.

Amma was in the front yard. I hid in the velvety dark of the verandah. The trees surrounding the house stood out like inkblots against the sky's deep blue, and the leaves were flocks of black bats lying in wait upon the branches. The low hoot of an owl sounded from somewhere above.

Amma looked unearthly in her pale, rustling sari. The night air felt lovely and warm upon my skin, but somehow I was afraid. She was walking across the lawn, wringing her hands, her steps light and deliberate, her eyes rapt. She moved with purpose, as if she had a specific destination in mind, although she was simply pacing, treading across the same white streak of moonlight over and over again.

Another figure emerged from the darkness of the front steps, another silent, unnoticed observer. I squinted through my glasses trying to identify the intruder.

It was Prem.

I knew then with utter certainty that it had been Prem who had been sending those letters to Amma. It was Prem who was taking Amma away from me and Aba.

"Chitra," he said, and Amma froze. Then she went to him, stumbling over the edge of her sari, wrapping her arms around his neck, and leaning her head against his shoulder.

He tipped her chin back and began to talk to her, softly, intimately—I could not make out the words. His fingers caressed the rope of her braid. I crouched in my hiding spot, transfixed, as if I were watching two actors in a play.

They spoke for only a few minutes. Prem kissed Amma on the mouth—a long kiss. I had never seen anyone kiss like that, except in movies that I wasn't supposed to see. Sometimes back at home, Aba kissed Amma in front of me, but it was always brief, and then Amma would turn scarlet, push him away, and say: "Vikram, not in front of Rakhee."

After a while Amma broke away from Prem, and ran back toward the house. I remained huddled in the corner, cloaked in shadows.

Chapter 9

Nalini Aunty was eagerly listening to Murthy, the mailman, perched atop his rusty bicycle, conversing enthusiastically in between sips from the metal tumbler of lime juice, which she had carried out to him. It had stopped raining and I was sitting alone on the damp top step.

"Really, Murthy?" Nalini Aunty's eyes were so wide with curiosity they practically bulged from their sockets, "Is Thara Thomas's husband really divorcing her? She was only one year senior to me in school—I still remember the wedding. Tut, tut, what a shame."

Murthy was the best source of village gossip, abusing his job by opening and reading everyone else's mail before making his weekly deliveries. His possession of coveted information allowed him to move freely from house to house, accepting tea and sweets, and sometimes whiskey, in exchange for the latest news. Nobody ever dared offend Murthy, and most people buttered him up in the hopes that he would keep their own precious skeletons locked up in their closets, safe and sound where they belonged.

He was short and rail thin, with a dark complexion

smooth and shiny as polished wood, an elaborate mustache, and a mischievous yellow grin.

"Yes, and this is only between us," Murthy continued, leaning toward Nalini Aunty and whispering conspiratorially into her ear, "but they say she was in the habit of taking drinks, and that is why he is asking for the divorce."

"No!" Nalini Aunty gasped, her face a mix of shock and thinly veiled glee. "I always suspected there was something off about that Thara. Poor woman, though, so sad, really. Her life is over."

"Are you through with all this silly talk?" Sadhana Aunty had appeared outside, her hands balanced on her hips, and her mouth pressed into a frown.

"Oh, Murthy was just telling me—" began Nalini Aunty, but Sadhana Aunty silenced her.

"Nalini, you forget yourself. I don't care to hear of it. Now, Murthy, if you have delivered whatever you were meant to deliver, please go. You are no longer welcome."

Murthy drew himself up with a haughty air and tossed a packet of envelopes onto the front step, where they landed in a heap at Sadhana Aunty's feet. Her frown stiffened and she eyed the letters in distaste.

"There you are—it looks like that Sardarji brother-in-law of yours wants your sister back, God only knows why. She's nothing but trouble, that girl." Murthy shook his head from side to side, then pedaled briskly away, the wheels of his bicycle kicking back swirls of dust.

Even though I was mad at Amma, Murthy's words made my blood boil and I glared after him.

Nalini Aunty reached out for the letters, but Sadhana Aunty swept up the pile and began to shuffle through it.

"Rakhee, your father has written a letter to you also,"

Sadhana Aunty said. She handed me a white envelope with my name printed across it in Aba's familiar reassuring scrawl.

"Can I bring Amma her letter, too?"

Sadhana Aunty paused and looked at me with a glint of distrust. To my surprise, she handed me another envelope. "Very well, but bring it to her at once. Do not loiter."

I carried the letters into the house and found Amma sitting on her bed. A book lay unopened in front of her and she was examining her knees. She looked as if she had not yet bathed even though it was late in the afternoon; her hair was greasy and unkempt. She had closed the curtains and a patch of light, dull and unflattering as dirty dishwater, squeezed through an opening and fell across her weary face.

"Letter from Aba," I said casually, and dropped it in her lap.

I wanted to wait and watch her read it, but as if sensing my intentions she said: "Thank you, molay, now run along."

I meant to obey, but I found that when I tried, I could not move from the spot. My mind kept replaying the scene I had witnessed the night before between Amma and Prem, how she had actually allowed that man to kiss her. The words seemed to spill out of their own accord, harsh and accusatory even to my own ears:

"You were never planning on going back to Aba, were you?"

"Rakhee." She stared at me with wide, blank eyes. "Why would you say such a thing?"

"Because it's true, isn't it? And you know what I think about that, Amma? It's stupid. Look how sad you are here.

If we could just go back home, I know it would all be okay and that you could be happy again."

Amma had been watching me speak in silence, but then her face changed and she spoke, spitting out the words: "Happy! When have I been happy? What do you know of my happiness?"

I stumbled back, startled by the bitter tone of her voice.

Amma covered her face with her hands and let out an anguished moan. Then she began to rub her temples with quick, manic strokes. After a few moments, she became still again, and sighed deeply. Her voice was hoarse.

"I'm sorry, molay, I don't know what I'm saying. Forgive me, I am not well right now. We shouldn't be discussing this. Why don't you leave me be for a while. I must rest."

I went back to my room and sat on the edge of the bed, overcome. Part of me was furious at Amma, but the other part still loved her, wanted to put my arms around her neck and protect her. I couldn't give up so easily. I needed to make Amma see reason.

A long time passed before I remembered the letter I was still holding in my hands. It was even more crumpled than before, and I realized I had been squeezing the paper in my fists. I smoothed it out and began to imagine Aba speaking to me, his familiar voice a balm to my injured soul.

> *My dear Rakhee,*
>
> *How are you? I hope you're enjoying yourself.*
>
> *I'm keeping fine, but I do miss you. I have been busy at work so I don't have much time to feel lonely. I think I might be on the verge of a really exciting discovery at the lab—I'll tell you all about it when you get back.*

Veena Aunty has been bringing food over once a week so I'm not starving to death, and she is almost as good a cook as your mother.

How is everything over there? Have you been settling in all right? How is your mother? Please let me know if you feel worried about anything at all.

It will be good to have you home again. Merlin says "hi" and that he misses you too (he sleeps on your bed every night).

Love, Aba

His words were simple, strong, unsentimental. I could almost feel Aba's hand on my shoulder and his wise, handsome face lost in thought, the way it was when he helped me with my science homework: *Well, this is quite a quandary, isn't it? But don't worry, there's always a solution, Rakhee. There's always a way out.*

I held the letter in my hands, rubbing my fingers across the paper. In a flood of emotion, I brought it to my face and inhaled deeply, the way Muthashi did when she embraced me. It smelled clean and fresh, like home.

~

Early the next morning, just as I began to rouse myself from the depths of sleep, I heard my bedroom door creak open and soft footsteps padding across the floor toward me. I shut my eyes and pressed my arms against my side, stiff and alert as a soldier.

"Are you awake?" It was Amma.

I opened my eyes.

"Me too," she said. "I can't sleep." She pulled the sheet back, crawled into bed next to me, and held me close. I felt her tear-stained cheek pressed against mine, and her hot breath in my ear.

"Please forgive me, molay. I'm sorry for shouting at you yesterday. I wasn't myself. You know how much I love you, don't you?"

I didn't say anything.

"Oh, you're still mad at me. I don't blame you. I've been awful, haven't I? Let me make it up to you—why don't we hire a car and drive into town today for ice cream? Meenu and Krishna can come along, too—would you like that?"

"I guess so." The idea of getting away for a few hours seemed too appealing to pass up.

My cousins were giddy at breakfast.

"Why are you not smiling, Rakhee? We are going for ice cream. Sweet, delicious ice cream!" said Meenu.

Gitanjali, who was joining us on our excursion, had dressed up in a fancy blue salwar kameez, and I detected a hint of unnatural red rubbed onto her lips.

"Why are you dressed like that? One of your simple cotton saris will do well enough for a trip into town," said Sadhana Aunty, glancing up from her cup.

Gitanjali ignored her mother and sat down. "Fine, I'll change after breakfast," she said.

Amma entered the dining room, wearing a pale green sari with her hair in a glamorous bun.

"Is Muthashi coming with us?" I asked her.

"No, I'm afraid not. She's getting too old to handle these long drives, especially in this heat," she said. "Is everyone ready?"

Muthashi stood up eagerly from her place at the head of the table.

Amma and Sadhana Aunty exchanged looks.

"But, you're staying here, at home, with Sadhana Chechi," said Amma in a soothing tone.

"Yes, I need you here with me today," added Sadhana Aunty, standing up and moving toward Muthashi.

"But I want to go. Why can't I go?" Muthashi's voice cracked. Again, she reminded me of a child.

"It's too far," said Amma. "You'll get tired."

"No, I will not. I'm going to go. I want to go! Let me fetch my shawl." Muthashi shuffled out of the room.

"You'd better all hurry up and leave," said Sadhana Aunty with a sigh. "Gitanjali, there's no time to change now—just go as you are."

"But what about Muthashi?" Krishna said.

"Don't worry about Muthashi. Come." Amma herded us out the door.

At the bottom of the front steps, a black car was waiting on the road, and the driver leaned against the door with his back to us, whistling a tune. When he heard us approaching he turned around and I saw that it was not a driver, it was Prem.

I grabbed Amma's arm. "What's *he* doing here?"

"Rakhee, stop being rude. Prem Uncle has kindly offered to drive us," Amma said in a low voice, and shot me a warning glance.

"Everybody in," said Prem, pretending he hadn't heard this exchange, and my cousins happily piled into the backseat. I squeezed in beside Krishna.

Before I could further indulge my anger by slamming the door, I heard Muthashi's frail voice.

"Come back," she called. "No!"

We all turned to see her struggling down the steps toward the car. "Wait!" she cried. "I want to go."

Before she could reach the bottom step, Sadhana

Aunty caught up, looped a firm arm around her waist, and pulled her back. "Go, go now," she said, waving her free hand at us.

"You'd better start the car, Prem," Amma said in a soft voice.

"No, wait for me!" I heard Muthashi wail as we drove off.

I turned around and through the back window I saw her standing, a pathetic figure in white. I watched her until we turned the corner and she disappeared.

We drove in silence. I stared out the window and watched an auto rickshaw holding two sari-clad women whip in front of our car at top speed and career around a corner.

Finally, Gitanjali spoke: "Thank you for driving us, Prem Uncle."

"You're very welcome," Prem said. "It gives me a chance to get out for a day. You know, it's been years since I've been back here, and after the madness of Trivandrum, the slow village life can be a bit too much to take in long stretches."

"Trivandrum? What's there to do in Trivandrum?" asked Meenu, leaning forward and resting her chin on the front seat.

"I teach English at a college there."

"Prem is a very talented poet," said Amma.

Meenu, who seemed bored by this response, reclined and began twiddling her thumbs.

But now I was curious. "Why did you come back here then? Especially if you like big cities?"

"Well…" Prem paused for a moment. Then he cleared his throat and said with his usual confidence, "My parents are getting old and I'm their only child. It's my duty to come back and see them from time to time."

"How *are* your parents doing?" said Amma. "I feel terrible. I've been so wrapped up in things at Ashoka that I still haven't had time to pay them a visit." Amma's tone rang false to me—I knew she had not been busy—and it must have sounded so to Prem as well.

"They are doing fine—though getting old and a bit lonely. They would love to see you. Why don't we stop by on our way back from town?"

Amma did not answer him. Instead she turned around and gave me a smile. "Rakhee, did you know Prem's father used to work with Muthashan at the hospital?"

"Yes, and they were the best of friends," Prem added. "So, it's settled, then, we'll visit them later this afternoon."

Amma opened her mouth as if to protest, but then closed it again and began to stare out the window.

When we arrived in town Prem let us out in front of a dress shop while he parked the car. An excess of stalls crowded the streets, which were clogged with mustachioed men and women swathed in bright saris and salwar kameez, their shiny black hair wound into pendulous braids that emanated the pungent scent of coconut oil.

"Let me just browse until Prem returns," said Amma. We followed Amma into the shop, and I marveled at the stacks and stacks of neatly folded fabrics in brilliant hues and various textures. The man and woman behind the counter who had been conversing casually leaped to attention when they saw Amma.

"Hello, madam, how may we help you?" said the man in exaggerated, saccharine English.

Amma sat down in a chair the woman offered her and waved away the tumbler of lime juice she held out on a tray.

The man immediately began pulling out the bolts of

fabric from the shelf, one by one, with the verve of a magician, destroying his carefully organized stacks. He spread them out one after the other on the counter for Amma to peruse.

"I'm going to get married in this," said Meenu, picking up a gaudy magenta-and-gold-bordered sari and wrapping it around her head with a flourish.

"If anyone even marries you at all," said Krishna.

Meenu dropped the cloth back onto the counter and went after Krishna, who let out a peal of laughter and began a game of dodging her irate sister.

While my cousins were thus occupied, I glanced out the shop window and saw Gitanjali standing outside talking with a boy. He was thin and well groomed, with a shy face and a shadow of a mustache on his upper lip; he was carrying a couple of books under one arm. I had never seen Gitanjali so animated before and wondered who he might be. She abruptly ended the conversation when Prem rounded the corner, then ducked into the store and began fingering one of the saris as if she had been there the entire time.

"Ready for ice cream?" Prem approached the counter and put a hand on my shoulder. I shrugged away from him and went to stand beside Amma, who was pulling a wad of rupees from her purse. The shopkeeper wrapped her purchase—a simple white sari with a wide gold border—in a plastic cover.

"This is a typical Kerala-style sari," Amma told me.

"It will look beautiful on you," said Prem, and while Amma did not look up or thank him, I saw her smile.

On the way home, after we had filled our bellies with ice cream, we stopped by Prem's parents' house.

"Why do I have to go? Can't you just drop me off at

Ashoka first?" I grumbled to Amma. She gave my ear a pinch and told me I had better be polite.

Prem parked the car on the road at the bottom of a hill not far from Ashoka, and we had to climb up a steep, wooded incline to reach the house.

"This is it," he said, when we made it to the top.

Prem's parents' house was small and shrouded in gangly trees. A thunderous bark erupted from a cage at the side of the house as we approached. A fierce-looking German shepherd bared his teeth at me through the bars.

"Quiet, Striker, quiet. These are friends," said Prem, and the dog, hearing his master's voice, flattened himself at the bottom of the cage and began to pant. Out of nowhere, a white-haired woman appeared and began to rattle a ring of keys in front of the dog's cage.

"Look, it's crazy Hema," Krishna whispered, nudging me.

Hema, with faded white widow's cotton wrapped around her shriveled frame and disheveled hair, shook the keys and made cooing sounds to the dog, as if it were a baby.

Prem's parents, roused by the commotion, came out onto the verandah. His father was tall and solemn, with a full head of gray hair and thick, Coke-bottle glasses. Although he looked as if he had once been a sturdy, handsome man, he now leaned heavily on a cane and his skin sagged on his frail bones. Prem's mother was short—about the same height as me, but rotund. She had curly gray hair with ragged bald patches the size of postage stamps spread across her scalp, and eyes blued and cloudy with cataracts.

"Hema, that's enough. Leave the dog be," said Prem in a firm but kind voice. Hema turned to examine us with unfocused eyes and muttered something under her breath.

"You can go now, Hema," Prem said. "Thank you."

Hema continued to stare with that vague, soft look in her eyes until Prem's father cleared his throat loudly and Hema slunk away behind the house.

Krishna and I exchanged looks.

Amma went over to Prem's parents as if nothing out of the ordinary had just happened, and bent down low to touch their feet.

"Uncle. Aunty," she said.

They each in turn put their arms around her and embraced her, like a prodigal daughter.

"Namaste Uncle and Aunty," said Gitanjali, bringing her hands together as if in prayer. Meenu and Krishna both did the same thing.

Prem's parents nodded their heads at them, and turned to me.

"Is this Chitra's daughter?" said the mother.

"Yes, this is my daughter, Rakhee," said Amma.

"What a nice child." Prem's mother smiled, and extended her hand to rub my cheek with a palm rough as bark. "Come, come inside," she said with great animation, and bustled into the house.

The sitting room was cramped and dimly lit by two small windows, but in spite of the shabby furnishings the floors were spotless and the wooden tables had been polished to an immaculate shine. The walls were painted blue and were spotted with stains. A photograph of my grandfather was prominently displayed in a gold frame.

"Sit, sit," said Prem's mother before disappearing into the kitchen. I sat down between Amma and Krishna on

the couch, which was long and hard as a bone. My backside began to ache.

Prem's mother returned with a large plate piled high
with an assorted selection of sweets. I wondered how long
the plate of sweets had been sitting in the kitchen, pa-
tiently waiting for guests to serve.

"Oh, Aunty, we don't need all this," Amma said. "We
just came to see you. You should save these for a special
occasion." But Prem's mother looked so horrified at the
suggestion that we each took a proffered sweet.

"Look at you both. How nice to see you together
again," said Prem's mother, beaming and glancing between Amma and Prem. "What friends you used to be!
Rakhee, did you know that when Prem went off to college,
your mother was so frantic she would not let go of his
hand and we had to tear her away. She cried so hard afterward she made herself sick."

Prem's father cleared his throat, and Prem looked
down at the floor.

"Well, it's probably time we head back to Ashoka," said
Amma, and I felt mortified by her brisk tone. "I'm sorry
this has been such a short visit, but Sadhana Chechi will
start to worry."

Prem's mother protested, saying how could we think of
leaving without eating dinner, but Amma was insistent, so
we left.

Chapter 10

I watched Amma wrap yard after yard of primrose pink silk around her waist. She was going out for the day, with Sadhana Aunty and Nalini Aunty, to visit friends in town. They were leaving us under the care of Gitanjali, who had been instructed by Sadhana Aunty to make sure Meenu and Krishna completed their two hours of study, and after that to see that we didn't spend too much time outside in the sun—we were already dark as it was.

"I've been dreading this, but it has to be done," said Amma, more to herself than to me, as she tucked the pleats of her sari into her beige underskirt. "People will talk if I don't go and see them and act as if everything is normal. Stupid gossips." She went over to the mirror and stared at her face—pale and tired, but still exquisite. She pinched her cheeks, blinked a few times, then took the round red bindi she had stuck on the smudged glass the night before and positioned it at the center of her forehead. Like a third eye, I thought.

I followed Amma outside, where Sadhana Aunty and Nalini Aunty were waiting near the front steps, both in stiff saris. Balu, who was perched in his usual spot on his mother's hip and playing with her braid, looked like a little man in his checked, button-down shirt with his tufts of hair slicked to one side.

Amma kissed my forehead with her cool, soft lips before she disappeared down the stairs. I went to join my cousins, who were assembled on the verandah.

"You all don't need me, do you?" Gitanjali looked around at the three of us as soon as the hum of the car motor grew distant. "I'm going to go read in my room, so don't do anything that will get us into trouble," she warned before stalking into her bedroom and closing the door.

We decided to go see what Muthashi was up to and found her in her bedroom, lying on her back with her bare feet splayed out to both sides. The top of her sari had unraveled, revealing the loose, defeated flap of her stomach. It looked as if she was just staring up at the rattling old ceiling fan without blinking, but then Krishna told me that Muthashi sometimes slept with her eyes open.

We spent the rest of the morning on the verandah, too exhausted by the growing heat to practice our play, or to even move. Swatting flies away was an effort. Janaki brought idlis and chutney, along with a pitcher of water, out to us on a round tray. By afternoon, the heat had become unbearable; it was by far the hottest day I can recall that summer.

"I can't sit around here like this—I'll go crazy," Meenu finally said, her body stretched across the swing. She wiped a ribbon of sweat from her forehead with the back of her hand and sighed. Krishna was slumped on a chair, with her mosquito-bitten legs spread out at an unladylike angle, fanning herself with a dust-laced comic book. I had laid myself down on the ground and pressed my cheek against the cool floor, for once not caring about dirt or bugs.

Vijay Uncle was down at the hospital, and Hari had taken the cows and goats out to the paddy field to graze. A thin cat with a mottled brown coat lay on the verandah step and licked the previous night's rainwater from a cracked flowerpot. Even the birds, whose various cackles and coos issued from the surrounding trees with unceasing frequency most days, had retreated, leaving the yard in silence.

"We have to do something." Meenu sat upright and a mischievous smile spread across her face. "I know! Let's go for a swim."

Sadhana Aunty had specifically forbidden us from swimming in the river because the monsoon rains had caused the water levels to surge. "The last thing I need on my hands is a drowned child," she had said.

"But what if the grown-ups find out?" said Krishna. "And won't Gitanjali Chechi worry if we disappear?"

"No one is going to find out. The grown-ups are not returning until evening. Who knows where Vijay Uncle is, and Gitanjali Chechi doesn't care what we do. I bet she won't even notice we're gone. She's too busy daydreaming about her boyfriend." Meenu emphasized the word *boyfriend* in a singsong voice and stuck out her tongue in disdain.

Krishna looked shocked for a moment, then giggled and glanced sideways at me.

"Anyhow," Meenu hopped off the swing, "no one ever said the two of you had to join me. I can go by myself." She skipped over the half-comatose cat, down the steps, and began strutting across the lawn. When neither of us made a move to follow her, she paused, her two braids swinging over her shoulders as she turned to face us. "Do you actually mean to stay here all day and burn to death? Stop being such bores—come along!"

I turned to Krishna. She shrugged her shoulders and grinned.

Together we scurried across the road, the giddy thrill of rebellion propelling our limbs through the sluggish heat. We decided to cut through the luxuriant overgrowth of bushes and trees behind the hospital to get to the river, but a gathering of people on the hospital's front lawn temporarily distracted us from our mission.

"What's going on?" Meenu pushed herself into the crowd and we followed. A young man was crouched on the ground in the center of the circle, clutching his gut and groaning. The women surrounding him were in various states of distress.

"Help him!" one of them sobbed, as the man's eyes rolled into the back of his head and he appeared to lose consciousness. "He's my son, help him!"

Vijay Uncle came running outside, accompanied by a young woman, and the crowd parted to let them through.

"What happened?" he asked the young woman, as he knelt beside the man and clasped his limp wrist.

"He had stomach pain all morning, but I did not think anything of it. We should have brought him in earlier," she said.

After asking the woman a series of questions about her husband's eating and bowel habits, Vijay Uncle hurried back inside and reemerged moments later with two glass bottles containing a bronze-colored liquid. He unscrewed the cap of one of the bottles, bent over the man, coaxed his mouth open, and released a few small drops of the liquid onto his tongue. Then he tilted the man's chin back and poured some more down his throat. We stood around waiting in anxious silence, and after about fifteen minutes the man's lids fluttered and opened.

"Thank God," a voice cried, and the crowd began to cheer. Vijay Uncle helped the man sit up and handed him one of the bottles.

"Take one ounce of this three times a day before every meal for five days. That should do it," he said. The man nodded and bowed his head in gratitude.

The mother and the young woman rushed forward and fell to the ground, touching Vijay Uncle's feet. "Thank you, Doctor, thank you," they wept.

Vijay Uncle's face flushed with pride. It was the first time I had seen Ayurvedic medicine being used to heal a patient. The whole scene had felt so magical, so foreign to anything that happened within the sterile white walls of the Plainfield Clinic. I could not fathom why Vijay Uncle, who had never looked more vigorous than he did in that moment, spent more of his time at the toddy shop than at the hospital.

"Come on, the fun's over. Let's go," said Meenu, grabbing both Krishna and me by our arms and leading us away.

When we reached the red banks we stopped to catch our breath and gazed down at the water. The prospect of entering the crisp churning waves below subdued the intensity of what we had just witnessed. Meenu pulled out her ribbons and ran her fingers through her hair, releasing the strands from the tight confines of their braids.

She looked at us. "Jump!"

Both my cousins laughed, tossed off their sandals, and left their dresses behind, as they leaped into the water with two great splashes.

"Come on, Rakhee!" Meenu doused me with a flush of water. "Don't be a baby." I peeled off my skirt, folded it, took off my glasses, and laid them down on top. Curling my toes, I hesitated at the edge of the bank.

"It feels so good, come in!" said Krishna.

I took a deep breath and jumped into the water, my limbs flailing as I fell. My long, loose T-shirt billowed out around my waist.

I ducked my head beneath the surface, ashamed of the tender nubs on my chest that the shock of cold water had exposed beneath the cotton.

I opened my eyes and even without my glasses I could see the perfectly rounded stones at the bottom of the river, the clouds of mud that puffed up through the cracks between the stones, the schools of miniature fish that flashed by like zippers. I thought I saw the white whip of a water snake, but when I blinked it was gone. I rose to the surface with a sense of panic growing in my chest.

"Are there any snakes in this river?"

"Don't be silly. Of course not," said Meenu.

I let myself relax, floating on my back and flapping my arms at my sides to prevent the current from carrying me off too far. The water lapped in and out of my ears; every now and then it covered my face. A network of spindly branches fringed with tapering leaves stretched out overhead like a swath of lace. The sky was a searing blue.

It reminded me of the feeling I got one summer afternoon when I ate two cartons of blueberries in a single sitting even though Amma had warned me not to. They were so juicy, so sweet as they slid down my throat, and even though I knew that they would cause me pain later, I couldn't stop sucking them down, one after the other, until my mouth was stained a grotesque purple and my stomach was full of pins and needles.

I wished I could stay in that moment, that I could drift like that forever, and that the sick feeling would never come. If I could somehow preserve it, then Aba would set all his mice free in a field and Amma would kiss *him* in a patch of moonlight. If I could lie like that on my back forever, staring up into the spotless cape of sky, then the cottage in the forest behind Ashoka wouldn't exist; there would be no garden, and most of all, there would be no monster inside it for Amma and Sadhana Aunty to hide.

"Rakhee, come back here." Meenu's distant voice broke the silence. "We want to have a contest. Who can stay underwater the longest?" Wheeling around, I found my footing on the river bottom and paddled back toward my cousins. It was harder than I expected, making my way through the water, swimming against the thick current, and I felt a twinge of fear about what we were doing.

We formed a circle of three, grasped hands, and plunged beneath the surface, sinking downward together, our cheeks puffed out, our hair flying upward like black jellyfish. Krishna did not last very long—I saw her pop up out of the water after about ten seconds. Meenu released my hand and stared me down. Her eyes and cheeks bulged, fishlike, and her hair swirled around her head; she looked like an underwater Medusa. I squeezed my eyes shut. Soon I began to feel light-headed, but I didn't want to give up. I tried to think of something other than my choking desire for air.

1,2,3,4,5, I counted in my head. Everything was still and quiet.

I opened my eyes and Meenu was gone. Again, I saw something white rippling through the water, past my head, and then brushing its slimy length against my arm.

I shot out of the water, my skin crawling. "Snake! It's a snake! Get out!" I yelled to Krishna, as I struggled through the water and pulled myself onto the bank. Gasping and with a spinning head, I scrambled toward where our clothes lay and heard Krishna, out of breath at my heels.

"Where's Meenu Chechi?"

We looked around. She was nowhere in sight.

"Meenu! Meenu!" We ran up and down across the exposed stretch of riverbank, the grizzled grass that poked through the sand nicking at our ankles. The current seemed even stronger now that I watched it flow furiously from above.

"Oh my God, she's drowned!" Krishna began to wail.

"Meenu!" I called once more. Even amid the sound of rushing water and Krishna's whimpers, an eerie quiet pervaded the air. Just as I was about to slink down beside my cousin, my body limp, I heard a loud splash and a gasping for air, followed by a triumphant laugh.

"I win! I win!" Meenu emerged from the river naked and dripping wet, waving her white slip in the air like a banner. "Rakhee, you should have listened to me. I told you there were no snakes in this river." She flashed her mischievous grin once more, and I realized that what had appeared to my impaired eyes to be a snake had actually been nothing more than Meenu's petticoat.

"Chechi, it's not funny! You frightened us—I thought you were dead!" Krishna's bottom lip quivered.

"Oh don't be so upset, it was just a joke," said Meenu, squeezing the water from her petticoat.

Now that we were over our immediate shock, Krishna and I became aware of Meenu's nakedness. We looked down at our feet, embarrassed by what we saw—the full, round breasts that she hid so well under her dresses and the thatch of dark hair between her legs. She was suddenly not Meenu Chechi anymore, she was a woman, like Amma, like Sadhana Aunty.

Meenu grew self-conscious and pulled her sopping wet petticoat and dress over her head.

"I'll give you one more chance to win," she said quickly, "How about a game of hide-and-seek?"

"No, I don't feel like playing any more games, I'm going back home." Krishna let out a sob, turned abruptly, and ran back toward Ashoka.

"How about you, Rakhee? Are you going to be a coward as well?" She arched one brow.

"I'll play. What are the rules?"

We agreed that Meenu would have ten minutes to find a hiding spot back at the house, and I had half an hour to find her.

Meenu ran laughing into the forest.

At first I thought about following her in stealth, discovering her hiding place right away, and humiliating her. But then I remembered how Aba always told me, "Never fight fire with fire." So instead I found a shady spot under some trees to wait. I examined my arms and legs, noticing that they had browned significantly over the course of the day; I hoped Sadhana Aunty wouldn't notice.

After the swim and Meenu's brush with death, my seat under the trees was as cool and comfortable as a bed. I pushed the pebbles that sprinkled the dirt out from under my bottom and leaned back against a tree trunk, resting my head against it. I closed my eyes.

When I woke up, the sun was already hanging low in the sky, an angry orange ball preparing to sink. Meenu was going to kill me. I started to get up, ready to run back home, hoping to make it before Amma returned, until I realized I was not alone. A group of servant women from Ashoka had gathered by the river and settled on their haunches next to heaps of clothes, some of which I recognized as my own.

They were washing the clothes in the river, roughly and efficiently, then standing and slapping them dry on rocks. Each time they brought a piece of cloth down upon the rock it made a resilient *thwack*. It was almost a dance: the women in their stained, monochromatic saris, their prematurely graying hair pulled back into frazzled buns, crouching, washing, standing, and beating, the rhythm of their movements imbued with a surprising grace.

There was no way I could slip away without their seeing me, so I settled back into my spot in the shadows, which was now no longer so comfortable. For a while they washed the clothes and folded them in tidy piles, quiet and intent in their work. When they had finally finished, streaks of pink and purple bruised the sky.

"Leave, leave," I said under my breath.

But instead the women sat down on the ground with their knees up and began chatting, so I had to remain in hiding until, finally, as it grew darker they stood, gathered up their stacks of clothing, balanced the piles upon their heads, and began to make their way back to the house, winding through the trees in a single-file line. I was about to slink away after them when I saw a lone figure still standing at the edge of the river. The color of the sky was now so deep that the figure was nothing but a forlorn silhouette. But I knew right away that it was Hema. I knew her by that wild white hair and those long, praying hands that trembled in the windless air. A brown sack lay in a puddle at her feet. A thrill of fear and excitement shot through me.

She remained by the banks for only a few moments before she picked up the sack, turned around, and began heading back. Quietly I followed, now no longer concerned about Meenu's being angry or Amma's getting home before me.

Hema made her way through the shadowy thicket of trees with unexpected agility, clutching the sack against her sagging breast. I was out of breath from the effort of trying to keep up with her without making too much noise. She paused at the front steps of the hospital, looked both ways as if she were a child about to cross a busy street, then went inside to the office where Dev usually sat, the office that had once belonged to Muthashan. She went in with such familiarity that I got the feeling this was something she had done before. I huddled in the long, unlit hallway and poked my head into the office. Hema's back was toward me, and she was standing before the portrait of my grandfather that hung high up on the wall, gazing up at it with such reverence in her eyes. There was something so alive, so piercing, about that look that she suddenly didn't even seem all that crazy to me.

She began muttering something under her breath, a prayer, perhaps. All the while muttering, she tucked the sack into the waist of her sari, and went over to the heavy wooden chair where I had seen Dev once sit. She dragged it over to the wall, removed her sandals, and stood upon it so that she was at eye level with the portrait. A garland of faded brown flowers encircled the frame. Hema removed the old garland and tossed it down upon the desk. Then out of the sack she had been carrying, she pulled a fresh garland of white jasmine buds, so fragrant I could detect their perfume from where I stood. Carefully she hung the garland around the frame, climbed down off the chair, returned it to the desk, and swept the old, crumbled blossoms into the sack. She was so wrapped up in her own private world that when she left she didn't even see me flattened up against the wall. For the first time I felt truly sorry for her.

Chapter 11

After Hema left, I went into the office and sat down at the desk. I felt very small behind it. An old phone—the only working one in the village—was perched on top of some books.

A few days before, Amma had overheard me asking Vijay Uncle if I could use the phone to call Aba and she had chastised me. "Rakhee, do you know how expensive it is to make phone calls to America? And besides, the connection is terrible. I told your father that we wouldn't be calling unless it was an emergency....He'll worry if you go phoning him now. Why don't you just write a letter instead?"

A letter was not enough. This was not exactly an emergency, but I wanted to hear his voice so badly, and I knew he would be happy to hear mine. I began dialing the number on the old-fashioned wheel.

"Please be home, please be home," I whispered. After several rings he picked up.

"Hello?" His voice sounded scratchy from disuse, but my heart leaped at the sound of it.

"Aba, it's me," I blurted, and to my annoyance, tears filled my eyes.

"Rakhee, is everything okay? Hello?" The connection was fuzzy and he sounded so far away.

"Yes Aba, everything's okay, I'm fine. I just wanted to talk to you."

"Thank goodness, you had me scared for a second. How are you? I can hardly hear you."

"Actually, Aba," and the tears really began to flow. I wanted to remove this burden I had been carrying around, to tell him all that was happening because he would know what to do. "It's Amma—" I stopped then because I heard my own voice bouncing back to me in an echo and Aba's voice saying, "Hello? Rakhee? Hello? Hello?"

"Yes Aba, I'm here—"

"Hello? Hello? Rakhee?"

"Aba? Aba?"

The line clicked and went dead.

I put my head down in my arms and was about to give in to my urge to sob, but the phone immediately rang again.

It was Aba.

"Rakhee, what is going on? I'm concerned. Are you sure everything is fine? Your mother, she is well?"

I paused. This was my big chance, but I choked. The words would not come and I heard myself saying, "Yes, Aba, everything is fine. Amma's doing great. I just got bored and thought I'd call."

"I'm glad you did, Rakhee," said Aba, before the line grew fuzzy again and finally went dead.

I clenched my fists, furious at myself for chickening out. Maybe I *should* write him a letter, I thought. Maybe it would be easier to explain everything that way.

Opening the top desk drawer, I searched for paper

but found only a few chewed-up pens and pencils. The next drawer was full of notebooks, but all the pages were covered in small numbers written in a meticulous hand. I took the notebooks out of the drawer, hoping to find some blank sheets underneath, but there was only bare, dingy wood.

The overhead tube light flickered, and a mosquito settled upon my arm. I slapped at it but missed, and it skittered away. An ugly red bump appeared in the spot where it had been sitting. I suddenly felt scared, sitting alone at night like that in the hospital. Reality came back to me, and I remembered that my cousins were probably wild with worry, and that Amma might already be home and that she would be furious.

It was time to go back.

Gathering up the notebooks, I started to put them back in the drawer, but as I slid them inside they bumped up against something hard. I reached in and pulled out the obstructing object—a small, carved wooden box, encased in a fine layer of dust. It looked as if it hadn't been touched in years. The lid opened easily and inside it was a pile of folded-up papers and letters. I flipped through them, one after the other. Most of them were letters and fragments of paper written in the funny, indecipherable curlicues of Malayalam script, but one of the letters, written on brittle yellow paper, was in English.

I hesitated, but the temptation was too strong. I stuck the letter into my T-shirt pocket and put the box and the notebooks back into the drawer. I turned off the light, and began to run with all my might back toward Ashoka, trying not to think too much about the darkness surrounding me and whatever might be lurking in that darkness.

When I got back to the house, my three cousins were

waiting for me on the verandah. Krishna's eyes were red and puffy, Meenu was pacing back and forth, and Gitanjali was sitting on a chair with her head in her hands.

"Rakhee!" Krishna jumped up.

Meenu stopped pacing and Gitanjali came swiftly toward me. At first I thought she was mad, but then she put her arms around my neck, pressed the side of my head into her stomach, and exhaled.

"Where have you been? I was just about to go find Vijay Uncle and tell him you were missing. Do you know how much trouble we would have been in? Where on earth did you go?"

I told them I had fallen asleep by the river—which was partly true—and had woken up only after dark. Even though I felt sorry to have worried them, part of me was touched that they cared so much, especially Gitanjali. I had always secretly wished for an older brother or sister, an ally who understood me and looked out for me, and for a fleeting moment Gitanjali's embrace made me feel that I did indeed have one.

Krishna sniffled and linked my arm with hers as we walked up the verandah steps.

"My mom's not home yet?" I asked.

"Thankfully no," said Gitanjali. "Now listen, all of you, we can't let on that anything went wrong today. For all they know, you spent the day reading and studying, okay?"

We all agreed, and by the time the grown-ups returned we were bathed and dressed in our pajamas, sipping milk at the dining table.

Amma stroked the top of my head. "Rakhee, I'm exhausted, I'm going to bed. You had a nice day?" She didn't wait for a response, just gave me a feeble kiss and left the room.

Nalini Aunty was uncharacteristically subdued. Balu

was sleeping in her arms, his small head nestled into her shoulder. "Where is your uncle?" she asked us. "Hasn't he come home yet?"

"No, Aunty, we have not seen him," replied Gitanjali.

Nalini Aunty sighed, and I wanted to tell her about what had happened at the hospital earlier that day so she would know that Vijay Uncle had done more than just drink at the toddy shop, but before I could say anything she left the room.

Sadhana Aunty clapped her hands. "It's getting late. It's time for you girls to go to sleep."

Krishna looked up at her mother. "What about you? Aren't you going to bed?"

"No," she replied, her mouth set into a grim line. "No, I have a few things to get done."

Sadhana Aunty was always the first one to get up in the morning and the last one to retreat at night. I wondered if she even slept at all. Somehow I couldn't imagine her lying down on that stiff bed, wrapping the thin cotton sheet around her exhausted body, letting her head rest on a pillow, closing her eyes, and surrendering to sleep.

"Good night, everybody," said Gitanjali. We all dispersed to our respective rooms without looking at each other, as if somehow making eye contact would cause the real events of the day to spill forth.

I turned off the light in my room and climbed into bed with the letter I had stolen. Clutching my keychain flashlight, I lay flat on my stomach and made a tent around my head with the sheet. In my little glowing shroud I read the letter the way I read books at home: late at night, under the covers, long after Amma had told me to turn off the lights.

The letter was addressed to my grandfather.

7 November 1950

Dear Dr. Varma,

My name is Charles Henry Holloway, Sr. I am a physician and faculty member at Yale University in New Haven, Connecticut. You have likely never heard of me, but you may be surprised to find that I have heard of you.

During my travels to your part of the world, a good two decades ago, I became acquainted with a former professor of yours at Trivandrum Medical College, Dr. P. K. Ramaswamy. I recently wrote him a letter, seeking his advice on a matter of a rather delicate and personal nature, and he referred me to you, assuring me that you were not only a skilled physician but also a man of impeccable character whom I could count upon for complete discretion.

With this in mind I am writing this letter in good faith that you will keep the information I am about to reveal wholly confidential.

Twenty years ago, when I was still a young man, I came to India as a tourist, having always held a fascination for your country. I spent the majority of my time in the North, visiting the grand old palaces of Rajasthan and, of course, the Taj Mahal. Toward the end of my journey, I went south to Kerala and visited Trivandrum, where I met Dr. Ramaswamy at the medical college. He was a kind, hospitable man who invited me into his home. His wife cooked us a wonderful meal, and afterward we sat on the hot verandah, sipping scotch and engaging in a delightful conversation. It was through this discussion that I first became introduced to and fascinated by Ayurveda. Dr. Ramaswamy insisted on accompanying me on a tour of the rural regions of Kerala, where I was able to witness the practice of Ayurvedic medicine firsthand. I must admit at the time I was skeptical, even disdainful, thinking what I saw was nothing more than quackery, than tribal shamanism.

Two decades later, when the memory of that visit had long since faded and I had along the way acquired a wife and two children, I was forced to see a doctor about a relentless pain I was experiencing in my gut. I was thunderstruck to discover that I had what was suspected to be an advanced case of inflammatory bowel disease. I was told that I may need a complete removal of my colon and even that may not cure me.

The treatments I have been receiving, the Western medicine I have believed in so strongly for my entire adult life, are failing. I feel my body withering away and am frail beyond my years. But even as my body slowly dies, my mind is sharp as ever, as is my will to live and continue my exciting research. My hope is now invested in the alternative medicine which has been time-tested in your country.

Now that you have heard the background of my predicament, let me tell you what I am proposing. I wish to know if your ancient Ayurvedic treatments can possibly cure me. Unfortunately I am too weak to travel, but may I persuade you to pay a visit to the United States to examine me and to offer whatever treatments you deem necessary? I would of course cover all your travel and living expenses. You would be very comfortable. Money is no obstacle. In addition, if you agree, I will also work with you and the Garrow Foundation to consider an endowment to establish a program at Yale dedicated to Ayurvedic research, and would champion you as the head of this program. Despite Connecticut being a much colder place than India, this would be an exciting and challenging opportunity for you and your wife.

I am almost ashamed at my desire to live longer. I am

*not a young man—sixty-five—and I have led a full life.
And yet, I am not ready to go. I want to live. According to
Dr. Ramaswamy, you are the best. You come from a long
line of Ayurvedic healers, and yet you also have modern
medical training.*

*I am willing to try anything, and my instincts are that
you could cure me.*

*Please consider my request and respond as quickly as
possible. As you now know, my time is limited.*

I anxiously await your response.

Cordially yours,

Charles H. Holloway, Sr.

I stared at the letter—at the thin, formal script written in blue ink, at the crisp, yellowing paper, at the network of creases, like the wrinkles on Muthashi's faded
cheeks. I imagined an old, sick man in a dark suit and
spectacles, huddled over a desk with an expensive foun-
tain pen. I pictured my grandfather reading the letter.
Somehow it was chilling to think that he might have
been the last one to have touched it, that my fingers
were on the very spot that his fingers had once been. In
spite of the heat, I shivered, and slid the letter under
my pillow.

The sound of shuffling feet and a chair being knocked
over on the verandah made me sit up. For a moment
there was silence. And then I heard the hollow, mournful
music of a solitary flute. It was a familiar tune, one that
Amma used to sing to me at my bedside when I was little.
She once told me it was a devotional song about Lord
Krishna. The melody was haunting, and I would hear it inside my head as I drifted further away from Amma's sweet
voice and deeper into sleep.

Following the music, I climbed out of bed and went out onto the verandah. Vijay Uncle didn't see me at first. He was sitting on the ground near the toppled chair, his back resting against the wall, playing a crudely fashioned wooden flute. I took one step back and the floor creaked.

Vijay Uncle dropped the flute and froze. "Who's there?"

"It's me," I said, stepping out into the moonlight. "It's just me."

Vijay Uncle sighed and placed his hand on his heart. "Rakhee, what are you doing up at this hour? You gave me a fright."

"Sorry, Uncle." I shifted my weight from one bare foot to the other.

"Well, seeing as you're awake, why don't you come and keep me company?" He patted the spot next to him.

I slid down onto the ground, and at once the heavy stench of alcohol draped itself over us like a cloak. I moved away a couple of inches but the smell did not dissipate.

"You are a night owl, I see," said Vijay Uncle. "I suspect that is another thing you inherited from yours truly. I'm glad of it. There's nothing sweeter than a clear, moonlit night. It's the only time I can really have any peace."

He seemed in a talkative mood, so I decided that this would be a good chance to find out more information.

"Vijay Uncle, do you know anything about a man named Charles Holloway?"

"Of course I do." He hiccupped and covered his mouth with his hands. "Please excuse me."

"Who was he? What do you know about him?"

Vijay Uncle laughed. "You really are a curious little monkey. I've never seen a child ask so many questions.

Good thing you're only here for a summer or we might have had a problem."

My heart thumped. "What do you mean by that?"

"Oh nothing, nothing at all, molay." Vijay Uncle ruffled my hair with a clumsy hand. "Anyhow, you were asking about Holloway. He was a friend of your grandfather's, well, more of a patron, really. He was extremely wealthy, and he brought Muthashan to America to cure him of some disease or other, and in the process grew fond of him and lavished him with riches. Muthashan was only there for six months but they grew very close during that time, a bit like father and son." Vijay Uncle snorted, rubbed his nose, and continued, "Holloway wanted Muthashan to move to America permanently—just before he died he offered him a position at Yale University, but Muthashan's family wouldn't allow him to take it. Not long before he sailed for America, you see, he had married Muthashi. She was still very young then, only a teenager, and he left her behind with his mother and three sisters. They were very resentful when he left, because his father had died a few months earlier and he was the only son. They relied on him for everything."

"Did they all live at Ashoka?"

"Ashoka? Heavens no. It hadn't even been built back then. No, they lived in our ancestral home, which is over four hundred years old. It's still standing today, and my three aunts still live there. The cranky old virgins. They never married."

"Where is the house? Why do we never see them?"

"It's only about a mile away from here. We do see them from time to time, but we were never close. Muthashan didn't much like having them around. Anyhow, after he wrote home telling his family of his good fortune and asking them to send Muthashi over to him, his sisters wrote him a letter, begging him to come home. Their mother was on her deathbed, they said, and was asking for him. So Muthashan came all the way back here to see his mother. She made him promise on the fate of her eternal soul that he would never leave again, that he would stay in Malanad and take care of his sisters, and that he would use his money and medical training to start a hospital in the village. She said his people needed him and he couldn't abandon his duty."

"So he never went back?"

"He never went back. Holloway died not long after he left. He did what his mother wanted but he never forgave his sisters for it. He was ambitious, you see, and had always dreamed of leaving the village behind. But his sense of duty was too strong, and ultimately he couldn't turn his back on his mother's dying wish. It turned him into a hard, bitter man, though. My grandmother may have thought she was doing the right thing by insisting he stay, but it was us, his children, that suffered for it, each in our own way."

His words had become increasingly slurred and now his eyelids were beginning to flicker.

"What do you mean?" I asked, hoping he wouldn't nod off just yet.

His head fell to one side and his lids shut, so I nudged his arm and he woke with a start.

"Huh? What?"

"How did you suffer?"

"Oh, yes, how I've suffered." Tears glistened in Vijay Uncle's eyes. "I hate him. I still hate him, can you believe it?" His head drooped, and for a second I thought he had fallen asleep again, but then he spoke. "Molay, the moon has grown dim. Creatures of the night as we are, I think it's time for us both to sleep."

"But Uncle, I'm not tired!"

"A young girl like you needs her beauty sleep, now off you go, off you go." He tried to stand and almost fell over. I quickly stood and tried to steady him but almost fell myself under the weight of his hand on my shoulder.

"There we go," he said, leaning against the wall, out of breath from the effort of getting up. "I'll stay here for a while, molay. But you? Off to bed." He waved me away with one hand, and realizing I wouldn't be able to get any more answers out of him, I obeyed.

Chapter 12

We set out for the ancestral house right after breakfast, hoping to get there and back before the afternoon sun grew too severe.

For much of the night I had stared up at the ceiling, turning over Vijay Uncle's words in my mind, wanting to know more. I wasn't sure why the house and Muthashan's three old sisters—my great-aunts—compelled me, but they seemed important. And Amma had never spoken of them—I had a feeling she wouldn't want me going there, and that only added fuel to my desire.

"But of all places, why *there?*" Krishna had asked, crinkling her nose at my suggestion.

"I'm curious, and besides, it's not as if we have anything better to do."

"That's true. But the old ladies—they frighten me."

"Maybe we won't even have to run into them," I lied. "I just want to see the outside of the house. I've never seen anything so old. Come on, it'll be an adventure."

"Well, all right, I suppose we can go," said Krishna, still looking rather reluctant.

"There's no way I'm stepping foot near that smelly old place," Meenu said, butting into our conversation.

We didn't try to convince her, but surely enough she came running after us, just as I had expected, as we made our way down the front steps.

"You two can't go by yourselves. You need someone older and wiser to take you. But you owe me a favor for doing this," she said, falling into step beside us.

We walked about half a mile down the main road, in the opposite direction of the village square. Along the way we saw a ginger-colored dog with a curly tail and a mangy coat lying on its side in the middle of the road. When it saw us it bounded up, its pale, saliva-coated tongue lolling.

It reminded me of Merlin, and I started toward it with my hand outstretched. Meenu jerked me back by the crook of my arm.

"Are you mad? You can't go around touching stray dogs. It's probably rabid, the disgusting beast. Shoo! Shoo!" she said to the dog. It whined and backed away, its ears drooping in disappointment.

We edged around it and continued to walk. After a few minutes had passed, Meenu stopped at the side of the road. "Ah, here we are."

"What do you mean?" I asked, perplexed.

"Don't you see the staircase? We have to climb this hill to get up to the house." Krishna pointed to a pile of stones wedged haphazardly into the side of a thickly forested hill.

As we climbed, a feeling of gloom settled over me. The unwieldy branches that formed a tangled archway over the path and the crooked steps covered in a carpet of moss told me that we were the first visitors the house had seen in a long time.

When we had reached the top of the hill we walked down another winding path, flanked on either side by shallow pools of tepid rainwater, and stopped only when we reached a clearing.

The house was dark and crumbling, with ragged eaves drooping down from the roof. It was made up of three different sections forming a U shape around a central courtyard. The lawn was overgrown with scraggly bushes and patches of weedy grass.

"I still don't understand why you wanted to come here," grumbled Meenu, leaning against the side of a ramshackle well to catch her breath.

"Yeah, it's even creepier than I remembered," said Krishna.

We heard a loud tapping sound.

"Who's out there?" said a gravelly old voice.

We froze.

The tapping grew louder.

"I didn't hear anything, Aunty," said a younger, softer voice.

"Well, I most certainly did hear something. Go out and see who it is. And don't call me Aunty. I am not your aunty," snapped the older voice.

"Yes, Aunty," said the younger voice.

"Quick, let's go," said Meenu, grabbing us both by the hand, but by then it was too late.

A young woman had come running outside and caught sight of us. She had squinty features, a low forehead, frizzy hair, and a wiry frame covered in a billowing floral housedress. Her frightened expression immediately softened into a jovial one.

"Ah, Aunty, it's only some children," she laughed, calling inside to the old voice within.

"Children? What children?" said the voice.

"Aren't you the girls from Ashoka? Gitanjali, right?

And Meenu?" she said, looking first at Meenu, then at Krishna.

"No, I'm Meenu and this is Krishna," said Meenu, drawing her brows together. "And this is our cousin Rakhee."

"Ah Rakhee, she is the one from America, no?" The young woman's eyes widened and she winked at me.

The voice from inside called out: "What? What are they saying? Who are they? Come inside and tell me at once, you impertinent girl!"

"Oh, she's angry, you'd all better come inside. She'll really give me a scolding if I send you away without at least inviting you in for something to drink. You are, after all, her brother's granddaughters."

"I think we'd better get home, actually," said Krishna, with a look of pure dread on her face.

"Oh no no, you mustn't leave. They'll kill me," said the woman, "Please, just come in, just for a little while."

The tapping started again, this time even angrier and more insistent.

We looked at one another. There was nothing else to be done, so we followed the young woman inside.

The room we entered was dark, so dark that for the second it took for my eyes to adjust I couldn't see a thing. A musty odor enveloped us, and slowly the room came into focus. It was relatively small and the windows were covered in rough brown fabric, thin enough to let in wan patches of diluted sunlight but thick enough to give the room a murky look. The ceiling was low and its broad rafters sparkled with cobwebs. Above the rafters was a cavernous space that rose up to a point at the rain-rotted roof. Three tattered sofas were arranged around a heavy stone table, and upon the sofas lay three very old, wizened women.

The woman lying on the sofa closest to the door was clutching a steel walking stick, and I realized that the gravelly voice belonged to her, and that the stick beating against the stone table had been the source of the tapping sound. She was the tiniest person I had ever seen, with shriveled skin and hair pulled back into a knot so sparse it reminded me of the small clumps of hair I sometimes left behind in the shower drain after a particularly vigorous shampooing, except hers was a dingy white. She didn't seem to have an ounce of fat on her body, only bones, jutting out sharply from her skin at odd angles, like gnarled tree branches.

"This is your Savitri Ammoomma," said the young woman. *Ammoomma,* I had learned, was another Malayalam word for "grandmother," like *Muthashi.*

The next woman, Sarojini Ammoomma, was also thin, with a curved spine and hunched shoulders. A marble-sized brown mole grew on her cheek, and bristly hairs swept across her chin. Her mouth was creased and sunken in, like a cave.

The last woman, Sharada Ammoomma, was significantly fatter than her sisters and had two pillowlike breasts so enormous they drooped down to her navel. Wispy gray hair danced around her head. She wore wire-rimmed spectacles and had a bulbous nose.

"So these are our little intruders," said Savitri Ammoomma, the old woman with the stick. "Come closer so I may see you."

None of us moved. The young woman gave us each a slight shove so that we were lined up in front of the sofa. Krishna was so close to me I could feel the hairs on her arms tickling my skin.

"Bend over," Savitri Ammoomma instructed, and this

time we obeyed. She ran her knotty fingers with their ridged, yellowing nails across Meenu's face and pushed her aside. She did the same thing to Krishna. When it was my turn, her fingers lingered on my face. They probed and examined every feature, they traced the frames of my glasses, they ran down along the side of my neck, and I couldn't help but shudder.

Savitri Ammoomma let out a dry chortle. "They're frightened of me, these children, frightened of their own dear great-aunt." She pointed a finger at me. "Sit, sit, won't you keep an old woman company?"

I perched beside her on the edge of the sofa.

"Won't someone sit beside me too?" said Sarojini Ammooomma, stretching out her trembling arms.

"And me too," Sharada Ammoomma called. Meenu and Krishna went and sat beside them, both with miserable expressions on their faces.

"Shanti, fetch some lime juice." Savitri Ammoomma ordered away the young woman with a weak wave of her wrist. "And how is your grandmother keeping?" she asked, turning to look at me with her cloudy yellow eyes.

"Um, she's fine, I guess," I mumbled.

"Eh? What in God's name are you saying? I cannot understand a word coming out of this girl's mouth. Didn't your mother teach you to speak Malayalam?"

I glanced at Krishna, then at Meenu, hoping one of them would step in, but the old women were already chatting away to them.

"No matter," said Savitri Ammoomma. "I can talk enough for the both of us. It has been a long time since we've had anyone to talk to but ourselves. Ourselves and that silly servant girl in there." She pointed her stick at the kitchen. "To think that we Varma women have sunk so low as to be cared for by that low-caste creature. When you see your Sadhana Aunty, tell her we are not happy with the girl she has sent to us. Not happy at all." She paused, shook her head from side to side like a little elephant, and puckered her withered lips in distaste. Then she turned to me again. "And how about your mother?"

I hesitated. "She's fine."

"Chitra. She was always such a beautiful girl. It's really too bad about that one. She could have made any match she wanted here. I suppose that is what happens when you let children run wild with no supervision. But your poor grandmother, I cannot think of blaming her, what could she have done? Such a sweet, simple girl she was back when she first married my brother. Sweet, yes, but cursed. Do you know that after Vijay she could never bear another child? She lost them, one after the other, one after the other. I suppose she didn't even have time to pay any attention to the children she did have, she was too busy losing babies."

I looked around the room to see if my cousins were hearing what I was hearing, but they were each involved in their own private conversations with Sarojini Ammoomma and Sharada Ammoomma. I was on my own.

"And your grandfather, my brother, he only cared about his oldest child, Sadhana," continued Savitri Ammoomma. "Oh yes, didn't care a whit about the other two, Chitra and Vijay. It was always 'Sadhana this, Sadhana that.' She was his pride and joy. 'She has the fire of intelligence in her eyes,' he used to say, 'not like the others. Her only fault is that she is a girl. But still, she will go far, she will marry well and run the hospital after I die. I can die in peace knowing it rests in her hands.' Chitra and Vijay were always running after him, trying to get his attention, but he would just brush them off, like insects."

Shanti came in with a tray of lime juice, and I took mine and gulped it down with relief. My throat had gone dry as the well in the yard outside.

"But all the blame cannot go on the parents, I suppose," continued Savitri Ammoomma after I had drained the contents of the glass. "There has to have been something wrong with Chitra from the start, some wildness in her blood that none of us could have ever predicted. I suppose it's all well and good that she escaped and a man would still have her after everything." She wagged her finger at me. "She has her mother to thank for that.

"The older one, Sadhana, now she wasn't nearly as lucky. Sadhana is just like her father, my brother— destroyed by pride. I used to have the Varma pride just as much as he did, we all did, but see where it has gotten us. What do we have to be proud of now? But Sadhana, as much as I dislike her, I do pity the girl. She never even had a chance at a good life. She disobeyed her father just once, and see what happened? She married that lazy cad she met at school and he abandoned her, just as we all knew he would. That is what happens when you send young girls to school, instead of marrying them off right away as God intended.

"I told my brother that, I warned him, but he wouldn't listen. Marry off the two girls, and educate the boy, I told him. But he wouldn't hear of it. As I said, he didn't care about the other two children. 'They don't have Sadhana's brains or her sense of family pride,' he said. 'No, Sadhana is the one who needs the education, and she will run the hospital after I die.'

"And then Sadhana defied him and married that low-caste villain, probably because he was the first man to ever cast a glance in her direction.

"Luckily he left her. Yes, it was a blessing, if you ask me. That man was worthless, just sitting around, smoking those cigarettes and reading nonsense, never lifting a finger to help out in the hospital. Clearly he was only interested in her wealth, and once he realized he would never see any of it, that it was all going to somebody else"—at this, Savitri Ammoomma paused and gave me a pointed stare so penetrating I had to look away—"he was gone. He left no trace. No matter, though, he was nothing but a burden, and Sadhana and the girls are surely better off without him.

"Little did she know she would spend the rest of her life trying to atone for that moment of weakness. Her marriage was her one act of rebellion and it broke her father's heart. She knew she had made a mistake right from the beginning when she returned to Ashoka with her new husband, her head lowered in shame, and fell to her father's feet, weeping. And he just looked down at her, then shook her away and went back inside. He didn't speak to her again. Not until he was on his deathbed did he forgive her. And his forgiveness did not come without a price." She gave a dramatic sigh.

"Alas, Sadhana has become what I call a hard woman—so proud, even prouder than her father, if that is possible. What I say is, if she would simply relinquish her pride, then maybe some of this family's troubles would end. But no, that will never happen, she will protect the Varma name until the day she dies, and by then, who knows what will have become of—"

Savitri Ammoomma stopped again, as if catching herself, then grasped my wrist with surprising strength and leaned forward. Her eyes grew clear as she stared right at me with a look that was at the same time knowing and searching. "We're all old and set in our ways, my child," she said. "It's too late for any of us. But you youngsters, you still have hope. Go and explore. Don't be afraid to search for the truth. There is nothing to fear."

I squirmed but she would not loosen her grip. "You know what I am saying, do you not? Just open your eyes and see what is before you." Her eyes grew cloudy again and she fell back upon the sofa cushion, releasing my wrist.

Shanti appeared at Savitri Ammoomma's side and placed her hand on her forehead. "Aunty? Aunty? Are you ill?" Then she looked at me, "She must be tired, she is not used to visitors. Perhaps we should let her rest now."

I was more than happy to let her rest, and so were my cousins.

"Come back and visit us again soon," Sharada Ammoomma said, as we stood in the doorway. Savitri Ammoomma had her eyes closed and seemed to be asleep; Sarojini Ammoomma was crying soundlessly.

"She hates saying good-bye," Shanti whispered to us in a confidential tone. "You'd better go quickly. It will be easier."

We went outside onto the lawn. The sun had disappeared behind a horde of clouds. "We'd better hurry," Meenu said.

Krishna eyed me with curiosity. "What was Savitri Ammoomma saying to you?"

"Oh, nothing. I could barely understand her," I said.

None of us uttered another word as we strode away from the house, but my mind was screaming.

Krishna had told me her father was dead, but really he

had abandoned them. Did Krishna know and just change the story out of shame, or had her mother actually told her that her father was dead?

Thunder lashed the sky and we quickened our pace to a run. The rain began to fall hard and heavy upon our heads, running down our shoulders.

What had Savitri Ammoomma meant when she told me to open my eyes?

"Hurry!" Meenu yelled.

As we ran, every now and then the darkness of the storm was broken by a streak of lightning that lit up the dripping trees and the red road that stretched out before us like a tongue. The thunder was deafening—I had only ever watched and listened to storms from behind the safety of a glass window. But I was part of the storm now, rain-whipped and shaking.

Savitri Ammoomma definitely seemed a bit crazy, and yet I could not forget the way she had looked at me, the way her eyes had seemed to see inside me, as if she was riffling through my thoughts, my secrets, like papers in a drawer.

"Come on," cried Meenu, and we ran even faster.

As I sprinted through that rain something peculiar happened. Even though the sky was still flashing and pounding with lightning and thunder, my mind went silent. I was filled with calm and a sense of purpose. The old woman was right. I couldn't keep hiding from what was right in front of me.

Aba's words drifted back: *There's nothing more thrilling than digging for the truth and finding it.* All this time I had been giving in to fear. What would Aba say if he knew what a coward I had been? Yes, there was no question, I had to go back.

When we arrived at Ashoka, nobody was around to see us sneaking inside, drenched to the bone. We dispersed to our respective rooms and I stripped off my clothes, laying them across the chair in the corner. I went into the bathroom and filled the bucket with cold water. Once the bucket was full, I used the plastic cup to pour it over my body and rubbed my skin with soap until it felt raw and clean.

My decision to go back to the garden made me feel both exhilarated and lonely. An invisible wall had been erected between me and my cousins. This was not an adventure that I could bring them along for, not even Krishna. I had to do it alone.

Chapter 13

The next morning I awoke just as dawn began to fill the room with a pink glow. I slipped my dress over my head, combed my hair, and polished my glasses. Just in case Amma woke up early and popped her head into my room, I stuffed a pile of clothes under the sheets on my bed and shaped them into a long, thin lump.

The morning was silent and I felt lucky—even the birds still slept. Rummaging through my suitcase, I pocketed the mango wrapped in a handkerchief, which I had stowed in one of the zippered pockets the previous night. I had stolen it from the kitchen when no one was looking. It might be unwise, I thought, to show up empty-handed.

Then I went over to the bed and slipped my hand beneath the pillow, pulling out the other thing I had stolen from the kitchen—a knife. I held it up and watched the sun flash across the polished silver blade. Carefully I placed it in my pocket beside the mango. My nerves pulsed as if fireflies were flickering on and off just underneath the surface of my skin. When I tiptoed outside, I breathed in the cool, light air. Pearls of fresh rainwater clung to the trees, and the wet sand was black and smooth beneath my worn soles. At that early hour everything seemed changed, bewitched. Feeling energized, my legs carried me quickly, effortlessly, over the stone barrier, into the forest, and down the narrow pathway.

It felt easier this time. My body instinctively knew when to turn, when to dodge an errant branch or a rogue thorn. In the early morning light, the green of the jungle was so hectic and brilliant, I felt as if I were in a dream. By the time I reached the stone wall, I could hardly feel my legs. A large banyan tree grew a few yards from the wall; I knelt atop a mound of roots, which gathered like a tangle of ancient fingers just before the door and once again peered in through the keyhole. The garden appeared untouched. Everything was exactly as I had left it except the flower petals were dappled with raindrops. An overwhelmingly sweet fragrance seeped from the crack below the door. I pulled the knife from my pocket and squeezed the wooden handle in my fist. Putting my mouth against the keyhole, I called:

"Hello? Who's there?"

The white peacock was sipping water from the pond. It raised its head at the sound of my voice and regarded me with a curious expression.

I waited, but when nothing happened I called out once more: "Please, let me in," and then, because I didn't know what else to say, "I come in peace."

Immediately I regretted the words. This wasn't a movie. I could actually be in danger.

Then—

"Who are you?" came a voice from the other side, and I lurched back as if the door had erupted into flame. The knife slipped from my hands, tumbling as it fell and grazing my shin before it disappeared into the mass of banyan roots. I pressed my finger against the bud of blood blossoming against my skin, cringing. But this was not the moment to back down in fear. I steadied myself.

"My name is Rakhee Singh. Who are you?"

"Why are you here? Who sent you?"

The voice was soft and feminine, yet tinged with hostility. And strangest of all, it spoke English. I had not expected this.

"Nobody sent me—I just decided to come here on my own." I prayed that I had not roused any sleeping Rakshasis, drunk and drooling, waiting on the other side with their clubs.

"But why have you come? How do you know about this place?" said the voice.

"I found it. I'm visiting for the summer and I'm staying nearby. My mother grew up around here."

"Are you alone?"

"Yes. Are you?"

"Does my teacher know that you are here?"

"Your teacher? I don't even know who your teacher is."

"I think she would be very upset if she discovered you here."

"Can you at least tell me your name?"

"Why should I tell you my name?"

The more I spoke to the voice on the other side of the wall, the less afraid I felt. Whoever or whatever she was, I was fairly confident she was not dangerous. But I wasn't getting anywhere by being direct, so I decided to try a new tactic.

"Okay then, I guess I'll go since I seem to have bothered you," I said, and turned. I walked only a few feet before the voice called out:

"Wait, don't go!"

I wheeled around. "What did you say?"

"Please, stay. I'll answer your questions, I promise. Just don't go." Now the voice sounded plaintive, almost desperate.

"All right, I'll stay, but only for a little while." I sat down on the ground and leaned my back against the door.

"My name is Tulasi," the voice offered.

"Are you alone?"

"It is just me, my peacock, and the garden."

"No one else lives there, then?"

"No."

Could it be that the terrible face I had seen belonged to this pretty voice? I had, after all, been sick that day. Maybe I had imagined it. I wanted to look through the keyhole again, but I wasn't sure how to do this without being obvious.

The voice put me at ease. I felt at home with it. The horror I had felt for so long was now all of a sudden laughable.

"May I come inside?"

"The door is locked from the outside and I do not have the key. My teacher has it," said Tulasi.

"Your teacher?"

"Yes, she comes to visit me every day."

I realized she must mean Sadhana Aunty. "You mean, you don't go to a proper school?"

"No."

"Don't you ever leave, then?"

"Never. It is for my own protection," said Tulasi.

"But don't you want to leave?"

"Why ever would I want to leave?"

I couldn't think of an answer. "Well, to see the outside world," I finally said.

"I have everything I need here—my garden, Puck,

and my books. Besides, I'm not like other people. I'm different."

"Oh," Again I was at a loss for words. "How old are you?"

"Sixteen, and you?"

"Almost eleven."

"So was it you who came here before?"

"Before? What do you mean?" I knew exactly what she meant, but I felt ashamed about my hysterical reaction.

"You ran away screaming. You gave me the fright of my life," Tulasi continued.

"Oh, that. Sorry."

"For a long time after that I was terrified. I could not stop wondering who you were and where you had come from. But it is funny, I am not afraid anymore. In fact, I do not think I ever was truly afraid. I remember I saw something very sweet in your eye."

I was embarrassed, but pleased. "Thanks."

"You have a funny way of speaking. I have never heard anyone speak like you before."

"I'm not from around here. I'm American."

"Do you have a mother and a father?"

I thought this an odd question. "Yes, but my father is back home in Minnesota. My mother and I are just visiting for the summer."

"My mother is a plant," said Tulasi in a matter-of-fact tone. "I'm named after her. She lives in a temple."

I started to worry. Tulasi sounded like she might be out of her mind.

"I like talking to you," she said. "I'm sorry that I was impolite. It is just that I have never had an unexpected visitor before. I did not know what to do. But I am so glad that you came. I feel very safe with you for some reason.

I want to show you my garden and introduce you to my peacock."

"Well, I can't exactly come inside."

"Perhaps you could wait for my teacher to arrive. She could let you in."

"No, no, I couldn't do that," I said. "Listen, you can't tell anybody about me, okay? We could both get into big trouble."

"You are right. Teacher wouldn't like it. But I do not understand why. I do not want to do anything bad. Why is talking to you bad?"

"No, it's not bad. It's just that I'm not supposed to wander this far away from the house. My mother would be worried. She doesn't know I'm here."

"It must be lovely to have a mother who worries."

Maybe she was insane, this Tulasi, but she was also nice, and we did have one thing in common—loneliness.

"I guess so," I said. In order to break the awkward silence that had sprung up between us I pulled the mango from my pocket. "I have a present for you. Can I throw it over?"

"Yes, please."

Scrambling to my feet, I shuffled backward, then hurled the fruit and watched it sail over the wall. It landed with a thud on the other side.

"A mango. How kind of you. Thank you, Rakhee Singh."

"You're welcome," I said, pleased that I had had the foresight to bring something along.

"You said you are from Minnesota? What sort of land is that?"

"Well, it's not really a land, it's more like a state. I don't know, it's not very interesting."

"But what does it look like? What sorts of people live there?" She sounded like a hungry child begging for food.

I tried my best to describe Minnesota—our house, Merlin, the Plainfield Clinic full of doctors, the cornfields and how they went from green to gold to brown to white as the seasons changed.

"How wonderful," Tulasi breathed.

She kept asking me questions, weird questions, and she barely took time to process my answers, just dove into the next question: "What does the sky look like in Minnesota? Is the moon white and does it change shapes? Can you see the stars from there, too?"

After a while I started to feel exhausted, and I realized by the distant crowing of the rooster that the morning was wearing on and my absence would soon be discovered.

"I'd better go now, but I'll come back," I told her.

"I have an idea," said Tulasi. "Do you think you could find a rope? You could climb over the wall. It would be like the story of Rapunzel, except my hair is not long enough. Once I tried to grow my hair out but Teacher made me cut it."

I wondered how she knew about Rapunzel. "Yeah, I think I could find some rope," I said, feeling excited again. "I'll have to come back tomorrow, though. Everyone will be waking up soon and they'll notice I'm gone."

"Will you vow to return?"

I hesitated only for a moment before I said, "I promise."

"At the same time?"

I swore to return with a rope at the same time the next day. "See you then," I said.

"Until tomorrow."

I turned and ran back through the forest, light-headed. I had done it—I had taken one step closer to figuring things out. There was no Rakshasi in the forest, only a sixteen-year-old girl; a nice girl who seemed like she could be a friend, even though she was kind of odd. But why was she there, and how did she get there? Why had Amma forbidden me from meeting Tulasi?

The longer I stayed at Ashoka, the more removed I felt from my regular life, from my regular self. Not long before, I had thought I was too old to believe in witches and monsters, but now I was not so sure. Part of me had wanted to laugh when Tulasi told me her mother was a plant, but another part believed her. What other explanation was there? The only reason I could think of as to why the grown-ups would keep her hidden was that Tulasi had some kind of magical powers. Either that or I was going crazy and had imagined the whole thing. I wondered if I would go back tomorrow and find that the wall, the garden, the cottage, the peacock, and Tulasi had all vanished.

I stole back into my bedroom, undetected, and changed into my nightgown. I walked into the kitchen a few moments later, yawning and sleep rumpled. Amma was sitting alone at the breakfast table, a satiny robe wrapped tightly around her shrinking frame, her eyes misty, and her hands pressed around a teacup, from which a thread of gray steam unraveled.

"Morning, sleepyhead," she said, blinking like a doll and changing back into smiling Amma, as if a switch had been turned off, then on.

"Good morning," I said, and slid into my seat.

Janaki appeared from the kitchen, carrying my breakfast.

"Now, Rakhee," said Amma, "I'm feeling a bit better this morning—is there anything you'd like to do together today? It looks like it won't rain for a while at least—we could go for a walk or something."

"No thanks." Why did Amma suddenly care so much about spending time with me, now that I actually had found something that interested me, something that I cared about? "We probably have play practice—Meenu's been working us pretty hard," I said.

"Oh, I see. Well, I'm glad you've found something to keep yourself busy and that you're getting along with your cousins." She fiddled with the chipped handle of her teacup for a moment, before saying, "You like it here, mo-lay, don't you?"

"Yeah, I guess so. I mean, it's all right and everything, but I miss home. I miss Aba." I emphasized the last part.

"Of course you do." Amma looked sad.

"By the way," I added. "Do you know where I could find some rope? We need it—for the play." How casually the lies rolled off my tongue!

"Hmm, rope? Hari must have some—I'll go and ask him for you." Amma got up from the table and wandered off. She seemed eager to do something for me.

She returned a few minutes later with a long, thick piece of rope encircling her arm. "Will this do?" She gave me a hopeful smile.

"That's perfect," I said, my lips twitching.

~

After lunch, Meenu and Krishna wanted to play four-square, a game I had taught them, and which we played using an old basketball that Muthashi had brought back from her visit to Minnesota years before. It clearly had never been used and barely bounced. But they seemed delighted to have discovered a new game and were deterred neither by the ball nor by the fact that we were only three people, since Gitanjali rarely agreed to be our fourth.

But this time my heart wasn't in the game. All I could think about was that I would finally be meeting Tulasi face-to-face. It was only a matter of hours now. This thought thrilled me but also filled me with a sense of my own disloyalty. My cousins bounced the ball back and forth, laughing, talking, teasing, as if nothing had changed. But things were different, so different now that their companionship seemed suddenly stale.

I also began to wonder what my real reason was for not confiding in at least Krishna. Was it because I didn't think she would believe me, or was it because I wanted to keep Tulasi all to myself? I had been angry at Amma for not telling me her secret, and now I was doing the exact same thing. But in spite of my guilt, I still knew I would not tell Krishna, not yet, maybe not ever. I was not ready to share Tulasi.

When it became clear that one-third of the party was distracted, our game dispersed, and I retreated to my room where I would have the privacy to daydream. I had stowed the rope that Amma gave me under the bed; I pulled it out, sat down, and held it in my lap. I ran my fingers across the glossy, hay-colored bristles. The rope was heavy, and I imagined that it was not a rope, but a snake coiled upon my legs. I held it there for a second, then shoved it off onto the floor and slid it back under the bed with my foot.

I went to the window, leaned my elbows on the sill, and looked outside at the cloudless sky. A ray of sun shone like a spotlight through the tops of the trees, as if some rare gem was hidden deep inside the heart of the forest. I wrapped my hands on the window bars and pretended that I was in prison, a game I sometimes played when I was alone in that room. I was the prisoner and Muthashan was my jailor, watching over me from the black frame on the wall.

As I stood there, I heard Amma's voice in the next room:

"Finally, we're alone. I thought she'd never let us out of her sight."

"Well, you can't really blame her after what happened the last time we were left alone, can you?" said another voice that made me clench the bars so tightly my knuckles went white.

"Prem, don't joke," Amma said. "We only have a few minutes before she'll notice I'm gone, and we have a lot to discuss. She's been watching me like a hawk. I've been going mad."

"Just tell me one thing: have you made your decision? I can't wait much longer."

"You've waited all these years, you can't wait another week?"

"Chitra, why did you come here? If you were just going to toy with me, you shouldn't have bothered at all. I can do this alone, you know, and I will, because it's the right thing, and I'm finally in a place where I *can* do it. But it won't be the same without you. I need your help. And you know how I love you. You say you've been going mad? I can't even tell you what hell these years without you have been for me. I haven't even really been living. With you, I could live again."

"You have to understand how difficult this thing you're asking me to do is, particularly for me. I've spent the last half of my life trying to forget, and then you come along with your sweet words, bringing it all back, as fresh as if it happened yesterday," said Amma.

"It's in our power to do what we want now. Our families can't control us anymore. We have a chance to be together, to—"

"I know, I know! Don't you think I've considered all of this?" Amma's voice rose to a shriek.

"Shhh, Chitra, keep your voice down. We'll be heard."

"I'm sick of keeping my voice down, I'm sick of hiding, always hiding." Amma's moan sounded muffled, as if she had buried her face in Prem's shoulder.

"I know, but this is your chance to come out of hiding, to be the woman you were meant to be. Just say yes, please, say yes."

"It's not that simple."

There was a long silence before Prem spoke. "You love him, don't you?"

"He's a kind man, Prem, and he's been good to me." Amma's voice faltered. "But I don't love him the way I love you. I was bound to you from the day I was born. I belong to you."

"Then say yes."

"I have my daughter to think about."

"Don't you think I know that? I'm always considering her welfare, always. I wouldn't have sent for you until I knew I could provide for a family. I have a full-time teaching job in Trivandrum now and I'm making decent money. It may not be what you're used to, but it's enough. The house I've found is small, but it's beautiful. The windows are large and they face west, and there's a small garden with a pond in the yard...."

Amma laughed—I couldn't tell if it was bitter or happy.

"Chitra, it's all there, ready and waiting for you. You'll love it, I know it. We'll be happy there, finally."

I heard brisk footsteps coming down the hall.

"I don't know if it's that easy," Amma said.

"Say yes, you know it's the right thing. Say yes now."

The footsteps grew louder.

"This is so hard."

"I know, but we have to do it. We must make up for the mistakes we've made. Say yes, please. Say yes now, I need to hear you say it."

"Yes, yes, yes," said Amma, and I felt myself going cold all over, from my head to the tip of my toes.

There was a sharp rapping sound on Amma's door.

"Chitra, are you in there? I need you." It was Sadhana Aunty.

"I'm here, I was just resting. I'll be right out," called Amma, then in a lower voice, "Wait here for five minutes after I go out, then you should be able to slip out without anyone seeing you."

I remained at the window for a long time after Amma and Prem had both left the room, my entire body trembling. All summer I had been disturbed by Amma's relationship with Prem, but I kept hoping that once we went back to Plainfield she would forget him and life would somehow go back to normal. After what I had heard, it was clear she was not going to forget. Amma had already betrayed Aba. Now she was planning to betray me, too.

~

Late that night I heard her sobbing through the wall. Wrenching sobs that made my own eyes water with their intensity and caused all the rage I was feeling toward her to melt away into the darkness. In the months leading up to our trip, I used to hear Amma weeping at home, but it had always been soft, subdued, somehow more bearable than this. I felt sick listening to her—I could stand my own sorrow, anyone else's sorrow, but not Amma's. Yet as much as I wanted to go to her, to climb under the sheets and put my arms around her quaking body, to tell her it was time to go home, I couldn't move. So I remained awake for much of the night, terrified and stiff as a mummy, listening to Amma weeping, and thinking about the knife, stained with my blood, which I remembered I had left trapped under the pile of roots outside Tulasi's garden.

Chapter 14

When I found myself standing again before the garden door, I looked down in search of the knife and with a pang of relief saw that it was still embedded beneath the roots, a barely visible sliver of blade, untouched. I knelt down to retrieve it and then, superstitiously, stood up and decided to leave it there, its sharp point facing out toward the forest like a guard.

"Good morning," came Tulasi's voice from the other side.

"You didn't tell Sadh—um, your teacher about me, did you?" I said.

"No, I did not. You were right. It is perhaps best we keep your visits a secret—just in case Teacher does not approve. She seems rather tense these days. I would be so disappointed if she prevented you from coming. Did you bring a rope?"

"Yes." I held the rope uncertainly. "What should I do with it?"

There was silence on the other side.

"Tulasi?"

"I thought you might know what to do," she admitted.

"I don't."

"Try throwing one side of the rope to me and I will secure it to the trunk of the Ashoka tree. Then you can climb over."

I began to uncoil the rope, while at the same time eyeing the wall that I was about to scale. The stones were unevenly stacked, with pockets of moss in between that I decided would serve as makeshift steps.

The first time I attempted to throw the rope it simply grazed the top of the wall and tumbled back down to my feet in resignation. I backed up and tried again. On my third attempt I managed to successfully get half of the rope over to the other side.

"I have it," called Tulasi. I heard her rustling around and grunting a little with the effort of securing the rope in a tight knot around the tree trunk.

But as soon as I tugged at my end of the rope, it slackened, came loose from the tree, and fell back over to my side of the wall.

"I don't think the rope will work," I said.

"What shall we do?"

I had to get over somehow. "I'm going to climb the wall."

"Can you do that?"

I thought of the many trees I had climbed down by the ravine in Plainfield. My skinny arms and legs were stronger than they looked. "I think I can!"

I dug my fingers high into the muddy spaces between the stones, feeling the dirt and clay seep under my nails. I placed my foot upon a protruding stone and tried to hoist myself up, but felt my body sliding back down, my palms scraping against the stones. I sat on the ground and looked at my hands, which were now covered in dirt and traces of blood where the skin had broken.

"Rakhee, are you all right?"

"Yes, I'm going to try again." I shifted down to another section of the wall, wiped my hands on my dress, and once more clutched at the stone. This time I made it halfway up the wall before I fell.

Finally on the third try, I made it to the top of the wall, which I clambered over with my back facing the garden. I gave one last look at the forest before I lost my balance and dropped down, landing on my bottom in a patch of soft grass.

"Hello." Tulasi was leaning over me and once again I saw her face. But this time I was not at all afraid. I was mesmerized.

A dusky pink cloud obscured more than half her face, beginning at the bottom of her chin, spreading up the right side of her cheek, and blurring into the hairline. Her upper lip was interrupted by a triangular gash that rose up to meet her nose and exposed her yellowish teeth. She was dressed in a simple beige cotton tunic and loose, baggy pants; and her hair, which was straight and black, hung down her back in a long braid. I had never seen anyone who looked like her before.

After a few seconds I realized I was staring, but just as I was about to turn away and apologize, it struck me that she, too, was staring.

I got to my feet and we stood face-to-face.

"Hi," I said.

"How interesting. You said you are an American, no? Is this the way all Americans look?"

"Um." I blushed, unsure of what to say. I couldn't believe that between the two of us, I was the one whose appearance was being scrutinized.

"Oh forgive me, Rakhee," she said quickly, sensing my unease. "I don't mean to embarrass you. It's only that I have not seen very many people—all I know is what I have learned from books, so anytime I meet a new person I am fascinated. You are indeed lovely."

Tulasi took my hand in hers, and an unexpected warmth flooded my limbs. She guided me down a narrow cobblestone path winding toward the cottage. Blue-and-white flowers shaped like conch shells bordered the path, and their satiny petals brushed against my ankles. The heady fragrance of frangipane lingered in the air. A rainbow of butterflies circled above our heads. The cottage's thatched roof winked under the sun. The peacock was lying on the front step, docile and languid as a Persian cat. He lifted his head to meet Tulasi's outstretched hand.

"This is Puck," she said, stroking his feathers.

"Aren't you afraid he'll fly away?"

"No, Puck would never do that. He's just as bound to this garden as I am."

She smiled serenely and opened the door, leading me inside the most wonderful room I had ever seen.

"And this," she said proudly, "is my home."

The room was circular and divided into sections—a sleeping area with a carved wood wardrobe and a four-poster bed, which was veiled in wispy white mosquito netting, a sitting room with elegant wicker furniture, a polished, compact kitchen, and an arched door leading to the bathroom. The most striking feature of the cottage was the sheer quantity of books. Floor-to-ceiling shelves lined nearly half the curved wall, and they overflowed with books. Books sat stacked in neat piles on the floor near the bed, on the coffee table, on the kitchen counter. The other half of the wall was taken up by windows—great, wide windows curtained in a gossamer material that let in swatches of warm morning light. A cozy window seat was piled with velvety fabrics and plush cushions.

"Shall I prepare tea?" said Tulasi.

Amma did not allow me to drink tea yet, only warm milk. "Sure."

She went into the kitchen and began to rummage around in the cupboard, pulling out a white china tea set, rimmed with a border of bright pink roses.

I watched as Tulasi, humming to herself, brought the water to a boil and poured it into the teapot. She fussed about the kitchen gathering milk, sugar, and spoons, and placed an orange tiger lily across the side of the tray with an artistic flourish.

"I never pluck flowers from the garden. I wouldn't dream of doing that," she assured me, "but I found this poor lily lying on the ground, and Puck might have trampled over it had I not rescued it first."

She seemed to derive intense pleasure from attending to these small domestic details. Carrying the tray over to the round wicker coffee table, she motioned for me to sit down on one of the chairs. Her hands were small and deft, at one moment capable and utilitarian, and the next graceful as a pianist's. She seemed so comfortable with herself, so self-assured. Taking in my surroundings, I noticed there wasn't a single mirror around the place, including in the white-tiled bathroom, which I poked my head into. Even the spoon she used to stir sugar into my tea was made of a dull, unreflective brass. Whoever had built and furnished this cottage had deliberately ensured that Tulasi remained ignorant of her appearance.

"So, how long have you lived here?"

"I have always lived here. Ever since Teacher found me as a baby in the temple."

"She found you in the temple?"

"Yes. You see, as I was telling you before, I am not like other people. She found me swaddled in the leaves of the tulasi plant, my mother. Teacher told me I was a special present from God and so I need special care. I cannot live in society like everyone else."

"So you have never left this place?"

"No, but I have no desire to leave. The idea of what lies beyond these walls frightens me and the thought of what would happen to me if I left is even worse." Tulasi shuddered.

"But aren't you even a little curious to see what it's like in the real world?"

"Oh, I admit I do get lonely from time to time. But really, I want for nothing—I am grateful that I even have this much. I feel safe here, secure and comfortable. Anything I need to learn, I can learn from Teacher or from my books. It's a peaceful existence."

"So what do you do all day?" I could not fathom staying cooped up in one room forever, to be a willing prisoner of your own house. I thought of the caged mice in Aba's lab.

"Teacher visits me every day to bring me food and go over our lessons. Otherwise, I work in the garden or read or play with Puck." She noted my face contorted in dismay. "You mustn't think I am unhappy, Rakhee. I enjoy my life. I have never known anything else, and I do not wish to."

I continued to probe. "So, who comes to visit you, besides your teacher?"

"Well, usually it is just Teacher. I believe there used to be some other ladies who cared for me when I was a baby, but I cannot recall their faces—they are such shadowy memories, I may have even imagined them. Sometimes

Teacher's brother comes around—he brought me Puck actually when he was only a chick, and I raised him myself. I named him after the narrator in *A Midsummer Night's Dream*. It is my favorite story—you must read it. It's written by a fellow named William Shakespeare. I asked Teacher if he had written anything else, but she said he hadn't, as far as she knew. Anyway, Teacher's brother always seems so sad when he comes here, I don't think he likes it very much. Then there is Teacher's sister. She is very beautiful, like a princess. But she also seems very sad."

I picked up one of the books lying on top of a stack on the floor beside me. It had a navy blue cover with *Grimm's Fairy Tales* written across it in gold lettering.

The books beneath it were *Hans Christian Andersen's Fairy Tales, Panchatantra, Aesop's Fables*, and *Arabian Nights*. All the books I used to read with Amma and devour with the aid of a flashlight long after she left me alone in the darkness. I got up and began to wander around, casually perusing the rest of the books in the cottage. They were all the same—fairy tales and magical stories. I wondered if these were the only books upon which she had built her conception of the real world, a world inhabited by witches and mermaids, a world where men beheaded their wives and animals spoke.

"Tulasi." I went back to the sofa and sat down. "You know how you said you couldn't live in the world like other people? What exactly did you mean by that?"

She looked at me and did not say anything. She took a sip of her tea and I took a sip of mine. The hot brown liquid scalded my tongue, but I swallowed it anyway.

"If I leave my garden," she said in a hushed, reverent tone, "then I will die."

"What?"

"We are dependent upon each other, the garden and me. That is why I spend so much time caring for it. As long as the garden stays alive and healthy, then so will I. But if I forsake it, then we shall both perish."

I couldn't believe what I was hearing. "Who told you this?"

"Teacher. She waited until my eleventh birthday to tell me, but I believe I have always known it. I have always felt the connection between myself and the garden. When I was a child, she helped me care for it, but now that I'm grown, it is my responsibility."

Tulasi lowered her eyes and began turning her teacup around and around in the saucer.

"So, what kinds of things do you learn in your lessons?" I asked, eager to change the subject.

"Oh, all kinds of things." Tulasi's face brightened. "Teacher is extremely clever. I've learned three languages—Malayalam, Hindi, and English. We read a great deal of poetry and stories together. Or she assigns me readings and we talk about them. She has also taught me some arithmetic and a little bit of science, but not much. There are certain topics Teacher does not like to tell me about and I am not sure why. I ask her so many questions but she avoids them. I am sure there is a good reason why. Teacher knows what is best for me."

It was getting late. I realized it was time for me to leave and I gulped down the rest of my tea. After promising Tulasi I would return as soon as I could, I ran back to Ashoka.

The house was just starting to rise when I slipped into my room to put my nightclothes back on. But instead of going to the dining room for breakfast, I got into bed. I wasn't hungry at all, and besides, I couldn't face the grown-ups just then. I couldn't shake the fear that they would know that I knew. They would take one look at my guilty face and the secret would be out.

So I lay there, replaying Tulasi's story over and over again in my head. She genuinely believed the tulasi plant was her mother and that she would die if she ever left the garden. She was so certain, and that otherworldly garden and Tulasi herself were so removed from anything I had ever experienced that I almost believed her, too.

There was a knock on the door.

"Rakhee, my mother is asking for you. She says to come out for breakfast." Even though it was only Krishna, I sighed with annoyance.

"I'll be there in a minute," I said, climbing back out of bed and slipping on my sandals.

I wondered if Amma would even be at breakfast. All that crying the night before might have given her a headache; perhaps she would spend another day in bed with the curtains closed.

I hoped the crying was a sign that she had been lying to Prem when she said yes. She had said yes but really she had meant no. And even if she had meant yes, Aba would never let Amma take me away to live with Prem in some house with a garden and a pond and windows that faced west.

Everyone, including a swollen-eyed Amma, was gathered around the table. Sadhana Aunty, standing at the head with the tips of her long fingers balancing on the surface, looked dark and somber. Two slanting bones protruded, bladelike, above the hollows of her cheeks. Purple bags sagged beneath her eyes. Dev was standing just behind her with a serious expression on his face.

"Muthashi is ill," Sadhana Aunty announced in a crisp voice.

Vijay Uncle's mouth fell open and Amma let out a quiet sob.

"It's nothing serious. Dev has examined her."

"Yes," said Dev, stepping forward so that he was now standing beside my aunt. "It's nothing but a f-f-f-fever, but at her age it's better to be ca-ca-careful."

"Dev would like Muthashi to keep to her bed for the next few days until the fever subsides," Sadhana Aunty said. Dev shot her a look, irritated that she had stepped in and interrupted his speech. "I'd like you all to make an effort to be quieter when you're in the house. I don't want you disturbing Muthashi with too much noise." I knew that this was directed at me, Krishna, and Meenu. "Also, Muthashi gets very lonely when she can't be around people, so all of us must take turns sitting with her and keeping her company." At this, I turned my attention to a cobweb shivering at the corner of the ceiling. "That means all of you. It's very important that we keep her spirits up." Sadhana Aunty's eyes zeroed in on me.

"But how am I supposed to keep her company?" I asked. "She can't understand anything I say."

"Rakhee," Amma said, "you don't have to say anything. She'll just be happy to be beside you and to know you're there."

"Okay, that is all." Sadhana Aunty backed away from the table. "You may eat now." She wiped her hands on her sari and left the room.

"Maybe we should just all go in together," I suggested to Meenu and Krishna as we ate.

"But that doesn't make any sense," Meenu said. "Then we have to sit in there for three times as long. Just do it yourself—what's the big deal?"

It wasn't a big deal to my cousins who had grown up with our grandmother, who could speak to our grandmother, who knew her before she became this helpless, childlike creature. Although my memories of Muthashi before that trip were hazy, I had always thought about her. Whenever the teachers at school asked us what we were doing over the holidays, we would go around in a circle and the other kids would say "I'm going to Grandma's house." Grandma's house became a vague, happy place synonymous in my mind with warmth and love—cookies in the oven, gifts under a tree, bony hugs that you shrugged away from but really looked forward to—images I had gleaned from movies or from overhearing postholiday conversations between the kids at school, images that I knew weren't necessarily real, but that I dreamed about anyway.

~

Muthashi's room smelled funny. It was hard to breathe with the dense curtains drawn over the windows, blocking out any light or air. I coughed as I stumbled over to the chair that Sadhana Aunty had placed next to the bed. My grandmother was lying asleep on her side with one arm stretched out under her ear and one arm resting on her delicate hip. From the meager light streaming in through the doorway, I could see that her gray hair, usually tied back, lay in scraggly disarray on the pillow. Her breathing was short and disjointed.

I settled down into the hard chair and thought about what Muthashan's crazy old sister had told me, about how Muthashi had been a teenage bride. Muthashan had married her, then left her behind in that old, rotting house to live with his mother and three sisters. Later, after Vijay Uncle, she had tried to have more children but lost them all. Her life had been filled with sadness, nothing but sadness. Krishna had said that there was something not quite right about this place, and I believed her.

I remembered the picture Krishna had shown me of Muthashi when she was young. Her face had not been beautiful, but even then there had been a kindness, a dignity to her round, placid features. The kindness was there still, but the dignity had gone, and I thought what a horrible thing it must be to grow old.

After a while Muthashi's eyelids opened. Instinctively I backed my chair away a few inches. Her eyes, blank as marbles, fell on me and slowly warmed with recognition. She reached out her hand. It trembled as it hung in the space between me and the bed. Reluctantly I took it and was surprised by the silkiness of her palm against mine. She closed her eyes again and smiled, and I felt a sudden rush of feeling that I hoped was love.

Chapter 15

Over the next week I juggled my visits to Tulasi with rehearsals for the play. My eleventh birthday was approaching, and my cousins and I had decided to put on a performance for the adults right after my birthday dinner, which Amma had taken upon herself to plan with surprising energy and determination.

In the early mornings I would sneak out of the house, quiet as a thief, and sprint through the forest to the garden, where Tulasi would be waiting, her excitement so palpable I could feel it radiating through the wall.

"It's me," I would say, and she would immediately begin moving about on the other side, so that I knew she had been waiting anxiously for my arrival.

Tulasi and I would sit together, drinking tea and talking until my hour was up and I would have to return to Ashoka. Usually during these visits she asked questions and I answered. She wanted to know all about things like school and other children. When I told her about them, a million more questions would follow. "Bus? But what is a bus?" She would reach out and grasp my arm in her hot hands and lean forward, her deformed mouth gaping, and I would do my best to explain. But it never felt enough. I could see the dissatisfaction growing in her face.

Once when we were out in the garden, she stopped talking midsentence.

"What is it?" I asked.

"Sssshhh," she whispered.

A bottle-green dragonfly was sunning itself upon a heart-shaped anthurium. In one deft movement, Tulasi leaped forward and captured the creature in her cupped hands.

"What are you doing?"

"Come and have a look," she said.

We went back into the cottage, where she placed the dragonfly into a glass jar and capped it. I watched it crawl up the side of the jar as Tulasi went over to the wardrobe and shuffled things around. She returned with a spool of silver thread and a pair of scissors. Picking up the jar, she motioned for me to follow her back outside and I recalled the mysterious dragonfly that had led me to the garden for the first time. Tulasi picked up a miniature rose, which had fallen to the grass, and poured the dragonfly from the jar back into her hand. Handling it with skilled delicacy, she tied one end of a piece of silver thread around its tail and the other around the stem of the rose.

Her face glowing, she released the dragonfly, and together we watched as it drifted over the garden wall with the rose trailing behind it like a comet.

"That won't hurt him, will it?"

"No, of course not, silly," said Tulasi. "It's very light and it will fall off soon. It's just a little fun I like to have."

I got into the habit of bringing her things—small presents—each time I visited. A bag of Skittles Amma had bought me at the airport, a tattered *Betty and Veronica* comic book, a Walkman with a Madonna cassette inside it, and headphones.

"Have you ever heard music before?" I asked.

"Teacher has taught me a few traditional songs."

I made her put on the headphones, adjusted the volume on the Walkman, and hit the play button. At first her limbs jolted and she stumbled backward as the music poured into her ears, but then she stood still and a warm light spread across her face. She smiled and began to sway back and forth with her eyes closed. After a few minutes the smile faded, and she pulled off the headphones and pushed the whole thing back toward me.

"Take it away," she said.

On the day before my birthday, none of the junk I could find in my suitcase satisfied me. I wanted to bring her something special, something that would really make her happy. I thought of the bookcase in the sitting room, dusty and unappealing, covered by an enormous yellowing doily, and decided that was where I would find the something really special for Tulasi.

I went into the sitting room, knelt before the two-shelved bookcase, and lifted up the doily, which gave off a musty odor. The books had an austere look about them, with dark spines and bronze lettering. I scanned the titles, most of which were unfamiliar to me, until I found the perfect book, *Shakespeare's Tragedies: A Complete Volume.* The book was thick and would be difficult to carry through the forest, but I knew it would be perfect, so I slid it off the shelf and tucked it underneath my arm, thinking of Tulasi's face lighting up when she saw that I had brought her an entire book of plays by her favorite writer.

As I arranged the doily back over the shelf, another book caught my eye. Unlike the thick hardbacks, this one was slender and frayed. I pulled it out. *The Poems of Mirabai.* Amma had been reading it that day when I had lain sick beside her. I opened the book to the first page; an inscription had been written on it in a familiar hand: "To my dear Chitra. Yours forever, Prem."

I felt that old tightening inside my chest at the sight of these words and automatically stuck the book into the pages of the Shakespeare before I rearranged the doily, left the room, and began to walk down the hallway clutching my stolen booty. Amma's door was open a crack, and I paused. I know I should have kept walking, that I should have run to hide the books, but I couldn't help myself, I had grown so accustomed to spying and eavesdropping that it was now second nature.

She was standing in front of the mirror wearing nothing but a threadbare brassiere held up by two thin straps and a beige underskirt, the kind she wore under a sari. Her scar, usually pale pink, seemed redder and angrier than usual. Her stomach was soft, brown, and flat. The long bones just below her throat were jutting out farther than I remembered, angled upward like a pair of eyebrows. Below them, her plump breasts rose and fell with the same steady, voluptuous rhythm of ocean waves on a calm day.

Her hair was loose and tucked behind her ears, and she was staring at her face while her fingertips were massaging her temples. They ran along the side of her face, down her neck, to her chest. They grazed the curving mound of one breast, then the other. There was a wild look in her eyes that I had never seen before.

The darkness of her nipples burned through the transparent white silk of her brassiere and her lips parted, letting a moan escape. A moan with a tumult of emotion behind it that I neither recognized nor understood, but that made me shrink away from the door nonetheless.

"God help me," I heard her whisper, before I turned away and went back to my room with heavy hands and hot cheeks, ashamed both by the scene I had witnessed and for having spied in the first place. I felt dirty, disgraceful.

I hid the Shakespeare book under a pile of clothes in my suitcase and took the little poetry volume out into the yard.

The midafternoon blaze wrung sweat from my pores. It trickled down my face in rivulets. Carrying the book in both hands I went and stood by the moss-covered stone well situated in the corner of the yard. I had never come so close to the well before. On one of my first days at Ashoka, Nalini Aunty had caught me eyeing it and told me with a smirk that the long grass fringing the circumference of the well was a favorite haunt for cobras. By now I knew that Nalini Aunty wasn't exactly trustworthy, but the damage had been done; the seed of fear had been planted.

I stared at the book in my hands, then down into the well, so black even the blinding sun flickered and disappeared like a dying bulb in its depths. My legs standing in that awful grass throbbed, but managed to stay rooted.

My parents had instilled the idea in me that books were sacred. Both Aba and Amma agreed on this one point. If I left books lying around on the floor of my room, Aba would pause in the doorway as he passed and frown.

"It seems to me you have more than enough shelf space, Rakhee, am I right?" he would say.

Amma taught me that if I ever stepped on a book, I should immediately kneel down, touch my fingers first to the book, then to my forehead, as a sign of respect. That motion had become a reflex to me now and I did it without thinking whenever my foot accidentally brushed against one. Books were meant to be revered, not destroyed.

How could something feel both right and wrong?

I heard the scratchy shuffle of cow hooves on sand. Soon Hari would be shepherding them onto the lawn and backing them into their pens. He would see me standing paralyzed and suspicious at the rim of the well.

It was now or never.

With a quick shove I sent the book over the edge. It seemed a long time before I heard a quiet splash but I forced myself to wait until I heard it.

Then I fled.

~

That night my cousins and I sat at the dinner table with Vijay Uncle and Dev, who had been over to check on Muthashi, while the aunts, Amma, and Gitanjali stood in silence against the wall. The creamy balloons of Vijay Uncle's cheeks seemed to have miraculously deflated into flaccid jowls over the course of the last week. He was making small talk with Dev, but I could see that every word that left his dry lips was painful, strained, and that he seemed to be using up every last ounce of energy he had to keep up his end of the conversation.

"Na-na-nalini," Dev said, turning finally to my aunt, who was standing behind her husband with a sullen expression on her face. "Your old friend Thara T-t-thomas. Did you hear, sh-sh-she has gone back to her parents' p-p-place in disg-g-grace?"

"Oh, that woman, she is no friend of mine," said Nalini Aunty in a subdued tone, though her eyes lit up at this piece of gossip.

"Her f-f-father should have thrown her out, but they h-h-have taken h-h-her in and she has no problems bringing sh-sh-shame to them all."

Nalini Aunty clucked and shook her head from side to side in agreement, and through the corner of my eye I saw Amma scowl.

When Dev had finished eating, Sadhana Aunty gave Gitanjali a nudge and she came forward with downcast eyes to reload his banana leaf. He leaned back and watched her as she ladled curry onto his leaf, his eyes flicking upward from her face down to the soft hands that served him.

"Sh-sh-she is a lovely girl, indeed, Sadhana Chechi, this d-d-d-daughter of yours. L-l-l-ike a full moon on a c-c-clear night."

Meenu let out a loud, involuntary snort, then clapped her hand over her mouth. Krishna's eyes widened and Sadhana Aunty's lips tightened.

A dull shade of red crept into Dev's neck and he turned to Meenu, who met his look with a mixture of fear and brazen amusement dancing in her eyes.

"Quite unlike this one," he said in a voice suddenly smooth as silk, "so dark, so homely." Dev tore off a piece of dosa from his plate, stuffed it in his mouth, and chewed. "I fear, my dear Sadhana Chechi, sh-sh-sh-she will be difficult to marry off. She was not b-b-blessed with the Varma beauty."

To my surprise, Meenu's face fell at these words. She had always seemed so tough, so uncaring. But now a shadow dulled the glint in her eyes, and the hand that had covered her mouth dropped to her lap, revealing the limp corners of her lips.

Sadhana Aunty cleared her throat. "I'm not concerned with that just yet, Dev. She is still very young." She moved to the table where she began to collect our banana leaves, before adding in a softer voice, "And she is a good, smart girl."

Dev opened his mouth as if he were about to say something, but then seemed to decide it wasn't worth it. "Vijay, shall we r-r-r-retreat and leave these l-l-ladies to their dinner?"

"Yes, let us do that," said Vijay Uncle uncomfortably, pushing back his chair with a squeak.

I looked at Meenu; something had changed in her face. The mischievous glint had returned to her eyes, but her nostrils were flared and her lips screwed up into a tight, bloodless ball. She didn't say or do anything—just stood and went to wash her curry-smeared hands in the sink, but my bad feeling was confirmed when she came up behind me as we left the dining room.

"Rakhee, switch parts with me," she said casually, but as she said it her fingers curled around my arm and she gave me a hard squeeze.

"What?" I said, turning to face her. "We're performing tomorrow. How can we switch now? I thought you liked your part. My character doesn't even come in until halfway through."

"I've changed my mind." She let go of my arm. "I already know all your lines and it won't be difficult to learn mine. You hated playing the villain anyhow."

Krishna furrowed her brow but didn't say anything.

Meenu stared at me.

"Fine," I said.

"Good. I'll give you the script, you can relearn your lines tonight, and we'll rehearse tomorrow. Just trust me, it will be better this way."

~

I stayed awake late into the night reading the script and only let myself close my eyes long after the net of sleep had settled over the house. A couple of hours later, I opened my eyes and it dawned on me that it was my birthday. I was eleven. Birthdays were still something exciting back then, so in spite of my lack of sleep I leaped out of bed, full of energy, and pulled my dress over my head, eager to get to the garden. I wrapped the Shakespeare book in a silk shawl I had swiped from Amma's room. I stuck it in my backpack and secured the straps around my shoulders.

Before I left I crept into the bathroom for a glance in the mirror, just to see if anything had changed. I thought that there surely had to be some kind of minor transformation to mark this passage into a new year. To my disappointment, however, my reflection was the exact same one that had greeted me the day before. It was a funny thing to look and feel identical to the way I did yesterday, but to suddenly be a whole year older.

When I got to the garden, Tulasi put her arms around me and wished me a happy birthday. "I've made a cake," she said with a smile. "Let me just finish watering these roses and we'll go inside and have some."

I knelt down beside Puck, who was curled up in the grass. He looked at me with his beady black eyes, then bent his head down, much in the way Merlin would do, and I realized he wanted to be petted. I ran my hand across his snowy feathers, from the rounded nub of his head down to the tip of his endless tail. I wondered if he ever danced, like the peacocks I saw in nature books, spreading out the intricate fan of his plumage. I was glad that Tulasi had Puck as a companion, but seeing him there, lying in the grass like a purring cat, also made me sad.

"I'm finished. Let us go indoors and have cake," said Tulasi, smiling at me and wiping her hands on her tunic.

As we ate the cake and sipped tea, Tulasi's eyes fell upon my backpack. "What have you got in there?"

"Oh, I almost forgot, I have something for you." My face warm, I unzipped the backpack and pulled out the book, still wrapped in Amma's shawl.

Tulasi took it from me.

"Rakhee!" she said, her eyes dancing, "I cannot believe you have been so kind as to bring me a book. You are the kindest girl in the world." Before she unwrapped it she held the book to her face and inhaled. She took the tasseled edge of the shawl in her fingers and stroked it.

"This smells delicious," she said in a dreamy voice, and then slowly began to remove the shawl. It fell in a silken rumple onto her lap.

She stared at the cover of the book. It seemed that she stared forever, her smile vanishing, her hands shaking. Where were the gushing words of gratitude, the effusive hugs?

She placed the book down on the table as if it were a repulsive object and turned her head to one side so that I couldn't see her expression.

"Rakhee, thank you very much. You are so very kind to think of me, especially on this day, your birthday."

"What's the matter? Don't you like it?"

"It's wonderful," she said lightly.

"It's Shakespeare, your favorite. You see, he's written much more than that one play. Now you can read everything he wrote. I'm sure I can find the rest—"

Tulasi cut me off. "I'm suddenly feeling a bit ill. I hope you will not find me ungracious if I end this visit now. I don't think I shall be very good company henceforth."

I still had half an hour left before I had to be back. Tulasi had always seemed so excited to see me. I couldn't understand her coldness.

"Okay, I guess. I'll see you tomorrow, then?"

"Yes, tomorrow."

I stood up and went to the door. Tulasi did not follow me, but as I opened it, I heard her say, "Please do come tomorrow, Rakhee. I live for your visits now."

As I walked through the forest back toward Ashoka, it hit me for the first time that maybe I wasn't helping Tulasi. Maybe I wasn't helping her at all.

~

I had forgotten all about the look I had seen on Meenu's face when Dev had taunted her. During the day she went back to being the regular old Meenu, making us rehearse for hours, ordering us around, tearing at her hair when we didn't infuse enough expression into our lines.

The servants had prepared my favorite meal for dinner: idlis and sambar. Dev and Prem were both there, but in spite of their presence I still managed to have a good time. Everyone seemed lighthearted, like their cares had dissolved into thin air for one night. Amma's face was rosy and glowing. Vijay Uncle was cracking jokes right and left. Even Sadhana Aunty, who usually got a distressed look on her face whenever Prem unexpectedly dropped by, was laughing. Muthashi's fever had finally subsided, and although she appeared a bit frail, she seemed otherwise healthy, her hair neatly pulled back, a smile on her face.

After we had finished eating, Amma disappeared into the kitchen, and emerged carrying a round white cake decorated with yellow roses and twelve burning candles.

"One for good luck," she said, setting the cake down in front of me.

Everyone sang "Happy Birthday," and I paused for a moment before I blew out the candles in one giant breath.

"What did you wish for?" asked Krishna.

"She can't say," said Prem, "or it won't come true." He smiled kindly at me and I averted my eyes.

Balu, who was so excited by all the activity, was squirming in his mother's arms and reaching for the cake. Nalini Aunty came up behind me so he could get a better look.

He dove forward and plunged his chubby little hands into the center of the cake, came up, and crammed fistfuls of sugary yellow rose in his mouth.

"Balu!" Nalini Aunty cried out in horror, but then everyone started to laugh and we couldn't stop, even though it really wasn't all that funny now that I think about it. We laughed and laughed. Tears ran down Krishna's cheeks, she was laughing so hard.

It was the last truly happy moment of that summer.

Chapter 16

Meenu, Krishna, and I went into Amma's room to begin preparations for our performance. With her permission, we rummaged through her cosmetics bag, which sat in a striped case on the dressing table, and pulled out various bottles and compacts, like candy on Halloween. Amma rarely wore any makeup, but she owned a lot of it. She used to wear it when Aba invited his colleagues to our house for dinner, but I didn't like the way the lipstick and powder made her look. She became more like the other wives, more common. I don't think Aba liked it, either, because he asked her to stop wearing it.

With little idea of what I was doing, I blotted powder onto my face and streaked blush across my cheeks, then removed my glasses and traced the outline of each eye with a black kohl pencil. I applied lipstick, which was the same bright red shade as the flowers blooming on the Ashoka trees outside. I was only playing a boy, but still I wanted to look nice.

When I had finished with the makeup, I examined my new face in the mirror. My cousins, who were now bickering over the same lipstick, faded into the background. The makeup had the opposite effect on me than it had on

Amma. For a second I wondered at the vivid, exaggerated features reflected in the glass. They were not mine; they belonged to someone else. I touched my face and the jolt of sensation made me smile.

We busily arranged our props and donned our meager costumes, culled from a heap of Sadhana Aunty's old saris.

I still have the photo that Amma snapped before we went onstage—my cousins and me with our arms splayed across each other's shoulders, looking more like a trio of beggars than the epic heroes and villains we intended to portray.

I carried the newfound sense of power onto the stage we set up in the sitting room, forgetting who I was for the brief window that the first act of our innocent tableau occupied. I let the sight of Amma and Prem, sitting side by side with amused expressions on their faces, blend in with the shadows the darkening sky cast about the room.

Everything went smoothly until Meenu came onstage. As Ravana, the evil demon king, she had made herself look repulsive, drawing raccoon rings around her eyes with kohl and smearing lipstick all over her face. I watched from the side as she staggered into the scene, opened her mouth, and paused. To my horror, she spoke her first lines, but not as we had rehearsed them. Instead, she spoke with a distinct stutter, just like Dev's. I looked into the faces of the audience.

Dev's nostrils had flared. Amma was biting her lip and Prem was shaking his head, trying to get Meenu's attention. But the look on Sadhana Aunty's face scared me the most. A white sheet of rage had descended upon her features, and her eyes were hard and ice-cold.

She stood up and I expected her to shout, but her voice was soft. "That's enough, it is getting late."

Krishna looked at her sister. Meenu's eyes filled with sudden angry tears. Her chest puffed up and she ran out of the room before it could deflate.

Balu, who had fallen asleep, began to stir and whine.

"I'll put him to bed, Aunty," said Gitanjali quickly, scooping him up and rushing out.

"Children!" Vijay Uncle remarked with a laugh. When nobody responded he wiped his hands on his trousers and went over to the table under the window. "Well, Dev, Prem, fancy a nightcap?" He picked up a half-drunk bottle of whiskey and began pouring out three glasses.

"One for me, too, Vijay," said Sadhana Aunty, and Vijay Uncle looked at her in surprise.

"Of course," he said, clearing his throat, and pouring the rich, brown liquid into a fourth glass.

Nalini Aunty made a disapproving shushing sound and covered her mouth with her hand.

The grown-ups sipped their drinks in silence.

"She's only a child, Sadhana," Prem finally said.

"She's nearly fourteen. That's old enough to have learned some respect." Sadhana Aunty's voice was cold.

"That's f-f-f-funny, Prem," Dev said, "that you should th-thi-think her age so very childlike."

"Why don't you girls go and get ready for bed?" said Amma, her voice cracking.

"But—" I began.

"No buts, Rakhee."

Krishna reached for my hand.

As we left the room together, she whispered into my ear: "Poor Meenu Chechi."

"Maybe we should go check on her."

Krishna nodded and we went and stood in front of Meenu's closed door.

"Chechi?" said Krishna, knocking.

There was no response.

"Meenu, come on, open the door," I said. "Please?"

We stood there for a long while, knocking and pleading, but Meenu neither responded nor opened the door, and eventually we gave up. Krishna, with tears streaming down her face, went to her room, but I lingered on the verandah in a pool of moonlight, thinking.

I knew Meenu shouldn't have mocked Dev, but I couldn't help feeling glad that she had. He was so unpleasant, and everyone was always fawning over and tiptoeing around him. I couldn't understand why. But I hoped things wouldn't be too awkward the next morning. I hoped the whole thing would be forgotten and we could go back to playing four-square and cricket as usual.

I began to feel sleepy, but my bed seemed so far away. I didn't have the energy to go wash my face and change into my pajamas, so instead I sat on the edge of the verandah step and rested my cheek against a pillar.

Birds sang in the Ashoka trees, and a soft breeze played the loose strands of my hair like a wind chime. The cows shuffled their hooves on the hay-strewn floor of their pen. It was a peaceful, soothing sound.

I wondered what Tulasi was doing at that moment. Was she reading the Shakespeare plays? Was she still sick? I wondered if she saw the lights of Ashoka through the forest and felt lonely.

For a while I sat there, undisturbed, half-dreaming. A man's voice interrupted my reverie.

"You were quite remarkable tonight, molay—a natural a-a-a-actress."

I looked down at my feet. "Um, thanks."

Dev came and sat beside me. I moved closer to the wall.

"B-b-b-but you envied your little cousin K-k-k-krishna, didn't you? You wanted the role of Sita." He chuckled, and I could smell the disorienting musk of alcohol on his breath. "At least you did not have to play Ravana, the v-v-villain."

I didn't know what to say.

"D-d-d-do not underestimate the v-v-villain, molay," he said. "It is only for the s-s-s-sake of the story that he loses in the end. If it were r-r-r-real life, he would get what he wants. The villain always h-h-has the bad reputation, but in t-t-t-truth, he is the most misunderstood c-c-character of all."

Dev didn't seem to be talking to me anymore; his eyes were fixed on the front gates, and his body was angled forward as if he was poised and ready to take off on a race.

He was silent for a minute, then he hissed, "D-d-d-do you know, Rakhee, that you m-m-might have been mine? That you sh-sh-sh-should have been my child?"

"What are you talking about?" I recoiled. The man was not only drunk, he had also lost his mind.

I stood up and so did he.

"Of course your m-m-mother would never t-t-tell you, but she was once b-b-b-betrothed to me—she was to be my w-w-w-wife. He promised her to me."

"Who promised?"

"Your g-g-g-grandfather, just before he died. B-b-b-but she ran away, she ran away from her d-d-d-duties and went to America." Dev gritted his teeth. "Oh! To think how differently life would have turned out had she st-st-st-stayed."

My head swam. "You're a liar." Amma could never have been engaged to Dev.

He swiveled to face me and grasped my shoulders. "You impudent child!" I squirmed beneath his painful grip. "How dare you talk to me in this way?" His stutter had vanished.

"Let go!"

He shook me hard. Yellow stars began to blink and flash in the space between us.

"Someone ought to teach you some manners. But then, I should not have expected much from the daughter of a h-h-h-whore."

I stopped struggling and my chin drooped to my chest. Blood flooded my skull and I thought I might faint.

"Take your hands off my daughter." I heard Amma's voice, cold with fury, and we both turned in surprise to see her standing before us. Dev released me and I fell against the railing, breathless. "Get out of here," Amma said, taking a step forward. Two wirelike veins stood out on either side of her neck.

Dev glared back at her. "I don't th-th-th-think you're in any position to tell m-m-m-me what to do, Chitra."

"I don't care who you are or what you know," said Amma with a fierce look in her eyes and a calm resolve in her voice that unnerved me. "If I ever catch you near my child again, I'll kill you."

Still, Dev did not move. He just stared hatefully at Amma for what seemed like an eternity. Finally he turned with a bitter laugh and stumbled off.

When he had disappeared down the stairs, I turned to face my mother, who was still quivering.

"Amma..."

"Are you all right?" she said.

"Yes, I'm fine."

"Are you sure?"

"Yes."

"Then go wash your face and change. I think you'd better go straight to bed," she said without meeting my eyes, and led me to my room.

I was so tired by this point that I could not argue. When my face was clean and bare, I sat on the bed and allowed Amma to run a comb through my tangled hair. She turned down the sheets and I lay beneath them. I couldn't remember the last time she had tucked me in. She tucked me in so tight I couldn't move.

"Amma?"

Muthashan was watching me from his portrait on the wall, his eyes dark and inscrutable.

"Yes, molay?"

"Can you stay until I fall asleep?"

Amma turned off the light and sat at the edge of my bed. I couldn't see Muthashan's portrait anymore. She stroked the hair off my face and kissed my forehead.

"I'm sorry, molay. I'm so sorry for all this. But I promise, it will be better soon. It will be better soon."

It would be better soon. For a moment I forgot where I was. Amma was my mother again and we were back in Plainfield. Aba was reading in his study, Merlin was snoozing at my feet, the stars were shining down on the cornfields.

Amma began to sing softly, the song about Lord Krishna she used to sing to me when I was a little girl, the one I had heard Vijay Uncle playing on the flute. I loved the story behind the song—the penniless scholar going to ask his prosperous childhood friend, Lord Krishna, for help and having nothing to offer him but a sack of puffed rice:

I am an orphan and I have only this humble gift to offer you, please accept this puffed rice which is soaked with my tears.

I fell asleep and dreamed that Dev was my father, and when I woke up my cheeks were wet, the sky was pink as a rose, and Amma was gone.

I got dressed and set out for the garden.

When I reached the wall I could hear Tulasi pacing back and forth. As I landed on the other side she hurried forward and threw her arms around me, pressing me close. She was wearing Amma's shawl.

"I have been thinking all night, Rakhee," she said. "I am sorry for not fully expressing my gratitude yesterday."

I was embarrassed. "It's okay, don't worry about it. We don't have to talk about it."

"No, but we should," Tulasi pressed on. "You are the only one I feel I can truly confide in now. Come inside."

I followed Tulasi into the cottage, and she went into the kitchen to prepare tea. The china cups made a tremulous tinkling sound as she handled them.

"The thing is," she said, when we had settled onto the wicker sofa and she had pulled the Shakespeare out from underneath a pillow, "the book is wonderful. It was the best, most thoughtful gift you could have possibly given. But it also shocked me. Why would Teacher have kept this from me? At first I thought maybe she hadn't known that William Shakespeare had written anything else, but according to the book's introduction, Shakespeare is famous in the outside world, and Teacher is an extremely learned woman. She must have known this. This means she deliberately lied to me, and I cannot understand why she would do such a thing. If she has lied to me about this, what other lies has she told? I have not been able to stop thinking about this. I am dreading her next visit. How shall I even look her in the eye now? Rakhee, I am so confused and ill at ease."

I had an idea. "Let me take you out of here."

"What are you talking about?" Tulasi's eyes widened. "You know I cannot do that."

"Why not?"

"No." She shook her head. "I cannot. I cannot leave the garden."

"Yes, yes you can." I knew what I was suggesting was crazy. Where would we even go? And what if something bad did actually happen to Tulasi if she left the garden? But I felt so consumed by adrenaline at the thought that I couldn't stop the words from coming out. "Just try it. Climb over the wall with me and you'll see. Nothing bad will happen to you."

"I couldn't possibly." The half of Tulasi's face that was not covered in a pink cloud turned a sick, yellow shade.

"Trust me. Nothing will happen. Just climb over the wall and then you can climb right back."

I knew that a week ago Tulasi would never have entertained my idea, but the Shakespeare book had changed everything. She hesitated.

"Do you promise I can climb right back?"

"Yes. Just see how it feels, then you can come back if you want."

Tulasi stared at me and said, "Okay, but only for a minute?"

"Only for a minute."

Tulasi walked over to the bed, knelt down, and slid the book underneath. "I'm ready." The yellow of her skin had been replaced by a waxy pallor.

We went outside and stood before the wall. Sunlight danced on the gray stone.

"I'll go first and you follow," I said, and scrambled up the wall. "It's easy, see?" I called out after I had jumped down to the other side. "Now, your turn."

I waited for a few minutes, shouting words of encouragement as I listened to Tulasi moving around on the other side, struggling to make it up the wall. Finally I glimpsed her white, terrified face at the top.

"Are you sure it will be okay?"

"I'm sure."

She dropped down beside me, and together we stood under the shade of the banyan tree.

An intense silence covered everything like a fresh blanket of snow. Gold filaments of sun flitted through the trees and lay on the forest floor like scattered beads. I glanced at Tulasi. Her knees were bent and her hands were outstretched, as if she were teetering at the very edge of a cliff.

I smiled, relieved. "See? Nothing happened."

Tulasi didn't speak. She was staring at the ground and breathing heavily, almost panting.

"Are you all right?" I placed a tentative hand on her shoulder.

"Let me go back, I have to go back," she gasped. Flinging herself against the wall, she began fumbling at the stone.

"But you just got here. You really want to go back already?" I was disappointed that our little adventure was ending so soon, especially now that I knew for sure Tulasi would be okay outside the garden wall.

"I am in earnest, Rakhee." She made a clumsy attempt to get her footing in between the stones, but slipped back down. She tried again, and again she slipped. She began to make an inhuman rasping sound.

I watched her try to climb up the wall and continuously slip down.

"Help," she croaked. "Help me."

But I couldn't get near her because her arms were flailing. "Hang on, be still for a second." I tried to grab her foot and boost her up, but she was thrashing about so much that I couldn't get hold of it. "You have to calm down and climb, Tulasi."

"I cannot breathe, I cannot—" She began to sob.

In the distance I heard the rooster's brassy crow.

I, too, started to panic. "Come on, you can do this, just concentrate." But it was no use. Tulasi continued to flap about like a fish on the deck of a ship.

What if Sadhana Aunty arrived and found us like this?

I couldn't let that happen. I pushed her aside and hauled myself up the wall. Draping my body over it, so that my stomach was flush against the top, my feet digging into the garden side, and my head and arms on the outside, I stretched my hands down as far as I could.

"Grab my hand," I said to Tulasi.

She reached up. "I can't."

"Yes you can. You have to jump."

She bounded up into the air and her fingertips brushed against mine. "I can't, Rakhee. It's too high, it's too high."

"You can do it. Come on, there's no other way. Take a deep breath and jump."

She jumped again, and this time our fingers latched. I grabbed her wrist with my free hand and felt my chin scraping against stone and my body falling backward with the weight of both our bodies. The next thing I knew I was on my back in the grass. Tulasi was beside me. Her breathing had slowed down and she was gazing up at the sky without blinking, blood welling on the underside of her chin.

"Teacher was right," she said.

"What?"

"I can't leave this garden or I will die."

I sat up and looked at her. "That's silly. She's not right, you just panicked. We can try again tomorrow."

"No, I can never try that again. She was right." Tulasi got to her feet and held her hand out to me, now calm.

I took her hand and she pulled me to my feet.

"Thank you for everything, Rakhee, truly," she said, drawing Amma's shawl around her shoulders. "Please come back tomorrow."

"I will."

I climbed back over the wall and ran as fast as I could through the forest, the scrape on my chin burning.

Ashoka was still swathed in the quiet of sleep, and I exhaled and paused on the verandah to catch my breath.

A howl of pain broke the morning's silence. At first I thought it was a cat fight. Then I heard a dull thud and another howl. It was coming from the abandoned shed that used to serve as a bathhouse, tucked into the trees a few yards away from the goat pen.

The thudding and the howling lasted for a full minute. Finally the shed door swung open and Meenu, her face red and swollen, limped out, followed by a haggard-looking Sadhana Aunty, who was carrying a wooden paddle.

I ducked so that they wouldn't see me. They went back into the house through the front entrance, and I heard Meenu's door close. A moment later Sadhana Aunty reappeared on the lawn, without the paddle, but this time carrying a notebook and a basket. She walked around the side of the house and disappeared, and I knew that she was going to see Tulasi.

From that morning forward, Meenu was different. For the rest of the summer she was haughty, sullen, and solitary. She no longer played or hung around with me and Krishna. Like Gitanjali, she rolled her eyes at our games and shooed us away when we approached her with the cricket bat. She had grown up.

Chapter 17

Not long after the incident with Meenu, Muthashi got sick again. Her fever spiked and she was confined to her bed, except this time nobody gathered us around the table and told us not to worry.

I heard Dev and Sadhana Aunty speaking outside Muthashi's bedroom.

"H-h-h-her heart is weak. P-p-p-preparations should be made." Dev's sleek stutter echoing in the corridor made my blood run cold. Nothing, it seemed, had been said about our encounter. He hadn't been around for a few days, but the moment Muthashi got sick, he arrived like clockwork, and nobody, not even Amma, said a word.

I looked inside Muthashi's bedroom when they left and saw not my neat, clean grandmother, but a mess of dingy white sheets and disheveled gray hair. There was that funny smell again, but this time it was more pungent. I covered my nose and ran to the verandah.

Krishna was sitting on the swing bouncing a small ball on the ground.

"I just saw your mother going down to use the telephone," she said in a flat voice.

"Really?" My heart thumped. "Who was she calling?"

"She had the big telephone book with her. I know what that means. She's informing people."

"Of what?" I asked, and as soon as the words left my lips I knew the answer.

A few tears rolled down Krishna's cheeks and dissolved in the lap of her dress. I had never seen anyone look so sad.

Later that evening, Sadhana Aunty went into Muthashi's room carrying a bottle of medicine and a spoon. A minute later she emerged with a fresh brown stain spreading across the front of her sari.

"She won't take her medicine," she said to Vijay Uncle, who was hovering outside the room. "She spat it out and swore at me. Our mother, Vijay. Our mother, who would rather let a mosquito feast on her blood than slap it. She is not herself."

"Let me try," said Vijay Uncle, taking the bottle and the spoon from his sister. But he, too, came out defeated, medicine dribbling from his chin onto his white shirt like dirty raindrops.

At the dinner table, Sadhana Aunty turned to Amma. "Did you speak to Veena? I assume she'll want to be here."

"Yes, she's trying to book a flight as we speak," said Amma.

"What?" I tugged on her sari. "Veena Aunty is coming here?" The thought of seeing someone I loved from Plainfield was too thrilling to contain my happiness.

"Muthashi is her aunt. We all grew up like sisters, you know. She wants to pay her respects." Amma's voice trembled, broke, and gave way to tears. She pushed away her banana leaf and buried her face in her arms.

"Chitra." Sadhana Aunty placed a hand on her shoulder but her face looked annoyed.

Vijay Uncle got up from the table and disappeared into the sitting room. My cousins all kept their eyes glued to the table, as if the knotty wood were the most fascinating thing they had ever seen.

~

I waited with morbid curiosity for Death to arrive. What would it look like? Dev had hinted at its arrival, but a few days passed and nothing happened, except a constant current of dread buzzed under my skin—that awful feeling of waiting for an unwanted but inevitable visitor.

I continued sneaking out of the house at dawn to visit Tulasi, and we never mentioned what had happened when she had climbed over the wall with me. Part of me wanted to try it again, and another part of me was afraid that maybe Tulasi was right. I did not want any harm to come to her, but at the same time, as the end of summer grew perilously near, I couldn't help fantasizing about setting her free and bringing her back to Plainfield.

She kept asking me what life was like in the outside world, and the more I told, the more I felt I should stop, for Tulasi was changing. She was no longer the happy, accepting girl I had met only a few weeks before. Caring for the garden was gradually becoming less of a priority for her. Instead she spent much of her time holed up inside the cottage, hovering over the Shakespeare book, devouring each play, one after the other, over and over again, as if the words on the page were now sustaining her life. The garden was still fragrant and exquisite as ever, but I noticed small changes, changes that pierced my heart with guilt. The grass was not so pliant beneath my feet. Petals from the Ashoka flowers pooled at the foot of the tree, waiting, like patient children, to be swept away. Weeds wound their way into the flower beds, and the magnificent roses began to droop.

Why couldn't I stop spinning my long, elaborate tales of life on the outside? The reason, I admit, was selfish. I told myself Tulasi needed to know these things, that I was telling her the truth, but really no one had ever listened to me like this before, had hooked themselves upon my every word as if their life depended on it. I felt bold, brash, and, for the first time, necessary.

Sometimes I woke up in the middle of the night and imagined I heard Puck's mournful call echoing through the forest and into my bedroom, a message for me alone, of sorrow or of warning. I shielded my ears with my hands and tried to put Tulasi out of my mind.

Death finally arrived around four o'clock one morning, accompanied by a chorus of wails. I ran out into the hallway, where my three cousins had already gathered in front of Muthashi's room.

"What's going on?" I asked Krishna, but she did not answer. Her mouth was agape. Sadhana Aunty, Amma, and Vijay Uncle were all huddled around Muthashi's bed. Amma and Vijay Uncle were clinging to each other and weeping. Nalini Aunty was standing with her back against the wall and her head bowed. Sadhana Aunty was not crying, but there was a haunted look in her eyes when she came to the door and told us:

"Muthashi is no more."

It was a funny way to put it: *Muthashi is no more.* Death had gathered up what was left of her in his black satchel and wandered off into the night. Muthashi had been snatched from the face of the earth. She was no more.

There was a loud collective cry, and my cousins were

all embracing. I stood apart. Sadhana Aunty put her arms around her daughters.

"There is nothing that can be done now. Her soul is at peace. Go back to bed and get some rest."

I did as she said, leaving my cousins to their grief. It was something I could not share.

I climbed back into my narrow bed and blinked into the ceiling, wondering if tears would come. The room was so dark I might have been lying on the lawn, staring up at a starless sky. I wasn't sure if what I was feeling was sadness.

I didn't get a chance to go to the garden in the morning because I fell asleep again, and by the time I woke up, the house was teeming with people. Murmurs and sobs emanated from the hallway outside my door. I sat up and listened, too afraid to go out. Eventually Amma swept in, her eyes puffy, with something green draped across her arm.

"Rakhee, have your bath, then put this on." Her voice was hoarse. She laid the material out on the bed. It was a long tunic with baggy pants and a shawl.

"Where did you get that?" I asked.

"It's Krishna's, but it should fit you all right, though you're taller."

Amma leaned against the door frame for a moment, sighed, and walked out, closing the door behind her.

I lingered in the bathroom, prolonging the process as much as possible. When I had bathed and dressed and could avoid it no longer I went out into the hallway, which was clogged with swarms of strangers. As I moved through the crowd, I felt all eyes upon me. Valsala, Veena Aunty's sister, was standing in one of the clusters, holding her baby, Parvathi, in her arms. Parvathi, who had grown considerably since I had last seen her that day at the hospital when she was a newborn, looked into my eyes as I passed and blinked, or at least I imagined she did.

The family was in the sitting room. Prem and his parents were there, too. In the center was a long white box that looked like a refrigerator except it had a clear glass lid and the words "Mobile Mortuary" printed across the side. Muthashi lay inside the box on a bed of chilly white satin. I had never seen a dead person before and instinctively turned away.

A hand came down upon my shoulder, soft as a falling petal. "It's okay to have a look."

Prem guided me forward toward the box. When I was only an inch away he removed his hand and left me alone.

I gazed down through the glass lid at Muthashi's face, which was illuminated by a fluorescent tube light. The withered moths of her eyelids were closed and her hands, fragile and wrinkled as crepe paper, were folded across her chest. At first glance she might have been sleeping, but the more I stared the more I sensed the difference death had wrought in her. There was a gray, iridescent sheen to her skin that hadn't been there in life, as if spiders had spent the night spinning webs back and forth across her face. She lay in that box, frozen and still as a slab of wood, and I knew that the Muthashi of my dreams, the one who sang the ant song to me, the one who pressed her face to mine and swallowed my scent, had disappeared entirely. Muthashi was no more.

"Come, Rakhee, you should eat something." Another hand came down on my shoulder; this time it was Amma's, and she steered me out of the room.

The rest of that day went by in a blur. Villagers trooped in and out of the house in a constant stream, some silent and subdued, others tearing at their hair and weeping, but all bearing food. I remember eating an uncomfortable amount because I didn't know what else to do, and by night my stomach was round and tight as a drum. It seemed the whole village came to pay their respects to Muthashi and our family that day. One woman pressed Sadhana Aunty to her ample breast and sobbed into her ear: "She was our mother, too. She was all of our mothers."

~

On the morning of the funeral Veena Aunty pulled up to the dirt road in front of Ashoka in a shiny black car, just as Amma and I had arrived only a couple of months before. I was waiting for her on the top step. It was the second day now that I had neglected to visit the garden. I knew Tulasi would be worried, but there hadn't been a single moment to slip away. Someone was always awake, up and bustling around, doing this, doing that. I was stuck.

The car door slammed. Veena Aunty was wearing a navy blue sari and had a maroon bindi on her forehead, but she was still the same Veena Aunty from Plainfield with her close-cropped black hair, her round face, her easy, gap-toothed smile.

I ran down the steps and hurled myself into her arms.

"Hey there!" she said, stroking the top of my hair.

"How's Aba?" I asked.

"He misses you like crazy. We all miss you like crazy."

I held her hand as she instructed the driver to take her suitcases to Valsala Aunty's house, which was another mile down the road. Together we walked up the steps to Ashoka, where Amma and Sadhana Aunty were waiting to greet her on the verandah.

Veena Aunty hugged Sadhana Aunty, then went over to Amma, placed both hands on her cheeks, looked into her eyes, and gave her a concerned smile. After a while Amma pulled away and Veena Aunty said:

"I want to see her."

Muthashi's body was still in the sitting room, but the mobile mortuary had disappeared. Now she was on a bed of banana leaves, laid out on the floor, with no barrier between us. She had on a white sari, but this one was slightly more formal than what she usually wore; the material seemed thicker and starchier, with a thin gold border. Someone had streaked her chalky brow with a red paste, and a constellation of bronze lamps flickered with smoky orange flames just above her head.

Veena Aunty knelt at Muthashi's side, folded her hands together, and pressed them to her forehead. She began whispering a prayer. I closed my eyes, waiting for her to finish, and when I opened them, Hema was standing in the doorway. Both Amma and Veena Aunty turned to Sadhana Aunty, who was watching Hema. Hema began to move forward into the room, her unblinking eyes never leaving Muthashi's face. Why did Sadhana Aunty not intervene? Hema sank to her knees beside Veena Aunty and continued to stare. Amma and Veena Aunty exchanged glances. Sadhana Aunty took a step forward, but still did not speak. Hema's face contorted into an expression of wild rage and she raised her hand as if she was about to strike Muthashi. Only then did Sadhana Aunty leap forward, grasp Hema by the arms, and pull her to her feet.

"Get out of here," she spat. "Who gave you the right to enter this house?"

The rage in Hema's face crumpled into despair.

Sadhana Aunty's back straightened and she looked

down at the feeble, shivering woman, who was clutching at the stained white cloth of her widow's sari and gathering it closer around her shoulders. "Leave now," she said.

Hema turned and shuffled out of the room.

Amma and Veena Aunty both had their mouths open.

"She is obviously unwell," Sadhana Aunty addressed us in a crisp tone. "Let us not mention this to anyone."

"But is it safe to keep her around here?" Amma's hand was at the base of her throat.

"She is too old and sick to be turned away. I will keep an eye on her. She will do no more harm to this family."

I left the room to find Krishna so I could tell her about what had just happened, and found her on the verandah steps, holding a striped cat in her lap, and watching something.

I sat down beside her and followed her eyes to Hari, who was holding an axe and standing in front of a mango tree near the well in the corner of the yard. The tree had a giant gash in the side of its trunk and was beginning to droop. Hari was shirtless, and his thin, dark chest was glazed with sweat. He twisted his palms around the handle of the axe, pulled back and struck at the gash with all his might. The trunk swayed and dipped.

"What's Hari chopping down that tree for?" I asked.

"They're going to use it to make a pyre for Muthashi—you know, for the cremation," Krishna said, stroking the cat's bristled fur. I had never seen Krishna, or anyone for that matter, holding that cat. It stalked around the yard, the fur along its spine raised in a perpetual mohawk of disturbance, its eyes wide, yellow, and unblinking. Occasionally it would turn its head to look at you and hiss. As far as I had known, it was feral. The servants fed it out of pity and the family tolerated its lurking presence, but nobody ever touched it. Now here it was, snuggled in the crook of Krishna's arm, its ears flattened against its head, meek as a gurgling baby.

"I pluck mangos from that tree every spring. They are so delicious," said Krishna. She nuzzled the cat against her cheek and it purred lethargically.

"Chee, get rid of that thing and wash your hands." Nalini Aunty was standing behind us. "You both must come with me. We are about to start."

Villagers began to arrive, moving up the stairs, across the lawn, and into the house. Eventually a single-file line of mourners snaked from the sitting room all the way to the lawn, spilling down the steps and onto the road. Krishna knelt in the doorway and I crouched above her. Amma, Sadhana Aunty, and Vijay Uncle were all standing near Muthashi's body and watching as one by one mourners stepped forward, each placing a magenta and gold cloth over Muthashi's head until a massive heap had accumulated, obscuring her face.

~

A miracle seemed to have occurred in the few hours since I had last been outside. Someone had strewn multihued petals—orange, white, red, pink—all along the ground from the edge of the verandah to the bottom of the steps of Ashoka, forming a pathway that was surrounded on either side by a border of lamps in full flare. Flames shivered and blazed, and the smell of smoke rose into the air, choking, intoxicating.

Women were not allowed to be present at the actual cremation site, so the last time I saw Muthashi she was being carried out of the house on a bamboo stretcher by

Vijay Uncle, Prem, Dev, and another man whom I did not recognize. I ran after them as far as I was allowed to go, across the lawn, through the wrought-iron gate, and down the steps, where I halted, slightly out of breath, watching as the men carried Muthashi through that path of flame and flowers as though she were a bride on a palanquin.

They brought her across the road and vanished into the grove of trees behind the hospital. Krishna had told me the land our family owned stretched far beyond the perimeter of the hospital, and that the cremation would take place about half a mile away from the house.

I stood at the bottom of the steps for a long time, even after the final scarlet streaks of sun had been erased by a shimmering blue twilight. In the distance I could see a thin plume of smoke curling through the treetops and into the sky like a sinewy black finger.

Veena Aunty came outside to join me. "Rakhee, are you all right?"

"Yes."

"Then why are you still out here, why don't you come inside? It's been a long day," Veena Aunty took my hand, but I resisted. I had been waiting to talk to her and now was the perfect opportunity. She was the one, out of all the grown-ups, who I could rely upon to tell me the truth.

"Veena Aunty, it's been a weird summer," I began.

"I'm sure it has been," she said with a laugh that struck me as uncomfortable.

"I have so many questions—"

But Veena Aunty interrupted me with a sorrowful expression. "Hush, not now. We'll talk about everything soon, I promise, but I just can't do it today." She wiped away a few tears that had begun to pool in her eyes. "You know, I loved your Muthashi like she was my own mother. When I was a kid I was over here even more than I was at my own house. It's different for my sister Valsala; she was too young, so she never really hung around with our group as much. It was always me, Sadhana, Chitra, Vijay, and Prem, and your grandmother treated us like she had given birth to us all, there was no difference." Veena Aunty sighed and rubbed her chest as if she were in pain. "Now that she's gone this place doesn't feel the same. She was the heart of this family. Even in these last years when her mind was starting to go, she never stopped being the heart of this house."

We began to walk back up the steps, but at the top step Veena Aunty paused. "Before we go in, let me ask you something, Rakhee. How has your mother been? Has she seemed—okay?"

"What do you mean, 'okay'?"

"Has she been acting differently, you know, from what you're used to?"

"She cries a lot now, and she gets these headaches," I said, "really bad ones. And one second she'll be happy and the next second she'll be sad." I didn't mention anything about Prem or about what I had seen that afternoon back in Plainfield when Amma had flushed all her pills down the toilet.

Veena Aunty's jaw clenched, and relaxed. "I'm sorry, this must be hard on you. But don't worry, it's going to be okay," she said, and then her tone went from anxious to playful. "Now let's get you something to eat. I thought a summer in India would fatten you up, but you're still way too skinny."

~

At dawn Vijay Uncle went into the backyard carrying a silver platter covered in newspaper. He placed the platter on the stone barrier that divided the yard from the forest, and bent his head down low. I saw him from my bedroom window and ran outside in my nightgown.

"Vijay Uncle, what are you doing?"

"Oh hello, Rakhee, aren't you up early," he said with a sad smile. "Just watch and see."

We stood there side by side in silence. Vijay Uncle kept acting like he was on the verge of doing something, but he'd suddenly chicken out. Finally, after a few minutes had passed, he leaned forward and whipped the newspaper off the platter with a quick motion, as if he were ripping off a bandage as painlessly as possible.

The platter was adorned with round, white balls made out of rice.

"Now"—Vijay Uncle took my hand—"we wait."

"What are we waiting for?"

"Sssshhh."

I was beginning to wonder if Vijay Uncle was going crazy, or if maybe he had been drinking, but then I heard a flapping sound coming from all directions. The sound grew heavier and more oppressive, and fear began to burn like a marching trail of fire-red ants up and down my spine.

"Ah," said Vijay Uncle, "they have arrived." He took my hand and guided me back toward the house.

We stopped and turned around when we were a safe distance away. A cloud of cawing black crows, larger than any bird I had ever seen before, had congregated on the stone barrier, wings beating, attacking the rice balls with a fierce appetite.

"This is good, very good," said Vijay Uncle. "This

means that our ancestors are blessing us, they are blessing this house even though Muthashi is gone. They are pleased with us."

He gave my hand a happy squeeze, but something in his voice made me think he wasn't at all convinced.

Chapter 18

R akhee, where are you?"
It was Tulasi's voice—there was no doubt about it.
I opened my eyes and sat up. The room was soaked in
moonlight.

"I waited and waited, but you never came, so I left the
garden to find you." Her voice was floating in through my
window, delicate and mournful. "Now I'm dying. Please
let me in. I don't want to die alone."

Tulasi's face, ghost-white, was gazing in at me, and her
two translucent hands gripped the window bars.

"Let me in, please," she said again.

I reached out to touch her hands, to reassure her, but
they were icy and wrinkled, like Muthashi's hands. I recoiled and flung myself facedown on the bed, pulling the
sheet over my head.

"I'm sorry, I couldn't come, it wasn't my fault," I
sobbed into the pillow.

She moaned and rattled the bars. "Let me in, let me in,
let me in."

I lifted the sheet; all the flesh had melted off Tulasi's
face and she was a skeleton.

"Now see what you've done! I'm dead, I'm dead," the

skeleton shrieked and stuck its arms, thin as tuning forks, through the bars, straining down toward me.

I cowered under the sheets. "Please, go away, just go away, I'll go to the garden tomorrow, I promise, just don't touch me."

I would do anything as long as those horrible hands didn't come near me.

The next thing I knew, I was being rocked back and forth, my head pressed against Amma's breast.

"Ssh, wake up, molay, you're having a bad dream," she crooned into my ear. "That's all it is, a bad dream."

I broke away from Amma and leaped to the window. There was no one there. The moon had ducked behind a murky bank of clouds, and the sky was black as a bat's wing.

"What happened?" I asked, climbing back into bed.

"I heard you shouting," said Amma. "Do you want to come and sleep with me?"

"No," I turned my face to the wall. Amma hesitated before leaning over to kiss my hot, wet cheek.

"As you like," she said, and left the room.

I was afraid that if I let myself fall asleep again the skeleton would come back, so I took a book out of my suitcase and began to read it under the covers with my flashlight. But despite my best efforts, sleep drew me back under its net. When I finally surfaced it was late morning and the house was alive.

All morning the skeleton danced a crazed jig in my head. I needed to go back to the garden, to see Tulasi and to explain my absence. So after lunch I made a lame excuse when Krishna asked me to play with her, and I recklessly slipped around the back of the house and through the forest.

"Tulasi!" I called, when I got to the wall. I waited for a few moments, but when I did not hear her usual rustling about on the other side, I climbed over, ripping open the newly hardened calluses on my palms.

The grass crunched beneath my feet as I landed in the garden, which appeared to be shrinking; the flowers were beginning to shrivel and sag; rotting fruit and dead leaves littered the ground.

I called my friend's name again with greater urgency in my voice. I walked up to the cottage door and knocked, but there was no answer, so I put my hand on the knob and turned. It opened with a low creak.

"Tulasi?" My weak voice echoed back at me.

I moved through the sitting area, the kitchen, the bed. I yanked back the mosquito netting and found the bed neatly made and empty. Even Puck was nowhere in sight.

I coughed and put my hand to my throat. She was gone. It was too late. I knelt upon the hard, cold floor.

"Rakhee," said a familiar voice.

My stomach lurched and I looked up to see Tulasi standing before me with Puck resting upon her outstretched arm as if it were a branch.

"You scared me," I said.

"I wasn't expecting you. I haven't seen you for days. I thought you had forgotten about me." Tulasi's voice was flat. She appeared to have lost weight.

"I'm sorry. I wanted to come, I really did, but something happened and I wasn't able to."

"What happened?"

"Somebody," my voice cracked, "somebody died."

Tulasi's eyes grew wide. "Oh, how wretched! Pardon my selfishness, Rakhee, that is terrible. Who was it that passed?"

"Actually, I'd rather not talk about it," I said.

Tulasi regarded me for a moment before letting Puck flutter to the ground. Moving to the kitchen, she began to boil water for tea, as if nothing had changed between us.

When we had settled down on the sofa, Tulasi bit her lip and said: "Rakhee, I have been thinking, and there is a favor I must ask of you, if it is not too much of a bother."

"What is it?" I said, my ears pricking up. "I'd do anything for you."

"Really?" she smiled, "Well, you see, I have been pondering a great deal over the last few days. I have learned so much about the world since you came into my life, and I realized—I cannot believe this never struck me before, but..." She paused, then continued, "I have no idea how I...look."

My mouth went dry.

"I mean, I have a general idea—I know the color of my hair and my skin. But I have only ever seen myself in the pools of rain that puddle in my garden, and the reflection is so distorted and blurry. I long to know how I *really* look. I asked Teacher if she could bring me a mirror, and she scolded me and delivered a lengthy lecture on the perils of vanity. I was so despondent because I feel awful going on without having a clue how I look. I mean, I know being vain is a deplorable quality, but I must know, Rakhee—am I beautiful?" She looked at me with expectant eyes.

"Yes, you are," I said automatically.

A glow of happiness lit up her face. "Really, you really mean that?"

"Yes," I said, "yes, I do." And I really did mean it. The first time I saw her I had been shocked and revolted, but the more I got to know Tulasi, the more her looks ceased to matter. In fact, I hardly noticed her deformities anymore. A teacher at school had once told our class, "Looks don't really matter, it's what's on the inside that counts," and I had scoffed at her. Of course looks mattered. I would have given anything to trade places with Lindsay Longren, to look into the mirror and see her long, flowing golden locks and blue eyes pure as the sea. But since meeting Tulasi, I understood for the first time what my teacher had meant. Tulasi was the most beautiful person I had ever seen, and I had never felt closer to anybody else. Sadness at the thought of leaving her consumed me, but I couldn't bring myself to tell her about my impending departure.

"I am so happy to hear you say that, because you are the only person I truly trust now and I simply could not bear to be ugly. Teacher has deceived me once. I do not know what else she may have been deceitful about. But still, as much as I trust you, I must know for myself. Would you please bring me a mirror? Teacher never has to know."

It would have been easy to bring her a mirror. I could swipe Amma's compact from her makeup bag and stash it in my pocket. But I did not want to be the one to show Tulasi the truth about her face.

"Um, there aren't really any mirrors where I'm staying," I said.

For a moment Tulasi's chin trembled. Then she brightened and said: "You have always talked about how much you love drawing. Perhaps you could draw my portrait?"

I wrung my clammy hands, not knowing how I could get out of this one. "Sure."

"Wonderful!" she exclaimed, and reached out to hug me. "You are my best friend."

"I'll be back tomorrow with my sketchpad," I said, worried about what I had gotten myself into. "I should go."

"I shall be waiting for you tomorrow."

When I got back to the house, Krishna was sitting on the verandah step.

"Where were you?" she said, her lips plumped to a pout.

"I just went for a walk," I said a little too quickly. "To the village square."

"Everyone's been mad with worry. You've been gone for two hours. They sent Hari out to search for you. You'd better go tell your mother you're back. She's in the dining room."

I ran to find her.

"Rakhee," Amma sprang out of her seat and clutched me to her breast as soon as she caught sight of me. "My God, where were you?"

I didn't answer. The material of her sari wadded and bunched up in my mouth. I couldn't speak.

Amma's face was red. She shook me by the shoulders. "Answer me, where were you?"

A dam burst inside me and I began to bawl. I wasn't expecting that. Neither were Amma or Sadhana Aunty. Amma let go and looked at me in shock. My body quaked and it felt so good that I couldn't stop.

"Rakhee, where did you go, what has happened?" said Sadhana Aunty, getting up out of her chair and taking a step forward.

Knowing I was in deep trouble and could not offer any ordinary excuse, I grasped at a story I had once overheard a girl surreptitiously telling another on the playground, a story that had haunted me for weeks afterward. I seized at the memory, which I had never mentioned to anyone, and made it my own. The words tumbled out, clear as if I had rehearsed them beforehand: "I just wanted to get some chocolate, so I went to the market. But on my way home I saw a tall shadow behind me. I turned around and there was a man standing there, a weird man. He pulled down his pants and showed me his thing." At this, I sobbed so hard I could barely speak.

Amma's face went white. "Oh my God," she whispered. "Oh my God, my darling, my poor darling." She hugged me and started to cry.

Sadhana Aunty pried us apart, sat me down on a chair, and gave me a handkerchief. "Yes, and then what happened?"

"I was scared, so I ran and hid behind a tree. I hid until I was sure the man was gone. I didn't know what else to do." Bringing the handkerchief to my nose I blew loudly and noisily.

"What exactly did this man look like?" she said, after I had wiped my face.

"I don't know. He was tall, he had curly dark hair and a moustache." I sniffed uncertainly. "He was missing some teeth," I added.

Sadhana Aunty made an impatient sound. "That could be any man in the village. Where exactly did this happen?"

"Um, by the corner of the road where...I don't know, I don't remember." I buried my face in my hands. The lie tied itself into a knot at the pit of my stomach.

"Corner? What corner?" She didn't believe me.

Amma stepped in. "Leave her alone. Think what she's been through."

"She—" Sadhana Aunty began to say, but then clenched her jaw and turned away.

Amma knelt down in front of me and took my hands away from my face. She squeezed them tight and looked at me.

"Molay, you must promise me you will never wander off like that by yourself again. Ever. Do you hear me? There are bad people out there, even in a small village like Malanad. It's simply not safe for a young girl like you to go off by herself. Will you promise me never to do this again?"

"Okay," I said, averting my gaze.

"Say, 'I promise never to wander off by myself again.'" Amma squeezed my hands even tighter.

"I promise never to wander off by myself again," I said, but in my heart I was crossing my fingers. No one could keep me away from Tulasi, not Sadhana Aunty and not Amma—especially not Amma.

~

I took my sketchpad out onto the verandah and sat next to Krishna.

"Want to draw together?" I asked. I knew that she was upset that I had chosen not to share my mysterious afternoon's adventure with her.

She shrugged and knitted her fingers into an elaborate web.

"Well, I'm going to draw," I said. "You can do whatever you like."

Krishna watched me for a minute, then finally extended her hand. "Me too," she said.

I smiled and tore out a piece of paper for her and placed my box of colored pencils in between us.

For a while we drew side by side in silence. I was sketching a hibiscus flower, but in my head I was planning out my portrait of Tulasi.

I decided I could not draw her as she was, with her misshapen mouth and discolored face. Beauty was so important to her, she had said so herself: *I couldn't bear to be ugly.* I just couldn't reveal this particular truth to her. So I would draw her as she would look had she been born without deformities. Where there was a strawberry splotch on her face, I would draw smooth, even skin. Where there was a gash in her lip I would draw a full, fleshy Cupid's bow. I would make her as beautiful on the outside as she was on the inside.

"Rakhee, you said you went to the market?" said Krishna, interrupting my thoughts.

"Yes." My face grew hot. Lying to the grown-ups was one thing, but lying to Krishna was another.

"But I saw you coming from behind the house," she said in a quiet voice. "Why is that?"

I did not know what to say, so thinking quickly I slammed my sketchpad onto the verandah ledge and exclaimed dramatically: "Why is everyone always interrogating me? Can't you all just leave me alone?" I stalked off to my room and closed the door, feeling instantly awful about how I had treated my cousin. I stayed in my room for the rest of the evening, refusing to come out even for dinner.

~

I crept outside earlier than usual the next morning, knowing I could no longer afford to be careless, and slipped over the stone barrier into the forest like a nymph dissolving into the dew. The sky, hovering between night and dawn, was both light and dark at the same time.

Holding my sketchpad between my teeth, I climbed up and over the wall, and landed in the garden, where Tulasi and Puck were both waiting for me.

"Come," said Tulasi, leading me with a solemn air down the cobblestone path and into the cottage.

Filled with excitement and anxiety, I drew back the curtains and positioned her in the window seat where an arrow of light fell across her face, giving her skin the same ghostly sheen it had had in my dream.

Two thick candles burned on the table.

"I thought you might need more light," Tulasi said.

"Thank you." I felt very proud and serious, like a real artist.

I settled down on the sofa, took a deep breath, and examined her face—the curve of her cheek, the point of her chin, the wave of her hair, the darkness of her eyes. My pencil began to move across the page. I had the sensation that my mind had detached itself from my body. Afraid of this new feeling, I struggled to yank myself back to reality and looked down at the indecipherable tangle of random lines I had created. Tulasi sat still and regal in the dawn light. She trusted me. It was in my power to make her happy. I bit my lip and made a few more tentative strokes. The outline of her face began to emerge. I let myself swim back into that feeling of detachment, and my hand grew more confident, darting back and forth across the page like a curious insect.

I cannot remember much else. Letting my hand do the work, guided by instinct, I entered a kind of trance. Gradually from within the mess of pencil strokes, a face came to life—a perfect, unmarred face.

As my thoughts drifted back to me, my heart began to pound so viciously I feared it would explode right through my chest.

"Rakhee, what is it?" Tulasi stood up, a V of worry creasing the space between her brows.

My hand was shaking, so I set the pencil aside and stared hard at the portrait.

Was I dreaming again? If I pinched myself would I be spirited through the forest back to my room, back to my bed, back into Amma's stifling embrace?

I closed my eyes and opened them again. This was not just any portrait. I had been introduced to this face for the first time only a few months ago, but I realized now that I had known it for my whole life, that it was as familiar to me as my own face.

"Rakhee, why did you stop?" Tulasi was watching me with a concerned and eager expression. "Are you finished? Can I see?"

I jumped up, holding the pad against my chest.

"Not yet," I blurted. "I have to go."

"But Rakhee, why can't I see it? It is early still. Why must you go so abruptly?"

"I can't explain right now, I just have to go." I ran out into the garden and clambered over the wall.

I sped through the forest as the sun rose, beating its heavy rays down on the top of my head and my back. Crows were everywhere, hovering in clumps on the branches of the trees, on the rotting stumps rising up from the earth, on the blankets of velvety green moss, the spirits of my ancestors guiding me, provoking me, protecting me, judging me. Who was Tulasi, really? A door had been unlocked, but still I struggled to open it. Twigs and sticks snapped beneath my feet as I stomped through the trees, back to Ashoka.

I half-expected to find Sadhana Aunty waiting for me on the verandah, hands on hips, but I was able to slip back into my room undetected. Panting like an animal, I tore the portrait out of the sketchpad, went over to my suitcase, unzipped the inner pocket, and slipped the sheet of paper inside.

I lay down on the bed, facing the ceiling, willing my ears to stop ringing and my heartbeat to slow down.

"Rakhee, are you awake?" My bedroom door opened and Krishna poked her head in.

I sat up.

"I am sorry for int-int-interrogating you yesterday," she said in English, pronouncing each word with practiced deliberation.

"I shouldn't have shouted at you."

Krishna grinned, "Let's eat breakfast. We're having dosas. Will you sit beside me?"

I smiled back at her. "Of course."

My body settled into a momentary calm as I followed Krishna into the dining room and sat down next to her. Janaki placed a perfectly round, crisp dosa onto my plate, and ladled golden sambar on top. Amma was wearing her nightgown, moving her forefinger in a circle around the edge of her teacup, and staring off into space.

"Would anybody like some fruit?" Sadhana Aunty came out of the kitchen holding a brass platter with a ripe red mango balanced upon it. She was surprisingly cheerful.

"Mmmmm, mango!" said Krishna.

Sadhana Aunty sat at the head of the table, and made a clean slice through the mango's flesh with a knife. Yellow juice oozed and trickled out through the crack.

Why was she in such a good mood? My heart began its uncomfortable dance again.

"Mango, mango, mango, my favorite fruit!" Krishna chanted.

"Rakhee, would you like some?" Sadhana Aunty's eyes

met mine and flashed. The dance in my heart came to an abrupt halt; everything inside me froze.

The knife.

It was the same one that I had brought with me that first morning I had gone to the garden; it was the knife that had grazed my flesh and drawn my blood. It was the same knife that I had left as a guard buried deep within the roots of the banyan tree.

Sadhana Aunty didn't look at me again, but she smiled as she peeled the skin off the mango in one long, endless stroke.

Chapter 19

The rain stopped. All summer long it had come down regularly, at least every other day, giving us respite from the sun, washing over the earth, making it new again. But now the sun reigned ceaselessly, blanketing the village in its cruel heat. Clay rooftops blistered and cracked, and sunstruck birds fell from the sky like charred stones.

I couldn't get back to the garden. Sadhana Aunty was always around. When I woke up at dawn I would hear her pacing the halls, knitting on the verandah, or on her knees scrubbing the floor like a servant. To my surprise, she hadn't confronted me, but she watched me the way bullfrogs in the river sat on their lily pads and eyed the black flies lathering just beyond the reach of their sticky tongues. Krishna and I were forbidden from leaving Ashoka unaccompanied by an adult, in case "that crazy man Rakhee encountered" was still lurking about, even though Sadhana Aunty and I both knew there was no crazy man.

When I wasn't lying in my room thinking about Tulasi or squinting at her half-finished portrait, Krishna and I sulked around the house trying to occupy ourselves with reading, drawing, or coming up with ideas for mini-plays. But it wasn't the same without Meenu, who, like Gitan-jali, had taken to shutting herself up in her room, coming out only for meals, and I suspected even that was only because Sadhana Aunty forced her. Nalini Aunty could usually be found staring at the fuzzy pictures on the tele-vision screen, popping a chili-coated snack mix into her slack mouth, while Balu crawled around on the floor or whimpered until he was lifted into her lap. Vijay Uncle was down at the hospital more often than not, but when he was at home, I could hear him muttering to himself. He had not shaved since Muthashi died, and a growth of unkempt beard blackened his jaw. Amma went back to sleeping away the days in her dim room, sometimes not even getting up to bathe, except when Prem stopped by for a visit.

"Rakhee, where's your mum?" he would ask, as he came swiftly up the verandah steps in his clean white shirt and khaki pants. The very sight of him brought the resent-ment rising up like bile at the back of my throat.

I would go into Amma's room, dark and hot with dan-delions of dust floating in the air. "Prem's here," I would say, trying my best not to breathe in the stuffiness.

Amma would sit up and regard me blearily as if I were a stranger for a few seconds before a light of recognition set her eyes aflame.

"Tell him to wait for me in the sitting room," she would instruct before springing out of bed and vanishing into the bathroom. After emerging more than half an hour later, fully dressed, her long hair swishing behind her back like a horse's tail, she would hurry to the sitting room, leaving behind a sharp scent and a trail of wet foot-prints.

One afternoon as Krishna and I sat fanning ourselves
with comic books on the verandah swing, the sound of
someone walking up the steps that led up to the lawn and
opening the creaky front gate punctured the restless sobs
of a baby goat alone in its pen. Slow, rhythmic footsteps,
not fast and eager, so I knew it wasn't Prem, who took the
stairs two at a time, just like Aba, which I hated to acknowledge.

I got to my feet when I saw Veena Aunty walking across
the lawn toward us. Veena Aunty hadn't been around
much since Muthashi's funeral, so I still hadn't had a
chance to talk to her. I had a feeling Amma didn't want
me to see her. A few times I asked for permission to go
over to their house for a visit and she said, "Why do you
want to go and bother Veena Aunty? She hasn't seen her
family in a long time."

"How are you, dear?" she said in a distracted tone,
and then without waiting for an answer, "Where is your
mother?"

"I'll get her," I told Veena Aunty, and started to go
toward Amma's bedroom. But she put a hand on my
shoulder.

"No, let me," she said.

She slipped into Amma's room and closed the door.
Of course I followed and pressed my ear against the warm
wood, but they were talking so quietly that I didn't hear
much. Only at one point did I catch anything as Amma
gave out a frantic yell:

"Don't you call him, don't you dare call him!"

"He needs to know, Chitra, he's your husband. Let us
help you."

"No!" cried Amma, and then everything was silent
again.

I tried to catch Veena Aunty on her way out, but she was even more distracted.

"What's going on?"

"Nothing you need to worry about, dear," she said in a hurry, as she passed me by, but then she paused, came back, and gave my shoulder a squeeze. "It's going to be okay, dear, I promise."

~

One day Dev, Vijay Uncle, and Sadhana Aunty filed into the sitting room, shutting the door and locking it behind them. It was daylight when they went in, and the door didn't open again until sunset, when Sadhana Aunty emerged with sweat on her cheeks and called for Janaki to bring them a jug of water. Taking the proffered jug, she went back in and closed the door.

Amma appeared after a while wearing a dingy white housedress, her hair loose and tangled, and, after grilling us about who was in there, began to pace back and forth outside the locked door.

"Why are they in there for so long?" she asked nobody in particular. Once or twice she tried to rattle the door-knob, but it didn't budge, so she gave up and went back to pacing.

At nightfall I heard a loud crackle and the lights went out.

"The current," said Krishna.

Janaki hurried around the dining room lighting candles, and everyone, even Meenu and Gitanjali, gathered around the table.

After the candles were lit, Janaki went and stood behind Amma and said: "The children must be fed."

Amma squinted at her, as if she didn't quite understand.

"The children," said Janaki in a louder voice. "They need their dinner."

"Oh yes, of course," said Amma, her eyes widening. "Go ahead and feed them."

"But madam." Janaki looked down at her scuffed feet, then shifted her weight from one to the other, her anklets jingling. "I don't know what to give them. Sadhana Chechi usually gives me instructions."

Amma pressed her palm to her forehead and closed her eyes. "I don't know, Janaki, give them whatever is in the kitchen, give them anything!"

Eventually we fed on the afternoon's rice coated in a dal so bland and soupy I suspected Janaki had watered it down to make sure there was enough to go around.

"What in the world could they be doing in there?" complained Nalini Aunty, as she shoveled the tepid mixture into her mouth. "I understand that Dev and my husband have business to discuss, but why must Sadhana Chechi involve herself? It's simply not ladylike the way she interferes with the hospital business."

"Maybe they'll sell the stupid hospital," said Gitanjali.

"*Chee*, don't talk that way, you silly girl. The hospital belongs with the Varmas. Think of the prestige it has brought this family. But I do wish I could convince that husband of mine to be better about collecting payment from patients. He is so lenient. At least Dev has some business sense. *He* doesn't treat people for free." Nalini Aunty's mouth curved downward. "Though we still never seem to have enough money. 'The Varmas are a prosperous family,' everyone told me when I was a young girl, but look at me now." She fingered the thin brown material of her sari and sniffed.

A muffled shout boomed through the door.

Nalini Aunty clicked her tongue in annoyance, but I saw fear in her eyes. Amma didn't say anything but she bit her lip so hard that a faint thread of blood trickled down from the edge of one tooth. Krishna and I exchanged looks.

A line of crudely crafted candles rose up from the center of the table like white fingers, and flames bloomed from their misshapen tips. Nobody spoke or moved. We sat glued to our chairs, waiting. There wasn't anywhere else to go.

Finally Nalini Aunty spoke in a voice that sounded different—softer, shakier.

"Chitra Chechi, won't you sing a song for us? I have heard stories about your voice. They say you sing like an angel."

I turned to Nalini Aunty in surprise, and for a second I thought I caught a glimpse of the girl in the photograph, the one with the hopeful smile, the one who had long been erased.

"A song?" Amma stared uncomprehendingly.

"Yes, please, sing us a song. Won't you?" Her eyes were wide and pleading.

Amma looked at Nalini Aunty and her face changed, as if, like Ashoka, the current had shut off inside her head for a while and then had been suddenly switched back on. "Of course," she said, smiling. "Yes, of course."

She took a deep breath, smoothed her hair, then folded her hands, like two pretty flowers, neatly upon her lap. As she began to sing, her sweet, clear tones wound a golden thread around the room, binding together its occupants, dissolving the thick tension, and replacing it with calm. She really did sing like an angel, my mother, and I closed my eyes, pretending it was like old times and she was singing only to me. Janaki emerged from the kitchen and crouched beside the table, her head cocked to one side. We all listened, entranced, until at last the door to the sitting room opened and the thread snapped. Amma stopped singing, Nalini Aunty stood up, and we all looked at Sadhana Aunty, who leaned in the doorway.

"Well, you are all still up," she said in a ragged voice. "Gitanjali, I must speak with you privately. Come with me, please."

Gitanjali, looking both concerned and grave, stood up and, cupping a candle in her palms, followed her mother into her room.

Vijay Uncle and Dev emerged next, Dev with a spark of triumph in his eyes and that familiar bottle of whiskey squeezed in his fist. Vijay Uncle staggered as he approached the table, the rims of his eyes raw and red.

"What is it?" said Nalini Aunty.

"Janaki, f-f-f-fetch lime juice for the l-l-l-ladies, and two empty glasses for Vijay and m-m-m-myself." Dev waved his hand.

Janaki jumped up and ran into the kitchen.

"Dev, I don't know if this is a good idea. It is late. Perhaps it would be best if you...came back tomorrow," Vijay Uncle mumbled, and stroked his beard.

"Nonsense, Vijay." Dev slapped his back. "We must c-c-c-c-celebrate this joyous oc-oc-occasion first."

Janaki bustled back into the dining room with the drinks. I drew the cup to my lips and sipped, wincing at the sourness; Janaki had forgotten the sugar.

An anguished shriek came from the direction of Gitan-jali's room.

Dev, who was pouring whiskey into two glasses, glanced

up and for a second the triumph in his eyes was blurred by a look of profound sadness.

"Vijay, what has happened? What is going on?" Amma stood up and gripped the edge of the table. The blood had dried and crusted into a red petal just below her bottom lip.

At the sound of Amma's voice, the sadness vanished, and Dev's mouth twisted into a smirk.

"C-c-c-congratulate me, Chitra," he said. "I have found the b-b-b-b-bride I was always meant to h-h-h-have. A young, beautiful g-g-g-g-girl, pure of heart, pure of b-b-b-b-body."

"What?" Amma turned to Vijay Uncle. "What is he talking about?"

Vijay Uncle lifted the glass, tipped his head back, and drained it.

"It is true," he said finally, his voice strained, as if he were being choked. "Dev has asked for Gitanjali's hand in marriage, and we have given him our blessing."

I dug my fingernails into my palms and pressed hard, the searing pain letting me know that this was not one of my nightmares.

Meenu's and Krishna's faces were blank.

Amma's lips went white.

"I am to be married to the f-f-f-f-f-fair Gitanjali." Dev took a sip of his drink, set it down on the table, and wiped his mouth with the back of his hand. "It is getting l-l-late, so we shall continue the celebration in the coming days. I wish to make her my b-b-b-b-b-bride as soon as possible. I do not believe in long en-en-en-en-engagements."

Vijay Uncle, without looking any of us in the eye, followed Dev, saying, "I will fetch the torch and accompany you home, Dev. Perhaps I'll nip by the toddy shop on the way back."

Nalini Aunty's chin wobbled as she watched Vijay Uncle, shoulders slumped, leave the room. She, too, got up and hurried out.

For a long time I had known something was "not quite right" about Ashoka, as Krishna had once told me, but the idea of Gitanjali marrying Dev was worse than anything I could have ever imagined.

The room had sunk into silence. Only at one point was it broken, when the door to Gitanjali's room swung open and Sadhana Aunty called out something unintelligible. Janaki went into the kitchen and came out with a small brown bottle and a spoon, which she brought to Sadhana Aunty.

"What is that?" I asked Meenu, who was sitting beside me, but she did not answer.

At last Sadhana Aunty came out of Gitanjali's room and dropped into a chair at the table.

"She is asleep."

For the first time that summer, Sadhana Aunty looked weak and insignificant, dwarfed by the frayed wooden chair into which she sank. She encircled her dry fingers around one of the untouched glasses of lime juice and drank it down in slow, measured gulps.

When she had finished drinking, she cleared her throat, but before she could speak, Amma said: "You can't do this. You *cannot.*"

"Chitra, please do not interfere. Haven't you already done more than enough?" Sadhana Aunty said in a sharp, cold voice. Amma flinched, then rose and left the room without a word.

"I am well aware of what I am doing." Sadhana Aunty addressed us now. As she spoke, her shoulders rounded and her spine straightened. "This is for my father and for our family. Gitanjali understands, or at least she will come to understand why this union is necessary. What you girls must realize is that family is everything and sometimes we must shoulder burdens and make sacrifices for the sake of our family."

"But why does Gitanjali Chechi have to marry Dev?" said Krishna.

"Dev Uncle," said Sadhana Aunty. "Soon to be Dev Chettan, your brother. You are all too young, it is too complicated, and it is not a story for children's ears."

Meenu glowered at her mother. "You ask us to understand but you won't explain anything to us."

"It is not my duty to explain, it is my duty to protect you and to protect this family. I have never wavered from that purpose. Gitanjali is young yet, but I am not blind. She has never cared much for her studies, and do not think I know nothing of that foolish boy from her class. Do you know that his father is a driver? A driver! If that is the future she dreams of for herself then I am saving her from a bitter fate. You may not like Dev, but he can take care of your sister in a way that I am no longer able, and he can ensure that the hospital remains in the Varma family. That hospital is our future, your future, it is your inheritance. Without it, you are just like everybody else." Sadhana Aunty paused and sighed. "Gitanjali will still be nearby, you will still get to see her often, and—I admit this is not an ideal situation, I never meant for any of this to happen. It was a last resort, but now it is unavoidable. So Gitanjali must make a sacrifice for this family. She must be strong and bear it and so must all of you." I had never heard my aunt speak so freely before with that defensive edge to her voice. She pushed her chair back, stood up, and began clearing off the table.

"Go to bed now, it is late," she said, dismissing us with a weary hand.

~

A candle was still burning in Amma's room. I pushed the door open.

She was not in bed, but pacing back and forth across the room, whispering loudly to herself.

"Savages," she said, running her fingers through her hair. "They're savages."

Nervous energy radiated from her skin, palpable as sparks. I leaned against the door frame, exhausted.

"Amma?"

"Rakhee." Amma rushed forward and embraced me. "You're still up?"

"I don't feel like sleeping."

"Me neither."

Amma held me, and with the side of my head pressed into her stomach it randomly occurred to me that school would be starting soon. Sixth grade. Middle school. But Amma had not yet mentioned anything about going back.

For so long I had hated Plainfield and dreamed of escape, but now all I wanted was to wake up with Merlin's silky black head nestled next to mine. I wanted to look out the window and see those familiar cornfields rolling off into the distance. I wanted the slippery ice beneath my feet and the sting of snowflakes on my cheeks. At least in Plainfield things made sense—I could run through the woods to the ravine and not be afraid of what I might find. In Plainfield, the lights didn't go on and off at random; young girls didn't have to marry old men; Amma took her pills and didn't frighten me; Aba loved Amma and Amma loved Aba.

I squeezed her waist. "Can we go home now?" I said.

Amma disentangled my arms and gazed down into my face. Her eyes were huge and sad in the candlelight. "Come on."

Holding my hand very tightly, Amma brought me to her bed and laid me down on the mussed sheets. The mattress was softer than the one in my room. I rolled over onto my side and curled up into a ball.

Amma lay down beside me, wrapped me in her arms, and kissed my hair. She smelled like sweat and lemons.

"It's going to be okay, molay, I promise. I have a plan," she whispered, and blew out the candle.

Chapter 20

Amma and I walked toward the hospital in silence, the sun radiating its merciless rays upon us. A dry leaf from an overhanging branch drifted down and crumbled on my hair; when I brushed the pieces away, it felt as if I had just pressed my palm against a hot iron.

I gripped Amma's wrist in my burning hand and squeezed. She looked at me but said nothing.

That morning she had casually mentioned over breakfast that she was going to call Aba and would I like to talk to him, too.

I told her yes, and butterflies began to soar and swoop in my chest. After that, I couldn't eat a thing.

Amma had transformed yet again. This plan, whatever it was, had given her a jolt of energy; she seemed nervous but at the same time happy. It reminded me of the way she had acted back in the spring when she first decided we were going to India. This worried me.

Amma peered into Dev's office, saw that it was empty, and smiled.

"Wait here," she said, and closed the door behind her so I couldn't hear anything. Sitting on the grimy floor with my back against the wall, I wondered how they could fit a whole summer of silence into one phone conversation.

Amma didn't come out of the office for a long time.

When she finally did, pink circles had appeared on her cheeks and her eyes were wet. I felt that sad, panicked feeling that wrenched my gut whenever Amma cried.

"I'll wait for you outside," she said, and hurried down the hall.

I went into Dev's office, sat at the desk, and picked up the phone. The receiver was hot and moist against my face.

"Hi, Aba." My voice quivered.

"Hi, Rakhee, how are you?" Aba sounded cheerful, but in a forced way.

"Ready to come home," I said. "I really miss you."

"I miss you too, but I have some good news. I've arranged to take some time off from work so I can join you and Amma there. We'll rent a cottage by the sea and relax for a few days before flying back. How about that?"

I had never been to the sea before. I closed my eyes and pictured an endless blue expanse bordered by a smooth ribbon of powdery white sand. The air would be crisp and salty on my face, and I would walk safe and sound along that sand with Aba and Amma on my either side, Aba's hand big and warm, Amma's hand small and soft. A fragile bulb of happiness began to sprout inside me. "That sounds good."

"Great," said Aba. "I will be there in a week or so."

"Can't you come sooner?" I needed Aba, but I didn't know how to tell him this. I hoped he would hear it in my voice.

"Rakhee, I wish I could, but I just have so much to take care of at the lab. Even getting any time off at all was a tricky business. You'll be okay for another week, won't you? After all, you've done beautifully all summer. Amma says you've been having a great time with your cousins. I'd just be getting in the way, isn't that right?"

My stomach dropped. "Yeah," I murmured. I didn't have it in me to plead anymore. Aba thought I had been brave and I didn't want him to think otherwise. "Aba?"

"Yes?"

"Will we be back in time for the first day of school?"

"Yes, Rakhee," Aba said. "Of course. We wouldn't want you to fall behind, would we?"

After I put the phone down, a couple of things occurred to me. One, that Aba had never taken time off from work for as long as I could remember; and two, that leaving this place meant leaving Tulasi behind. I had always known this fact, but somehow hearing Aba say that I would be back in time to start school made the prospect of our separation alarmingly real. If Aba found out about Tulasi, I wondered, would he want to help her? Maybe he and Amma could adopt her and bring her back to Plainfield with us. My fantasies began to run wild. Maybe we could adopt all of them—Krishna, Meenu, and Gitanjali, too. I wanted to take them away from this place, and if they lived in Plainfield with me, I knew I would be happy. I would be strong enough to face school because I would have something better than friends, I would have sisters.

~

That evening Amma put on a deep pink sari that rustled as she wrapped it around her body. We were going to the temple to ask the goddess Lakshmi to bless Gitanjali's upcoming marriage. Amma's face was flushed and dewy from her bath, and with the sari on, she reminded me of a hibiscus, vivid and striking against the dull green bush upon which it bloomed.

Beside her I felt like a ridiculous bird. Vijay Uncle and Nalini Aunty had presented me with a new dress, and Amma had insisted I wear it that night. It was made of a stiff, white material with red, blue, and yellow balloons embroidered across the chest, and a thick white sash that tied in a bow at the back. My skinny arms and legs stuck out from the mess of frills like bamboo shoots. It was clearly a dress made for a much younger girl, but I could not say anything without offending my uncle (I didn't care what Nalini Aunty thought, and I had a sneaking suspicion that the dress had been her selection).

The sun had set by the time we left for the temple, so we brought along flashlights. Clouds of insects hummed around our ears and in the treetops night birds just emerging from their nests whistled and cawed. The market had shut down for the evening, but all the shopkeepers were gathered in their little huts beneath fluorescent bulbs wrapped in colorful star-shaped lanterns. As we passed, they put down their cigarettes and playing cards, and gawked at our grand procession, especially at Gitanjali, whose tiny, stooped frame was enveloped in a stunning magenta fabric. She stared down at the ground as she walked, and Sadhana Aunty seemed to be dragging her along by the arm. For the first time I noticed a white stone on Gitanjali's ring finger. It flashed coldly in the dark.

At the temple gates I removed my sandals, but this time, as I stepped into the courtyard, my feet didn't feel so exposed above the stones. A summer of running barefoot across rough sand had hardened my tender soles. I tasted the familiar musky scent of incense and hot oil I now associated with God on my tongue and in my nostrils.

Craning their necks to look inside, a throng of people clogged the pathway directly in front of the shrine. A pair of insistent hands pushed me forward.

"Can you see her, Rakhee? Can you see the goddess?" Amma's voice was anxious and desperate in my ear. "This is the auspicious time."

"I can't see."

Amma pressed down on my back so that I was leaning over the iron railing that guarded the long aisle leading up to the shrine. All around me people were shoving one another, hoping for a glimpse and a blessing. The scent of God now mingled with the stink of sweat.

"You must look at her," said Amma. "You must get her blessing."

With my body pressed against the railing, I stood on my toes and stretched my neck out as far as it would go, so that I was able to see into the shrine, where an intricately carved sandstone idol was surrounded by blazing lamps, garlands of orange and white flowers, and bowls overflowing with sumptuous fruit—bananas, apples, mangos. The thin, bearded priest, who was naked except for a frail white cloth wrapped around his waist, looked as if he were about one hundred years old. He was reciting verses in an unfamiliar language and tossing red petals into a spitting flame that shivered and bowed in front of the goddess.

"Pray to her and she will bless you with good fortune and success," said Amma. "Pray to her and she will keep you safe."

Next to me I could feel the heavy fabric of Gitanjali's sari rubbing my arm. Someone had pushed her, too, to the front of the flock of worshippers, and she leaned against the railing as if it were the only thing holding her up. Black tears were running down her face, washing away the kohl Nalini Aunty had painted across her lids.

I closed my eyes and tried to pray, but my mind and heart were blank. Maybe Aba was right; maybe there was no God. If there was a God, then he would do the right thing and save Gitanjali. If there was a God, Aba and Amma would adopt Tulasi and take her away from the garden. *God, if you exist, then you'll hear me. Please help us.* I squeezed my eyes shut and prayed for what could be the last time. If my prayer didn't work, then maybe I, like Aba, would stop believing.

The priest picked up the lamp and descended the steps of the shrine toward us. He held the lamp out. Amma reached over my head and swept her hands over the fire, then passed them across her face and hair, as if she were washing herself with the light. She instructed me to do the same.

Gitanjali also waved her hands over the flame. She covered her face with her hands and left them there.

Amma leaned over and whispered into her ear, "It's going to be okay, I promise. I'll see to it."

The priest handed Amma a small leaf with jasmine flowers and a clot of red paste folded inside. She dipped her finger into the paste, smeared it across my forehead, and tucked a jasmine flower behind my ear.

Arms and elbows began to jostle me, and without moving my limbs I felt myself drifting through the bodies, like a wave on the river, until I had been ejected. Amma, Gitanjali, and the rest of the grown-ups had moved on with the crowd to pray to the other idols.

I found Krishna and Meenu waiting nearby. I eyed

their clean foreheads; no one had bothered to make sure they were blessed.

"This is boring," Krishna said, yawning.

"Come with me, both of you," said Meenu, the devilish look I hadn't seen for a long time back in her eyes. "I want to show you something."

Krishna and I followed her through the shadows and past the various shrines, unseen by the grown-ups, to the decrepit brick wall that stood at the back of the temple courtyard.

We stopped when we had reached the point where the wall came to a ragged halt, and turned into a grassy field, empty save for a crumbling old well covered in a tangle of vines, and an Ashoka tree, whose petal-encrusted branches rose up toward the bone-white moon like magnificent jeweled arms.

"See that well? It's haunted," said Meenu in a whisper that made the fine hairs on the back of my neck prickle. "It's haunted by a *yekshi*."

"What's a yekshi?" I asked.

"A yekshi"—Meenu gave me a penetrating stare, and I could feel Krishna begin to tremble beside me—"is a ghost."

"A ghost," repeated Krishna with a shudder.

"Her name was Rohini and she lived two hundred years ago," Meenu began. "There used to be two houses in this field. Rohini lived in one house and another family lived next door, on the other side of the Ashoka tree. They had a son who Rohini was madly in love with. The two families were very close, and soon Rohini and the boy were engaged to be married. But a few days before the wedding, the two fathers quarreled—nobody knows what it was about—and the boy's father declared that no son of his would ever marry a daughter from his rival's family, and the wedding was called off.

"Rohini was devastated, but what really broke her heart was that only one month later, the boy was engaged again. She watched him marry this other girl, then bring her home with him, and she had to see them together every day. Finally she couldn't take it anymore, so one night she threw herself into the well. But that wasn't the end of the story. She came back as a yekshi and began to haunt the married couple. Terrible things started to happen. The wife was never able to give birth to a live child. The boy's father died suddenly of a heart attack. The boy got some disfiguring skin disease. Eventually the family left the village, and Rohini's family was so ashamed that they destroyed both the houses. Only the tree and the old well survived the fire. Rohini's ghost still guards the well to this day. Some say that if the well were destroyed, so too would be the yekshi, but nobody wants to risk her fury."

"I don't believe you," I said.

"It is true. Every word," Meenu pronounced. "In fact, they say Rohini was a distant relative of ours."

This final revelation made Meenu's story even worse.

"There's no such thing as ghosts," I said, but felt myself begin to shiver alongside Krishna. I wanted to be a nonbeliever, I did, but then why was I suddenly so afraid?

"If you really think that there is no ghost, Rakhee, then why don't you go and see for yourself?" said Meenu.

"What do you mean?"

"If you don't think there is a yekshi guarding the well, then there is nothing to be afraid of. Go and touch the well, hold your hand there for one minute, then come back and prove us all wrong."

I took a step forward.

"No," Krishna whimpered.

Meenu folded her arms across her chest and leaned against the wall.

I took another step and paused. *There's no such thing as ghosts,* I reminded myself.

What would Aba think if he saw me, his own daughter, cowering like a baby, when all I had to do was walk across a field and touch some stupid well? I suddenly remembered that day at the beginning of the summer when Meenu and Krishna had told me that a demon woman, a Rakshasi, lived in the forest. They had been so wrong. And if I had listened to them, then I never would have met Tulasi, and she might have been stuck in the garden forever because I would not be there to rescue her.

Meenu and Krishna had been wrong. Or had they? Maybe Tulasi wasn't a Rakshasi, but that didn't mean there wasn't a demon living at Ashoka. A blackhearted demon that poisoned everything around it.

I felt myself falter, and as I was about to turn around to face Meenu's mocking smile, Amma's voice saved me.

"There you are. Come, girls, it is time to go home."

~

The story of the yekshi was not the most chilling thing I heard that evening.

The first thing came after dinner. A celebratory feast had been laid out on the table when we returned to the house. But Dev was the only one who seemed in a celebratory mood, in spite of the fact that Gitanjali had gone straight to bed without even greeting him.

"No m-m-m-matter," he said with a wave of his hand,

when Sadhana Aunty told him he would not be seeing her that night. "All brides are b-b-b-b-bashful."

We shoveled the food into our mouths in grim silence, punctuated every now and then by a comment from Dev about the wedding or his beautiful young bride.

Prem was there, too, much to Sadhana Aunty's chagrin, and he kept shooting glowering looks in Dev's direction. At one point I heard him say "You sick bastard" in a low voice, and Amma placed her hand on his arm and said, "Prem." Later, as Prem prepared to leave, Amma walked him to the door and I went with her.

"Chitra, we have to act fast," he said in an urgent, intimate tone, as if I were not standing right there between them.

"I know," Amma said. "No more wavering, I promise. I'm ready."

Prem paused, then a slow smile spread across his face. "Good."

"What are you talking about?" I said loudly.

"Don't worry about it, molay," Amma replied, but she did not look at me. She was looking into Prem's eyes, and they were both smiling.

"Amma, when does Aba get here? Soon, right?"

Neither of them responded.

"Chitra." Sadhana Aunty's voice came from the dining room. "What is taking you so long? Please come back in here."

I heard the second thing in the middle of the night. For what seemed like hours, I lay awake, tossing and turning. The ceiling fan had stopped spinning, and the air was stale and hot. I kicked off the sheet that covered me and lay on top of the mattress, with one arm dangling off the edge and the other arm pressed against my sweating forehead. The white balloon dress was hanging over a chair in the corner of the room, and through my blurred vision it looked like a ghost. I thought about Rohini. The night swirled with familiar sounds—cicadas singing, frogs croaking, owls hooting. I sat up and looked outside, wondering if I could see a light from Tulasi's cottage glimmering through the trees, but there was only darkness.

She must hate me for not going back. If I had known how impossible it would be to get back to the garden, then I would not have run out like that, without a word of explanation. I put on my glasses, climbed out of bed, and went over to my suitcase, which was leaning against the wall near the door. Bending down, I flipped it open, reached in, and pulled out the portrait of Tulasi. Holding my pocket flashlight over the drawing, I scrutinized the face staring up at me, tracing each line and curve with my finger, as if I were a girl lost in the forest and this was my map. Just looking at the picture filled me with a sense of warmth. The face seemed to say "You are not alone. We are in this together."

As I crouched in front of my suitcase, I heard a sound that made me freeze. Someone was crying. But the dry, crackling sobs were unfamiliar, and somehow even more horrible and piteous than Amma's tears. Tucking away Tulasi's portrait, I opened the door and stood in the hall. It must be Gitanjali, I thought. I walked toward her bedroom; the crying grew louder.

It surprised me that Gitanjali should cry like that, a guttural cry that sounded as if it came from a very old, broken woman. But who else could it be? I kept walking toward the sound, and only when I passed Gitanjali's door did I realize it was not Gitanjali but Sadhana Aunty who was crying, as if her heart were breaking behind that closed door.

Chapter 21

I searched for traces of grief on Sadhana Aunty's face in the morning and saw nothing but a cold mask. She had gone back to being the impassive Sadhana Aunty I had met on the verandah when I first arrived at Ashoka.

As I came into the dining room for breakfast, she was in the process of sorting through a heap of gold jewelry spread out across the table.

Nalini Aunty sucked in her breath as she lifted a heavy necklace encrusted with green and pink stones.

"I had no idea we owned all of this," she said, more to herself than anyone else. "Think what we could sell it for. See how heavy it is? It will drown the poor girl if she wears it."

"It belonged to our mother," Sadhana Aunty said without looking up. "It was a wedding gift from our father. All of this is hers—I would never sell it. Neither Chitra nor I had a chance to wear any of it. It is only right that it should go to her eldest granddaughter on the occasion of her marriage."

Nalini Aunty sighed and laid the necklace back down on the table.

Watching my aunts fingering the gold and setting aside

pieces for Gitanjali, while Amma and Veena Aunty sat on the other end of the table talking softly but not objecting, drove a spike through my insides. This wedding was going to happen. They were really going to force Gitanjali to marry Dev.

I had to get away from that room. I pushed back my chair so that it scraped against the floor and ran out, no longer harboring any delusions that anyone would follow me. I sat on the verandah swing and pumped my legs hard so that it wobbled on its chain. I knew I was pushing it higher than it should have gone, but the breeze on my face created by the vigorous motion soothed me, and the pulsing heat that had rushed to my cheeks began to subside.

My legs grew tired and I stopped pumping. The swing slowed to a sway. I lay down with my knees up in the air and let myself be rocked back and forth like a baby.

My legs, two brown twigs, were covered in a network of angry mosquito bites. I hadn't even noticed them until now. I pulled my skirt down over my knees and began to hum, willing myself to fall asleep. If I could sleep, then I could escape, at least for a little while.

But sleep would not come. I spent an hour lying with the solid wood of the swing agitating the wings of my shoulder blades, thinking and thinking, my frustration rising with every passing minute. Amma said she had a plan, but she didn't seem to be in any hurry to put this supposed plan into action. And even Veena Aunty, the one grown-up I had always been able to depend on, was not doing anything. The wedding date was barreling toward Gitanjali like a bullet. Two days, to be exact. I thought of her kohl-dyed tears the previous night, and how they had stained her cheeks the color of night.

The sound of shuffling footsteps disrupted my vision and I sat up. Veena Aunty was hurrying down the verandah steps and across the lawn. I leaped up and followed her, my palms aflame.

"Veena Aunty!"

"Oh, Rakhee, I thought you were asleep. I didn't want to wake you," she said, turning around.

"Where are you going?"

Veena Aunty was looking at me with a funny expression on her face. She took a step forward.

"Rakhee, are you okay? Your face is all flushed. You don't have a fever, do you?" She came closer and pressed a hand across my forehead. I batted it away like a petulant cat.

"I'm fine."

"Maybe you should go back inside and lie down for a while."

"I don't need to lie down. I need you to tell me what the hell is going on!" I added in the word *hell* for extra emphasis, and it worked, because her mouth fell open.

"Rakhee! Since when have you used language like that?"

"Please, Veena Aunty, stay for a minute. Explain to me why all this happening. I'm sick of it. I deserve to know the truth."

Veena Aunty's eyes darted from side to side before they settled upon mine, and their soft brown irises seemed to darken.

"What do you mean by 'all this'?"

"The wedding, the secrets—everything! Everyone keeps saying I'm too young to understand, but why can't they just try? I'm not blind."

Veena Aunty sighed. "I know this is hard on you,

Rakhee. I wish there was something I could do or say. But it's all so complicated. It's just such a horrible mess."

"There *is* something you can do. Try to explain it to me. Maybe I can help."

"Oh, darling." Veena Aunty reached out and took my hand, her eyes pools of sadness. "Your mother never should have brought you here. I knew it was a bad idea. I should have insisted. And I've been so preoccupied since I've been here, I didn't even stop to think about how confused and scared you must be."

Veena Aunty glanced around once more before guiding me through the front gate and down the stairs. We sat down together on the bottom step, facing each other with our backs against the stone railing and our knees touching.

"You're right. You do deserve an explanation. It's just that I don't even know where to begin."

"From the beginning."

"Let me think." Wrinkles pleated the space between her brows. "Do you remember that summer when your mother…went away for a while, and I came and stayed with you?"

I nodded.

"So you know that she is, well, troubled. After that… episode, we had things under control. The doctors gave her medicine that helped. But she has stopped taking her medicine recently. I know that you've noticed some changes in her. I've taken the liberty of telling your father because she wouldn't do it herself. Hopefully when he gets here he will be able to reason with her. There's only so much that I can do."

"But what does this have to do with Dev and Gitanjali?" I asked.

Veena Aunty looked up, as if she were hoping she would find the answers written across the sun-streaked sky.

"I just don't understand," I continued, and then I remembered a conversation I had had with Dev, the night he had shook me by the shoulders and called Amma a whore. "Dev said he used to be engaged to Amma. Is that true?"

Veena Aunty's lips parted and closed again. She was silent for a while before she finally said, "Yes, it's true. Dev was in love with your mother for a long time. It was sick and selfish, but it was the only way he knew how to love. And I can't say that I fully blame him. He had it rough as a child."

I narrowed my eyes. Was Veena Aunty actually defending Dev? "What do you mean?"

"Well, he lived alone with his old widowed mother in a run-down little place a few miles from here, and they were dirt-poor. His mother had him later in life, and her health was not so good—she could never get any work, and his father had left nothing when he died. He had no siblings, no cousins. It wasn't easy."

Veena Aunty's body alternately tensed up and relaxed as she spoke, as if telling this tale was both painful and comforting.

"We're the same age, Dev and me, and I still remember him as a sickly little thing. Mind you, his stutter was even worse back then. The village kids used to tease him like anything. I wish I could exclude myself from that group, but I'm ashamed to say I did it, too. Me, Vijay, Prem—even Sadhana. Dev used to follow us around everywhere we went in spite of the teasing, hoping one day we might include him. God, I even remember a time when we drove him away from one of our games by throwing stones at him. Only your mother was kind—to his face, at least. Behind his back, she was just as cruel as the rest of us, maybe even more so. She followed him after the stone incident and apologized for our behavior. She comforted him because even though she looked down on him, she still wanted his adoration. Then she came back to our group and laughed at how he had run away like a dog with his tail between his legs. But Dev adored her. She was incredibly beautiful even back then as a child. And Chitra, she liked the attention. Even though we never let him join in our games or adventures, we always knew he was there, watching us, watching her."

Veena Aunty stopped talking and regarded me uncertainly, as if she realized she had gotten carried away with her story. I urged her on.

"But why would Muthashan have agreed to let Dev marry Amma?"

"I got married and moved to America when I was twenty. Your mother was fifteen at the time, so I wasn't actually here when—" Veena Aunty paused and I could tell that she was struggling to find the right words. "Let's just say something…happened. Dev saw something he shouldn't have seen, and he used that information to his advantage."

"What do you mean? What did he want? What did he see?"

Veena Aunty ignored my questions. "Dev's mother had passed on by then, and he had nothing. He confronted Muthashan. He promised not to reveal to anyone what he had seen, but he wanted two things in return—to inherit the hospital and to marry your mother. Your grandfather was an incredibly proud man. He wanted Dev to keep the secret, so he agreed under the condition that after Dev, the hospital would always remain in the Varma name and that it would never leave the family."

So Amma's father had betrayed her to protect some secret? Thinking back to what Vijay Uncle had told me, about Charles Holloway and all that my grandfather had been forced to give up for the sake of his family, the strength of his pride and desire to protect the hospital made some sense. But what could Dev have seen that would be so bad he would sacrifice his own daughter? I felt as if the wind had been knocked out of me, but I needed to know more. "Is that why Amma left?"

"Yes. She was so distraught when she found out about what her father had agreed upon that she ran away. Muthashi helped her escape—made the travel arrangements with me, gave her the money—even though she knew that her husband would be furious and that he might never forgive her. I didn't know the circumstances until Chitra arrived on my doorstep in Plainfield."

"But what were the circumstances?"

Veena Aunty continued speaking, as if she hadn't heard me. "Your mother stayed with us for a few years. Eventually we introduced her to your father. On the outside, they seemed like an unlikely pair. He was older and so accomplished, and she was just this simple village girl. But they were both lonely and...running from painful memories. They stumbled upon each other at the right time. Your father knew that Chitra couldn't stay with us indefinitely without a green card, so he married her. He would have married her anyway. He loves her, he really does. And she loves him, too. Unlike Muthashan, your father encouraged her to use her brain, to take classes, to read. And Chitra was so caring in the beginning, until she got sick. I still remember how happy they were." Veena

Aunty smiled. I liked hearing about Aba and Amma being happy and in love, but at the same time, it pained me.

"What happened when Muthashan found out that Amma had run off? Why didn't he come after her?"

She cleared her throat with an air of finality. "He never did find out. The night before your mother left, he had a stroke. He was in a coma for two weeks and then he died. Dev was enraged when he found out that Chitra had broken the deal, and I think that is when he truly changed. As a child, he could be sweet, I remember, but this experience hardened him. So he moved on from bribing your grandfather to bribing Sadhana. He threatened her and he has been blackmailing this family ever since. Bleeding them dry. He may not appear so, but he is a wealthy man now, and the Varmas, who were once the richest family in the area, are practically destitute. That is why he wields so much power over this family, and that is why they agreed to this wedding. Sadhana made the same deal with him that her father once made regarding Chitra. There is no money left, and if they marry Gitanjali off to him, then they think this will all finally end."

My breath was coming in short gasps, but I tried to stay calm for fear that she would stop talking, thinking I was too young to hear what she was telling me. I did not have to worry, however, because she no longer seemed to be addressing me. Her eyes had a distant look. I had melded in with the green vine that crept over the stone railing and tumbled over my shoulder like Rapunzel's braid.

"I can't help feeling that some of this is my fault," she continued with a sorrowful shake of her head. "I should have set a better example. If I had been nicer to Dev, then the others would have followed my example. And if we hadn't been so awful to him as kids, maybe he wouldn't have blackmailed our family. If I had been a better person, maybe he wouldn't have turned into such a monster. If I had only..."

"It's not your fault, Veena Aunty," I said, "You're a great person. I mean, you saved Amma's life. I would have never been born if it hadn't been for you."

Veena Aunty's confused eyes met mine. "What are you talking about, Rakhee?"

"You know—how Amma got her scar...when you were both in the jungle together and Amma got bitten by that snake. You carried her to the hospital so that her father could give her medicine. She would have died without you."

Veena Aunty stared at me. "That wasn't me, Rakhee," she said, then pressed her fingers to her lips with a sharp intake of breath.

"Who was it, then?"

"Oh God, I've opened up a can of worms here." Veena Aunty's fingers migrated to her temples.

"Tell me, please?" I grasped her wrist. "If you don't tell me, then I'm just going to go ask Amma, and think how much it will upset her."

"It wasn't me." Veena Aunty let out a long sigh. "It was Prem."

My grip on her wrist tightened.

"Prem was with her. Prem carried her home. They used to go running around in the forests together all the time, just the two of them—" She broke off abruptly, and I knew without her having to tell me what the secret was, what they had been trying to hide all this time.

My moment of revelation was surprisingly quiet, as if I had known all along, known somewhere deeper than my mind—in my blood, in my soul.

251

"Tulasi is my sister," I said.

Veena Aunty drew away from my feverish, clinging hand. "Rakhee, how do you know about her?"

"I found the garden. I've been visiting her all summer. We're friends."

The portrait had been so disconcerting because it had been like looking into the mirror and seeing another side of myself.

"Does anyone else know?" Sweat had formed beads on Veena Aunty's upper lip. "Have you told your cousins?"

"No, no one knows, but I think Sadhana Aunty suspects." I closed my eyes as I felt the rage beginning to build up inside me. "How could Amma have kept this from me? I have a sister and nobody bothered to tell me?"

"Rakhee, I know this is hard, but you have to understand it's complicated. There's no easy way of dealing with such things. I know there's nothing I can say to justify it. This really has to be something your mother explains to you herself."

"No!" My anger was temporarily replaced with desperation. "Please don't tell her I know. You can't tell anyone, not yet. You won't tell on me, will you, Veena Aunty?" I didn't want anyone finding out until I had figured out a plan for setting Tulasi free. Amma clearly didn't want her. But surely Aba wouldn't just leave her behind. If Amma found out that I knew about Tulasi, though, she might do something. She might hide Tulasi someplace where I would not be able to find her. I leaned forward and pressed my head against Veena Aunty's bosom. Aba was not here yet. I had no one else to turn to.

Veena Aunty stroked my hair, but the gesture was surprisingly discomforting. I felt the cautious fear trembling in her fingers, as if she were petting a tarantula. "Rakhee,

I can't make that promise. You don't know what you've gotten yourself into. This isn't something you can handle on your own. This is an adult matter."

Veena Aunty had been the one grown-up I thought I could rely upon and now this final illusion was shattered.

"Are you listening to me, Rakhee? Just don't get any more involved, and let me handle this. I'll take care of it. And your dad will be here soon. We'll figure out a way."

I withdrew my head from Veena Aunty's breast.

I had a sister.

A real sister.

I knew with certainty that I couldn't depend on any of them to save her. It was up to me.

I cleared my throat. "Okay. But since I know this much already, can't you tell me the rest of the story?"

"I suppose there's no keeping it from you now, though God knows I wish I could. I wish I could have protected you from all this." She shook her head back and forth before continuing. "Chitra got pregnant at fifteen. When your grandfather found out, he was furious and mortified. He convinced Prem's father to send him away to school at his expense. Then he forced your mother into seclusion. She wasn't allowed to leave the house or to see anyone. He went so far as to tell Prem and his father that she had miscarried. They never even told Prem's mother about the pregnancy because they didn't want to upset her. The only people who knew were Chitra's immediate family and, soon after, me. Nalini Aunty, the girls, no one living in this house knows except for Sadhana, Chitra, and Vijay. And I believe Muthashan's sisters know, too, which is why he kept them away all these years. That's it."

I imagined Amma as a young slip of a girl in a white nightgown, with a grotesquely inflated belly, humming a tune through the bars of her bedroom window, the lonely notes floating into the waiting forest. My own stomach bucked at the image, and I had to swallow hard to find my voice. "What happened then?"

"Your grandfather had decided to bring the baby to an orphanage and then go on as if nothing had ever happened. But when the baby was born and he saw that it was—she was—deformed, he took pity on her, knowing that she would have no chance of ever being adopted. He also knew there was no believable way they could keep the child openly or explain her existence. So instead he brought builders down from the north, and had the cottage and the wall constructed deep in the forest. They fitted the house out beautifully, sparing no expense, to cover their guilt."

Veena Aunty peered at me through the corner of her eye. Hearing the story of Tulasi's birth and the plot to keep her hidden intensified the twisting pain in my gut, but I forced my features to remain composed.

"It was the perfect plan, your grandfather thought, except that Dev found out about the baby," she continued. "When Chitra went into seclusion he noticed she wasn't out and about anymore, and he took to hanging around the house, waiting for her to come out. One day he saw her sitting on the verandah with her belly all swollen. When the baby was born, he was lurking outside. He saw the poor child with his own eyes. He agreed to keep the secret as long as your grandfather gave him what he wanted. Your mother ran away shortly after, and then the baby was cared for by Muthashi, Hema, and Sadhana. As Muthashi got older and Hema grew more deranged, Sadhana took over almost completely. And Sadhana is just like her father, proud and stubborn, maybe even more so.

She will give up everything before she betrays the secret. She feels that she owes it to him after she married against his wishes and broke his heart."

"But what about Prem? Why didn't he do anything? Amma didn't care, but what about him? It was his baby, too."

"Rakhee, it's not that your mother didn't care. She was young and scared. She was a child herself who didn't know what she was doing. And Prem—he didn't even know Tulasi was still alive until recently. It was Vijay who wrote to him finally, telling him everything. Vijay was getting desperate, so he went behind Sadhana's back because he knew she would never agree to it. He hoped that by writing to Prem and revealing the truth about Tulasi, Prem would do the right thing and come back for her. He hoped Prem would take Tulasi away and that their financial problems would finally be over. But it wasn't that easy. Sadhana doesn't want to give her up. She'll fight tooth and nail to keep that girl right where she is, even if it means forcing Gitanjali to marry Dev. You see, she has grown quite fond of Tulasi, perhaps even more so than her own children. She was the one who named her Tulasi, after the holy plant. I think she feels more like the girl's mother than Chitra, and I don't blame her. After all, she has been her main caretaker for all these years."

So was that the big plan? Were Amma and Prem plotting to take Tulasi away in stealth, and me along with her?

"When Prem got the letter, he immediately contacted your mother. Until then, he wanted to let her move on with her life, but when he found out about Tulasi, all the memories came back. I think he had always planned to return to Malanad when he was finished with school to marry your mother. He wrote her letter after letter telling her to wait for him and that his love for her had never wavered, but your grandfather intercepted and destroyed them. At least, that's my only guess as to why they never made their way to Chitra. She thought he had forgotten about her or that he had lost interest because of the pregnancy. When Prem's parents told him that Chitra had run away and that she eventually married someone else, he was devastated. He stayed away, barely even coming back to see his parents, because being here reminded him too much of her. It breaks my heart to remember all of this. Those two were so perfect for one another, they were so in love, even as children."

Just then, Krishna came tripping down the stairs.

"There you are, Rakhee! I've been looking everywhere for you," she said before stopping in her tracks. "What is wrong?"

I wiped my face with the edge of my dress. I hadn't realized that I was crying.

"I was just telling Rakhee a sad story," said Veena Aunty.

"Can I hear it?" Krishna snuggled up next to Veena Aunty, who smiled.

"I'm just about done. Why don't I tell you girls another story?"

"Okay, then," said Krishna.

Veena Aunty began to spin some fairy tale or another, but I didn't hear a word. My stomach ached and my mind was numb.

Finally Veena Aunty stopped talking and stood, telling us she had to get going because Valsala would have lunch waiting. She leaned down to hug each of us, and at my turn, she whispered in my ear: "You're okay, right? I know this is a lot to digest, but I'm just asking you to leave it to me and not do anything rash, all right? We can talk as much as you want when this is all over and done with."

"I'm fine, Veena Aunty."

After she had disappeared around the curve in the road, I told Krishna I was taking a nap. I waited in my room for a while, and when the coast was clear, I dashed around the side of the house, over the wall, and into the forest, my body propelled by a new delirium.

My sister.

I ran as fast as I could because I needed to see her and also because the wind waving through my hair and the twigs scraping my ankles distracted me from the tumult of emotions. Happiness that I had a sister, shock at Dev's story, and, most of all, hurt at the thought that Amma had once had a child and abandoned it. She had not wanted it, not cared for it, not loved it. If she was capable of such an act, then how did I know that she had ever wanted me, that I wasn't just a mistake, a regret, like everything else?

When I got to the wall, I dug my fingers and toes into the dry stone, heaved myself up, and jumped over, expecting to be greeted by the cushiony lawn. Instead, my knees fell hard upon rough grass that peeled away a thin layer of skin. But I could not dwell on the fast, sharp pain or the weak dribbles of blood that snaked down each knee. It was not just the grass. The entire garden had transformed into a crumbling shell of its former self. The tender, sculpted roses and wide, bright peonies sagged on their stems, shriveled up like the wasted fists of old women, and the pollen of the stooping gray hibiscus was ashed upon the crusted soil. The ground was strewn with crunchy leaves and dead fruit that sent sweet, rotten fumes swirling up into the air. I picked my way through the wreckage toward the cottage.

Inside it was cool and dim. Shades had been drawn down over the windows. I went over to one and tugged at the string, letting in a shock of golden light.

"Tulasi?" I called.

Everything was clean and in its place.

I walked toward the bed, suddenly feeling very drawn and tired, as if all my energy was being siphoned away. Even breathing was a chore. What was happening to me?

Raising a weak arm, I drew back the netting and saw the outline of Tulasi's thin form coiled beneath a white cotton sheet. The top half of her face peeked out from the sheet and rested on a pillow. Her skin had a yellowish-gray tinge. I looked down at my own hand and saw that it had taken on a violet hue that was almost unearthly. My veins were clear as blue rivers.

Why was I so tired? What was wrong with me?

Puck was curled at the foot of the bed, his wings tucked beneath his body, like a nesting hen. He examined me with his round black eyes, but did not move or make a noise.

"Tulasi, are you awake?"

She stirred, moved her face from side to side, then opened her eyes and pulled the sheet down away from her bloodless mouth.

"Rakhee," she whispered. "Is that really you?"

"It's me," I said, and felt the tears start in my eyes. "I'm sorry I didn't come back, I'm sorry it has been so long—"

"It does not matter, you are here now. I wish I could make you some tea, but I am so terribly tired—"

"I don't want tea," I said, and climbed onto the bed. I bent down and hugged my sister with trembling arms.

"Come under the sheet, you are so cold."

I lay down beside her, the sheet molding to me, and

held her close, with my cheek pressed against her. Her breathing was slow and labored, and as I lay next to her I realized so was mine.

"What's the matter? Are you sick?" I asked.

"I am not well. How about you? Are you sick?"

"Don't worry about me. What's happened to you? What's wrong?"

"Rakhee, please just lie here with me. Let us not talk of sickness."

There was so much I wanted to tell her, so much I wanted to say, but I didn't have the energy.

"Tulasi—"

"Rakhee, just lie quietly here with me, please. Stay with me."

"I'll stay," I said. No one could separate us now.

We lay together like that silently, and even after she fell asleep I continued to lie there, unable to let go, until I, too, fell. A heavy sleep swept over me and I succumbed without a fight, as if it were the first time that summer I could really rest.

My mind was undisturbed by dreams. I don't think I have ever slept so well since.

When I finally opened my eyes, I realized with horror that night had come and gone, and the warm, rosy light that lapped in through the open window was the light of dawn.

I looked down at my hands. They still had a pale, mottled look, and my body felt hollow, as if someone had scooped out my insides. I could have easily closed my eyes and slept for another day, another night.

But I had work to do, so I gingerly disentangled myself from Tulasi's arms.

"Tulasi?" I touched her shoulder and her eyelids fluttered, but did not open.

I said her name again, but still, she did not wake, so I kissed her cheek and took one last look at my sister.

~

I made it back to the house, stumbling, heartsick. The first thing I saw when I got to the doorway of my room was Amma kneeling on the floor, sobbing. She was holding something white in her hands.

Sadhana Aunty was standing near her and turned when she heard my footsteps.

She stared at me for a moment with her unreadable eyes, then slowly, deliberately began to move toward me.

"What's going on?" I said.

Sadhana Aunty did not respond, just kept walking.

She was going to hug me. For some reason, Sadhana Aunty was going to hug me.

Was it Aba? Had something happened to Aba?

It was only when I felt my face stinging and my body falling that I realized she had slapped me.

Chapter 22

My cheek burned and my ears rang from the force of Sadhana Aunty's slap. I fell to my knees. Through the haze I heard Amma cry out: "Chechi, don't!" But she made no move to help me.

I looked up. Sadhana Aunty's fists were clenched and her elbows stood out at angles, like wings. She was a wild bird whose nest had been plundered.

"How dare you," she said in a voice strangled with hate.

I tried to stand. At the same time, she yanked me up by the shoulders and gave me a shake.

"I don't know what you're talking about!" I gasped. Had Veena Aunty betrayed me? My teeth pierced my tongue and I tasted blood.

Sadhana Aunty glared at me, then released my shoulders and went over to Amma, who was still kneeling on the floor, weeping. She snatched the something white out of her hands and held it up for me to see. It was Tulasi's portrait.

"You've been seeing her, I knew it. Who gave you the right? Were you intending on showing this to her? To lie and make her believe that she was beautiful?" Sadhana Aunty began to shred the portrait with the scruple of a

261

butcher, strip by strip. The portrait that I had poured so much of myself into creating, the portrait that had revealed so much to me, the portrait I had planned to keep with me forever should Tulasi and I ever be separated again. Each tear felt like another slap. She crumpled up the pieces, opened her fist, and let them fall like snowflakes.

"Do you understand the consequences of your actions?" She was quiet now. "For the first time in her sixteen years on this earth, I have seen sadness and distrust in her eyes, have seen her body weakened by sickness. You have broken down everything I have worked so hard to build up, destroyed the life and the world that I have given her."

"She's a prisoner!" I shouted. "And you're a horrible person for lying to everyone and keeping her locked up like that for all these years!"

"You call her a prisoner? Foolish girl. What would she find out here that could be any better than she has in there? Pain, sickness, greed, evil. I was sparing her all of that. I made a beautiful world for her, I kept her safe. You say that I am the horrible one, but it's you who have taken that all away from her, and for what? For some childish summer adventure, and then you'll leave us here to pick up the pieces?"

"No, I'm not leaving her! She's my sister!"

"Rakhee," I heard Amma rasp, "how do you know that?"

Sadhana Aunty silenced her.

"Let me handle this, Chitra. It does not matter how she knows. What matters now is making sure this does not get out."

"I'm going to take Tulasi away," I cried, "to bring her

out into the open. She is not something to be ashamed of or to be kept secret."

"Rakhee, stop talking like that," Amma warned. I ignored her.

"You will do no such thing." Sadhana Aunty clenched her fists.

"Yes, I will, and you can't stop me. I'm going to tell everyone about her. Everyone!" Hysteria washed my veins with adrenaline.

"You are a silly, selfish girl. Your mother has been far too lenient with you, but do not think I'm going to let this kind of behavior go unpunished." Sadhana Aunty took a step forward. Without stopping to think, I brought my foot down hard upon my aunt's and she stumbled back, cringing.

"Don't come near me! Stay away!"

Sadhana Aunty's eyes narrowed, and she advanced again. I tried to dodge her, but this time she was too fast; her hand encircled my arm in an inescapable grip, and she dragged me out of the room and down the hallway with surprising strength.

"What are you doing? Where are you taking her?" Amma was behind us.

"She needs to be disciplined."

"Don't you dare hit her again!"

"She must think about the consequences of her actions." Sadhana Aunty's voice was calm. "She needs to learn some respect for her elders."

We passed Krishna's bedroom, and I saw one wide frightened eye through a crack in the door.

"Rakhee, baby," Amma cried and reached for my hand, but Sadhana Aunty jerked me away. "I'm so sorry, I'm so sorry."

Sadhana Aunty shoved me into a room, closed the door, and slid the lock into place from the outside.

I took in my surroundings and recognized the room where Muthashi had died.

"No!" I hammered the door with my fists. "Let me out!"

"Is this really necessary?" came Amma's voice from the other side.

"You heard her, she said she is going to tell everyone. The girl is hysterical. She needs some time to calm down and think about what she has done."

"Rakhee, I'm sorry, I'm sorry, I'm sorry," Amma said over and over again through her sobs, and as her voice got quieter I knew that she was leaving me.

"No, Amma, don't go! Let me out! Please!" I screamed and banged my fists against the hard wood until I thought they would bleed.

"Stop that, do you hear me?" Sadhana Aunty said. "The longer you shout and make a fuss, the longer you will stay in that room."

I gave one last bang and slumped to the floor with my back against the door, listening for the sound of Amma's advancing footsteps. I waited with my ears pricked for a long time. The footsteps never came.

Finally, exhausted, I dropped my forehead to my knees and began to cry, my heart swollen with fear and, beneath that fear, something more ominous: the realization that Amma was not coming back. I was alone.

Ever since that first blue letter had arrived in our mailbox in Plainfield, a new Amma had been emerging, one who was mysterious, infuriating, and sometimes frightening. But in spite of these changes, there had been lingering pieces of the old Amma to which I had clung all these months. Now, after Veena Aunty's story and the events of the last day, the new Amma had taken over, extinguishing any remnants of the old one whom I loved desperately, the one who sang and read to me, cooked me delicious meals, knelt beside me as we poured seeds into the earth, and banished my night demons with her warm embrace. I couldn't reconcile her with the one who laughed as her friends threw stones at a young boy, the one who said things she shouldn't to men who were not Aba, the one who was letting Gitanjali be sacrificed, the one who had abandoned not only me, but my sister. My sister!

At least I had found Tulasi, and for her, I had to stay strong, I had to keep going.

But the longer I remained in that room, watching the sun dance across the sterile white sheets of the bed where Muthashi had breathed her last, the harder it was to stay calm. I kept remembering the last time I had been here, the memories slicing through my courage with haunting precision.

The darkness. The wasted body on the bed. The hand reaching out for mine, searching for comfort that I could not give. The smell. The smell.

I couldn't breathe. I half-lay, half-fell on my side, with my legs splayed out in front of me, and closed my eyes. Something other than sleep slipped over me then, a shadow, dark and protective. The room grew hazy and dissolved.

~

A strange light was streaming into the room, a color I had never seen before. I got to my feet and stumbled to the window.

How much time had passed? The last thing I knew, it had been early afternoon.

Now the sky was a mixture of pink, blue, and gold, bolting across the horizon. The sun was preparing to set. But something was not right.

Fear began to seep back in like ink staining a cloth.

Over the trees, deep in the forest, the sky was neither pink, blue, nor gold. It was black.

Black as night.

Black as the sky above Muthashi's pyre.

A drum started beating inside my ears, swift and terrifying. I ran back to the door and pulled at the handle. Nothing. The drumbeat got faster. I rattled the handle and kicked at the door.

"Help!" I called.

My cheek still throbbed from Sadhana Aunty's slap. I thought of the cold look in her eyes as she had yelled at me, brutal and inhuman. Who knew what she was capable of? And the rest of the grown-ups—Vijay Uncle, Nalini Aunty, even Veena Aunty—they were just as bad. They, too, like Amma, had idly sat by, letting Sadhana Aunty keep my sister a prisoner. I could not trust any of them. If I did not get out of here, who knew what they would do to Tulasi?

I banged and banged at the locked door.

No one was coming.

And what could I do from here? How could I save my sister when I was locked in this room like an animal?

Then—

"Rakhee?" came a small voice from the other side.

A burst of joy temporarily blocked my despair. "Krishna, open the door, please, hurry!"

"My mother said to leave you in there." Krishna

sounded uncertain. "She said you did something evil and that I would be punished if I let you out. What did you do, Rakhee?"

"Where is everyone now?"

"In the sitting room with the door closed. My mother and Vijay Uncle just came home. They were out all day. I don't know where they went. Rakhee, I'm afraid."

"Krishna, I'll explain everything, but the grown-ups, we can't trust them. You have to let me out. There isn't any time."

A crushing silence. Then at last I heard the sound of the lock being unlatched and the door opening.

I stumbled into the hallway and grasped my cousin's hand. "Krishna, we have to run. I'll tell you everything on the way, but just believe me, we have to run."

Her eyes gleamed with fright, but still she said,"I believe you, Rakhee." Relief and love steadied my racing heart.

I wished I had told Krishna everything sooner and that I hadn't been so intent on keeping Tulasi all to myself.

Krishna returned my grateful smile with a brave one.

I wanted to throw my arms around her neck and thank her for taking my side, but there was no time, so I looked both ways, pulled her down the steps with me, around the house, and into the backyard.

When we got to the barrier, Krishna balked, and I knew I had to tell her the truth right then, before we could go any further.

"Krishna, there's nothing to be afraid of." As the words came out, I realized they weren't true, but I pushed on. "Your mother lied to you. They've all been lying, this whole time."

"What do you mean?"

"There is no Rakshasi living in the forest."

"Then...what is there?"

"There is a cottage and a garden, and..." My voice faltered.

"And what?"

"A girl."

Krishna's eyes narrowed, causing wrinkles to form at the edges, and making her appear, for a moment, much older than she actually was. "A girl?"

"Yes," I said, "a girl." The story of Tulasi—who she was and how she came to be—spilled forth.

"I can't believe it," Krishna whispered, when I had finished.

"I know, I'm sorry," I said, and even though I knew that every second we lingered at the barrier we risked getting caught, it felt so good to confess everything to Krishna that I couldn't help but blurt, "I think my mother is planning to run away with Prem."

Krishna was quiet. "But Prem Uncle is gone."

"What do you mean, he's gone?"

"I overheard your mother telling my mother that he left."

"When?"

"This morning."

"Did Amma sound sad?"

"No, she sounded happy." So there was hope! "But *my* mother got very upset when she heard."

My smile faded. "Why would Sadhana Aunty care if Prem left?"

"I don't know. She kept asking your mother where he had gone. She sounded really angry. She said she never believed he would have the nerve to go through with it, and if she had, she would have banned him from our house. I've never seen her like that, but your mother would not tell her anything. Then my mother finally stopped asking and said, 'Maybe it is for the best, after all.' She sounded so sad. That is when she and Vijay Uncle disappeared. She was even more upset when they came back, and their hands—Rakhee, their hands were all...black."

As much as I wanted to continue probing, I knew we could not afford to waste any more time. "Krishna, will you come with me? We have to hurry. We have to save Tulasi and hide her from the grown-ups."

She hesitated for only a moment before throwing her legs over the barrier and climbing over to the other side. She turned to look at me, her silhouette framed by a backdrop of trees whose branches were spangled in sunset light, as if in preparation for a festive event.

I climbed over, too, and reached for her hand. "Let's go," I said, and together we entered the forest.

We began to run, me in front, pulling Krishna along with one hand, and batting away the leafy branches that brushed against my face with the other. Even in the fading light, I could make out fresh footprints in the dirt.

The pounding of drums pulsed in my ears. Behind me Krishna was panting and stumbling.

The sun had not yet set, but its vibrant glow dimmed as we delved deeper, and a thick gloom began to gather us in. The black haze seemed to be simultaneously drifting down from the sky and rising up from the ground. The smell of smoke furled in my nostrils. We ran faster.

When we arrived at the wall, I stopped short, and let my cousin's hand fall. It still stood where I had last left it, but in place of the locked door, there was a charred, gaping hole. The smoke swept over my face and head like a hood. The fumes filled my lungs and I choked back a gasp. Krishna hesitated and glanced at me.

I tried my best to sound brave. "Come on."

Krishna followed me through the hole. We coughed and covered our mouths with our hands.

Everything slowed down and went quiet.

It was gone. All gone. There was nothing left but a singed circle of grass and a mess of blackened rubble. Wisps of smoke curled up from the burned earth and enveloped us. I was light-headed. Through the clouds I could almost see the flowers, the cobblestone path, the cottage, hovering like phantoms. But Tulasi herself had vanished. I could feel no trace of her.

The silence was thick. I tried to walk but could barely move.

Sadhana Aunty and Vijay Uncle had been out all day. I shivered. Of course they had.

It was so quiet I could not even hear myself breathe. Was I breathing? Had I, too, died along with the garden? Was that what this silence meant?

But I was not dead.

I must have screamed, because Krishna clapped her hand over my mouth. "Sssh, they might hear you."

"She's gone," I croaked.

"Do you think they—killed her?" Krishna could barely get the words out.

"They can't have, they couldn't, they wouldn't." But I didn't know anything anymore. All I knew was that Tulasi was gone, and Krishna and I knew too much. We were not safe. We could not stay here. We had to run. Far away.

I started to move back the way we came, but Krishna grabbed my arm. "We cannot go that way. They will know we are gone by now."

So we turned and plunged deeper into the forest

as the sun vanished and night opened its black flower around us.

"Do you know where we're going?" I said.

"No, I have never come this way."

"Well, wherever we're going, it is safer than where we came from."

We began to run again, hand in hand, until we reached a clearing, which opened onto a paddy field.

By now the darkness was impenetrable. The moon had abandoned us behind a heavy bank of clouds.

Nalini Aunty had once mentioned something about how snakes loved to curl up in the paddy fields at night.

"We can't go this way," I cried.

"There is no other way," said Krishna, bending down. "If we turn back, it will just lead us toward Ashoka. They'll find us. They might have already come after us. Think what they'll do if they catch us." I heard her rustling around on the ground, and when she stood up she was holding a long stick in her fist.

She was right; we would have to go through that paddy field, snakes or no snakes. Here, we at least had a chance of making it through. If we turned back, we would be heading straight into the snake's nest.

Our limbs plastered against each other in fear, we began picking our way through the high stalks, with Krishna beating the stick on the ground and making a shooing sound with her tongue.

It was so dark I could not see my own body. The only thing that reminded me I was alive and not drowning was the sensation of Krishna's warm, pulsing arm entwined in mine.

The stick rasped against the earth. With every step, I prepared to feel the sting of fangs on my leg. Krishna would never be able to carry me out of here. I would not be saved, like Amma. The poison would slowly suck out my life and I, writhing in pain, would die there in the darkness.

I tortured myself with such thoughts until I heard Krishna's relieved sigh. "We made it."

It was true. I moved my foot to feel the ground below me, and it was hard and flat. We were on the road.

The darkness began to lift. The clouds had dispersed, and we could see the moon paving the red road with light.

"Wait," said Krishna, "I think I know where we are."

"Which way should we go?"

"We haven't gone very far. We just made a big circle. We are just past the village square, not far from Ashoka. We had better hurry."

All around us the air rattled with a chorus of sounds, ushering us through the night.

But after a while I became aware of a sound that did not belong. A hectic rustling in the trees that bordered the road. Krishna heard it, too, because she came to an abrupt halt. The rustling intensified.

Someone else was sprinting through the night.

"Maybe it's them!" I hissed.

"No, I don't think so."

Growls, barks, and yelps mixed in with the rustling.

"Dogs!" Krishna's hand gripped my arm.

At first, I did not understand. "Oh good, it's just dogs."

"They're coming straight toward us. Run, Rakhee, run!"

I remembered then what Meenu had said about stray dogs, about how they were dangerous and rabid.

Behind us I heard an explosion as their thrashing bodies broke through the trees, followed by the sound of barking and paws slamming into the earth.

My legs spun and I breathed in knives. But even as I fled I knew we could never outrun a pack of dogs.

Nobody outruns a pack of dogs.

So it would end here.

I was almost relieved. Amma would find us lying on the road with our throats open, and she would know that it was all her fault.

A thorn broke through my sandal, piercing the bottom of my foot. I fell forward but caught myself before I hit the ground.

My right sandal went sailing through the air and landed faceup several yards away.

I froze and blurted: "My shoe, my shoe."

"Leave it, Rakhee, just run!" cried Krishna from up ahead, but somehow I could not move.

I stood rooted to the spot, blood seeping from my foot onto the road, watching the dogs approach.

"Rakhee!" Krishna shrieked, but still my limbs would not budge. Even my eyelids were paralyzed.

The dogs were getting closer and closer.

I felt a rush of wind as something streaked past my head.

Krishna.

She grabbed my sandal in one hand and my wrist in the other. "I know where we'll be safe."

My body came back to life.

The road veered off to the right and tapered into a thin pathway. I recognized it immediately.

The temple.

The iron gates of the temple were unlocked. We pulled them open, hurled ourselves into the courtyard, and pushed them shut. The barking grew louder, then faded just as fast.

We paused, leaning our backs against the gate, letting the relief wash over us.

"Come." Krishna led me through the courtyard, past the goddess, past the shrines, and toward the brick wall.

"What are we doing here?"

"Rakhee, there is nowhere else to run. We will be safe under the Ashoka tree."

I limped after Krishna, following her to the end of the brick wall, through the long grass, and to the tree, where we both collapsed against its trunk.

As my breath came back to me, I reached for my cousin's hand.

"Thank you. You saved my life back there with the shoe. I don't know what happened to me."

"You are welcome." Krishna gave me a wan smile.

After that we were quiet for a long time, huddled together, watching and waiting. For what, I don't know.

Neither of us could sleep, but I was so exhausted that everything seemed distorted and exaggerated. The thrum of insects, the crying of birds, the faint breeze singing—they were all sinister sounds, and the grass was so green under the moonlight it hurt my eyes to look at it.

The well loomed in the near distance. The lair of the yekshi. I tried to pretend it wasn't there, but my eyes kept falling upon its smoky gray silhouette.

"Krishna, do you think that story about the yekshi is really true?" Just saying the word made my skin prickle, and yet I couldn't help asking, as if talking about it would somehow make it less scary.

"There have been stories," said Krishna, "of strange things happening near the well. People say they have seen...her."

"What does she look like?" The air was warm, but still my teeth chattered.

"I don't know, Rakhee. I don't want to know."

"It can't be true," I said.

A soft wind began to whistle in my ears. It ruffled the branches of the Ashoka tree, which showered us with red petals. I held out my arms and caught them in my palms and Krishna sat up and gazed at the curtain of petals, her mouth hanging open in awe.

I closed my eyes, consumed by a sense of peace. "Nothing can touch us here."

Krishna did not say anything.

I opened my eyes. Awe had been replaced by an expression of horror.

"Krishna?"

She pulled me so close to her that I could feel her breath on my cheek and her ribs bearing into mine.

"What is that?"

"What is what?"

"The yekshi." Krishna was shaking so hard that my body, too, began to shake.

"Krishna, stop it, you're scaring me!"

"Rakhee, it's her. It's the yekshi!"

I saw her, too, then. A figure dressed all in white running through the field toward the well.

"It's real, she's real." The words fell from my dry lips, and the song of the wind turned back into a terrible drumbeat.

Beside me I felt Krishna slump over and fall into the grass.

Let me faint, too, I begged. *Or let me be dreaming.* But I was awake and I could not look away.

The yekshi reached the well and paused before climbing up on the stone rim, where she crouched like an animal. Slowly she rose, stretching out her arms on either side of her willowy figure. I watched her hovering there, a faceless form with a black flag of hair. Her body began to sway back and forth. I opened my mouth and tried to scream, but no sound came out. At the same time that her knees buckled, my breath caught in my chest. The yekshi let out a great, throttled cry, then lurched off the edge of the well and plunged down into its depths.

Chapter 23

I was drifting.

My entire body ached. I was cold and wet, but my head was nestled against something soft and wonderfully strong.

A light rain misted my cheek, the sort of drizzle that follows a downpour.

I tried to open my eyes a crack and saw a slender crescent of light. I lifted my lids a bit further, even though it hurt to do so. Up ahead, a man was carrying a limp rag doll in his arms.

My eyes fluttered.

Then came a voice, concerned and questioning, close to my ear. "Rakhee?"

Hope, radiant as morning, filled my chest.

"Aba!" I tried to call out, but I could not get the sound to rise up past my throat. My eyes closed again and I had no choice but to continue drifting.

The next time I awoke, I was lying in bed, clean and dry, with a bandage across my foot. Amma and Aba were sitting in chairs on opposite ends of the room.

"Krishna?" My throat was so parched that I did not recognize my own voice.

Amma came forward with a glass of water and held it to my lips.

"She's fine. But she has a high fever. She's asleep in her room. Thank God Vijay and your father found you when they did."

"Aba," I said next, and water dribbled out of my mouth.

He came over to the bed, sat down next to Amma, and put his arms around me. He had finally come. I could not help myself. I started to cry.

"Rakhee," he said, stroking my hair.

I tried to choke out the story of Tulasi and the garden, but it came out more in a jumble of senseless words strung together.

Aba shushed me. "I know. Amma has just now told me everything."

"Where is she? What have you done with her?" I turned to Amma and felt my strength coming back, along with my anger.

"Tulasi is safe," Amma said. "She is with her father. She is with Prem. We went together to fetch her from the garden. We told her the truth. She's very confused but she'll eventually understand. We'll get her the help she needs."

Aba flinched. I started to speak but Amma interrupted me.

"Rakhee, Aba and I need to talk to you." She paused and we both turned to Aba.

Now that the initial excitement had died down, I was able to really see him for what he had become over the course of the summer—a shadow of the man we had left behind in Plainfield. Thin with hollows in his unshaven cheeks and tortured eyes.

Amma bit her bottom lip. "Rakhee, I'm so sorry that I

haven't been honest with you and that I let things go as far as they did. I will never forgive myself for that. When I saw that you had run off, when I thought that I might have lost you—" Amma's voice cracked and so did something inside me. Bringing my knees up, I hugged them to my chest and buried my face. I could not even look at her.

"I never wanted you to find out about Tulasi in the way that you did. It's just that I've been so confused and so sad. It was only when I heard what they were making Gitanjali do that I realized I had to make things right again. I can't keep running away from my past. Rakhee, your father and I, we both love you very much, but—it simply isn't working between us anymore. And if we stay together unhappily, it will be even more miserable for you. Rakhee, molay, won't you please look at me?"

I shook my head and Amma sighed.

"Aba and I have decided to separate. I want you to come to Trivandrum with me. We can start a new life with Prem and Tulasi. And you can visit Aba whenever you want and spend the summers and holidays with him. I've already promised him I'll go back on my medication. Things will be better, I swear to you."

The mattress shifted and I raised my head. Through the screen of my tears I saw that Aba had stood up and strode away. His back was facing me and he was leaning against the wall with his head bowed.

Amma kept talking, though her voice wavered. "Prem has built a house for us. And he has found a doctor who can help Tulasi, and a great school for you. We can send Merlin over on a plane. I know it will be a huge change, but I think you'll grow to like it. I know we can be happy together. I can't erase my past mistakes, but I can at least try to make up for them now."

As Amma spoke, the horror of the choice I had to make became increasingly clear. If I went with Amma and Prem I could be with Tulasi, and we could grow up together, side by side, as we were meant to. I could never get back the years that Amma had stolen from us, but at least we could have a future. This possibility sent a surge of indescribable happiness through me. I could handle moving to India; I could even handle Prem, if it meant Tulasi and I could be together. But could I handle leaving Aba behind and becoming a part of Amma's betrayal? For a fleeting moment, the prospect of a life with my beloved sister hovered in front of me, a glittering bubble of temptation. But even though it felt as if I were severing a limb in doing so, I knew I had to turn away from it. In truth, I had no choice. Whether Aba knew he needed me or not, I could never abandon him, even if it meant that I had to give up Tulasi.

A numbness began to spread through me. I had expected that if the moment of our family's separation ever came I would shout, stamp my feet, sob, and make a fuss, but my body seemed to understand that it had outgrown such tantrums. I looked into Amma's eyes and said: "No."

"What?" Amma took my hand but I pulled it away.

"No, I'm not coming with you. I'm going back to Plainfield with Aba."

"Rakhee, I know you're upset, but that's not possible. Aba can't take care of you by himself, and I need you. I need you with me."

"Aba, I can come back with you, can't I?"

Aba turned around; a light had entered his eyes. "Of course you can, Rakhee, if that's what you want. I just assumed you'd choose to stay with your mother. I mean,

I don't have much to offer you. Are you sure you'll be happy with just me?"

"Yes, I will, I know I will. I want to stay with you."

"You don't mean that, molay." Amma's lips trembled.

Before I could tell her that yes, I did indeed mean that, Sadhana Aunty came into the room.

"Good, you're awake," she said crisply, as if all of what had passed between us had been a bad dream. Her face was paler than usual. "Rakhee, where is Gitanjali?"

I wanted to turn away from her, to ignore her, but I found that I could not do it. She looked too sad, too broken. I was not the only one, after all, who had lost Tulasi.

"I don't know. Isn't she here?"

"No, if she was here, I would not be asking you this. She disappeared last night. Did she not run away with you and Krishna? I expected all three of you to be found together."

"No, she wasn't with us," I said.

Sadhana Aunty's face went a shade paler. "Now that we don't have to hide Tulasi anymore, there is no need for the wedding to go on. Vijay and I have seen to it that any evidence of her existence has been destroyed. And Dev is gone. He took all the money and ran off to God knows where. But I cannot tell her that because she is nowhere to be found."

Gitanjali had disappeared.

As I processed this fact, the previous night replayed itself across my mind with the clarity of a film.

The temple.

The tree.

The white figure running through the field.

Her long black hair.

Her piercing cry.

In the light of day it was so clear. How could I not have known? There was no yekshi. There never had been.

At that moment, with everyone looking at me, I wanted nothing more than to shrink under the sheet and stay there forever.

But I could not.

"Rakhee, what is it? Are you feeling sick?" said Amma.

I swallowed the nausea and cleared my throat.

"Is there something you are not telling us, Rakhee?"

Sadhana Aunty stepped forward and I took a deep breath.

"Yes," I said.

~

They fished Gitanjali's body from the old well that same day, and almost immediately the stories began to spread. The villagers said that her spirit had come back to haunt them, that she had returned in the form of a white peacock and had been seen in the forest, roaming and wailing. "They say it was a *suicide*," they whispered.

The funeral was simple and private. Mourners left parcels of food at the front gate, but no one dared venture beyond. After the funeral, Sadhana Aunty went into her room and did not come out for two days. Vijay Uncle shut down the hospital and spent hour after hour in the toddy shop. Nalini Aunty and Meenu watched television as if their lives depended on it, and Krishna was still too sick to get out of bed. A few times I tiptoed into her room hoping we could speak, but she was always tossing and turning in her bed, and even though it was a fitful sleep, I did not want to wake her.

Because things were so strained with Amma, Aba was

staying in the spare bedroom at Veena Aunty's sister's house. He tried to convince me to stay there, too, but I refused. Despite everything that had happened, I could not bear to leave Ashoka.

I floated through those last days alone, bereft and empty. Aba came and visited me every day but we did not talk. He would bring his work along and sit on the verandah for a few hours each day. During that time, Amma would make herself scarce. I sometimes sat with him, but other times I retreated to my room where I would lie on the bed and stare at the ceiling. All summer long I had yearned for his presence, and now that he was here I did not know how to talk to him or be with him. Even though he was trying, I sensed that he felt the same way about me. Without Amma there between us, everything was different.

This was not how I thought it would end. I had vowed to spend the summer bringing our family together and we had never been more separate.

I found my sister, then lost her. Gitanjali was dead. Amma and Aba were getting a divorce. And I was too tired to fight anymore.

On the afternoon before we were scheduled to leave—Aba and I back to Plainfield, Amma to Trivandrum—I found Amma in her room, packing.

"We'll take the first train tomorrow," she told me with tears in her eyes, refusing to believe that I was not coming with her.

I slept badly that night, and in the morning I rose early, bathed, and dressed. I packed the rest of my clothes, zipped up my suitcase, and dragged it out onto the verandah, where Aba was already waiting.

"We have to get going soon. The driver is here," he said. "Let's go see your mother."

Amma, too, had finished packing, and she was sitting at the dressing table in a yellow sari, her hair in a braid, staring at her face in the mirror. She looked like a young girl. I saw two train tickets lying out on the table.

"Chitra," said Aba.

Before any of us could speak, Sadhana Aunty entered the room.

She was completely different from the queenlike woman I had first encountered a few short months ago. Her face, stripped of its pride, was haggard and had never looked so old.

"You all are leaving now?" she said, her voice hoarse.

Amma blinked up at her sister. "Yes, I'm afraid we must."

"And you are going to him?"

Amma paused. "Yes."

Sadhana Aunty looked at Amma. "You cannot."

"I have to. He's waiting for me. Vikram and I have talked about it, and we agreed it's the best thing for us both."

"Chitra, you cannot go to him," Sadhana Aunty repeated.

Amma stood and her cheeks reddened. "I have to. It's all been decided. He's waiting for me."

"No," said Sadhana Aunty, "he is not waiting for you. I have already telephoned him."

I felt Aba's hand tense up on my shoulder.

"What are you talking about?" There was an hysterical edge to Amma's voice.

Sadhana Aunty passed through the doorway and sat down on the edge of Amma's bed. She began to smooth the coverlet with her fingers.

"Our father told me something before he died. He

284

told me in the strictest confidence. Only I and one other living person have known about this, all these years. Prem is not who you think he is."

"What are you talking about?" Amma repeated.

"His parents adopted him as an infant. He really belongs to Hema. Many years ago, when she was a servant in this house, she became pregnant but refused to name the man responsible. Prem's parents, who were themselves childless after many years of trying, took pity on her. She was young, low-caste, and penniless, with no husband. They agreed to take her in and raise the child as their own. They have kept her on as a servant out of pity, but they never told Prem he was not of their blood and they never let her take on any sort of role beyond that of a servant. And even they never knew who the father was. Hema may have lost her mind, but she never lost her loyalty, I will say that much for the woman."

"Where is this going? Why are you telling me this?"

Sadhana Aunty paused and turned to me, as if she had forgotten I was in the room until now. "Rakhee, why don't you go and wait outside? We will be out in a moment," she said.

I started to protest, but Aba patted my back. "Do as she says, Rakhee."

He steered me out of the room and closed the door.

I stood outside for a long time, scuffing puffs of dust around with my foot, unable to hear anything but muffled voices coming from the other side of the door. Finally Sadhana Aunty came out and peered down at me. I had seen many emotions whirling in those sharp black eyes—hatred, disgust, contempt—but now I saw something new and confusing: triumph. Sadhana Aunty's lips curved up into a smile.

"What happened?" I wanted to sound nonchalant, but my voice betrayed me.

"Your mother won't be going to Trivandrum after all," said Sadhana Aunty before she turned and walked away, leaving me alone.

A swell of unbridled hope consumed me. I did not know what had caused this sudden change. But all I could care about in that moment was the thought that if Amma did not go to Trivandrum, then she could come back to Plainfield with us. And maybe Prem would let Tulasi come and live with us, too.

After everything I had been through with Amma that summer, in spite of all the anger I had felt toward her, I still loved her. I knew this the moment I realized I would lose her. She had meant well. She only wanted to make up for the mistakes she had made in the past. If she came with us, Aba and I could help her find her way back to happiness. We would return to gardening and reading stories together, but this time Tulasi would be with us. My face was wet with tears. I loved Amma so much it hurt my insides. Without her, I would be lost.

The door opened and Aba came out. I was so caught up in my own thoughts that I didn't notice the look of devastation on his face.

"Rakhee, Amma would like to see you."

"Aba, can we still go to the sea?"

"I had completely forgotten about that," said Aba, his voice gruff. "You actually want to go?"

My dream could still come true—Aba, Amma, and me, all together, walking by the sea, a real family. We could even pick up Tulasi on our way.

"Yes, Aba, please can we?" I said. "I think it will be good for us."

Aba pressed his lips together in what I took to be a smile. That must have meant yes.

"I'm going to bring our suitcases out to the car," he said. "You go see your mother now."

I went inside Amma's room. She was sitting at the dressing table again and her face was flushed but dry. She seemed calm, which I thought was a good sign, and she gave me a radiant smile as I came forward.

"Rakhee." She reached out and took both of my hands.

"Amma, it's going to be okay. I'm sorry about the way things have turned out, but Aba and I will take care of you. I promise we'll make you happy."

"Of course you will." Amma rubbed the back of her hand against my cheek and I leaned into its softness. "You have always made me happy."

"And Aba says we can still go to the sea. That will cheer you up, won't it?"

"That sounds wonderful."

"We'd better hurry, then. The driver is waiting."

"Before we go, Rakhee, since I have you here alone, I want to tell you I'm sorry. And I want you to know how much I love you. I may do terrible things, I sometimes act out of my mind, but just know that I will always love you, that you are the most precious thing in the world to me, and that will never change." Amma pulled me forward and pressed her hot lips to my cheek. "Now go to Aba."

"Aren't you coming?"

Amma's smile wavered, and for a moment my heart stopped. But then she patted my arm and said: "I'll be out soon."

I drew away from her.

"Okay, see you in a minute," I said, and walked out of the room. Vijay Uncle, Nalini Aunty, Balu, and Meenu were all gathered on the verandah. I had not expected this final courteous formality, but there they were, lined up stiff and polite as if they were posing for a photograph, as if they were sending me off at the close of a pleasant, uneventful summer.

I scanned the line. "Where's Krishna?"

Sadhana Aunty, I noticed, was also not in the line, but I did not ask about her.

"Krishna is still unwell. We will tell her you said good-bye," said Vijay Uncle.

"Rakhee, hurry up, we have to go now!" Aba called from the top of the steps.

It pained me that I would not get a chance to see Krishna, but I would write her a letter. I would invite her to come visit us in Plainfield. This was not the end.

Nalini Aunty gave me a perfunctory pat on the shoulder.

"Keep in touch," said Vijay Uncle, and he slipped a dusty, unwrapped candy into my hand with a wink.

"Don't forget us," Meenu said, giving my arm a pinch.

"I won't," I told her. "I won't forget."

I looked at them all once more before turning away for the last time. "Bye!" I called, and ran across the lawn toward Aba.

"All set?" Aba said without looking me in the eyes.

"Amma will be right down," I said, and followed him into the car.

"We're ready," Aba leaned forward and told the driver, as we settled in and shut the door.

"Not yet," I said, "Amma's just coming."

"Rakhee—" Aba started to say something, but was interrupted by a shout.

"Wait!"

Krishna, barefoot and in her nightgown, was running down the steps. I opened the car door and jumped out.

"Rakhee!" she cried, and flung her arms around my neck.

"Krishna!"

"Rakhee, come back for me," she whispered. "Please come back for me."

"I will," I touched my cool forehead to her burning one, "I promise."

"It's time," came Aba's voice.

I gave Krishna another kiss on the cheek and got in the car. Aba leaned across me and pulled the door shut.

The engine roared.

"But wait, Amma—" I said, and my heart flared with panic and confusion for only a split second before it hit me. Just now, in her room, she had been saying good-bye.

The car began to jog down the bumpy road.

My eyes filled up, and a huge feeling of emptiness opened in my chest. I turned around and looked out the back window.

Krishna was still at the bottom of the steps of Ashoka, waving. But she was not alone. A snow-white bird was strutting out of the trees, dragging his plumage behind him like a bridal train. He was crossing the road and heading toward her. Krishna stopped waving and turned her head to the bird.

I pressed my hand against the glass and watched Krishna and Puck grow smaller and smaller. The afternoon sun blazed into a frenzy of gold, blinding me.

Ashoka melted into the distance, and with it, so did Amma.

I sat back down on the seat and covered my face with my hands.

"Rakhee." Aba took one hand and held it in his. "Amma will come back to us when she is ready."

The empty feeling deepened, and I leaned my forehead against the window to hide my face. Around us, on either side, the forest was green and lush with life.

Aba squeezed my hand.

I knew that he would take me home.

Chapter 24

A few days after we returned to Plainfield I went out into Amma's garden. It had survived the summer and that fall was unseasonably warm, so it continued to thrive. Even though the leaves were still green and the sky was summer blue, the air had taken on that distinct fall scent, crisp and sharp, the scent of new beginnings. I spent the whole afternoon yanking the flowers and the rosebushes up from their beds, making sure to get the entire root. I gathered the refuse into a giant wheelbarrow and made several trips back and forth to the ravine, where I dumped everything and watched as the piles and piles of vibrant blooms tumbled down the hill.

Aba never said anything about my act of vandalism, but not long afterward a landscaper arrived, and eventually a layer of fresh green grass carpeted the space where her garden once grew. No one ever brought up the idea of planting a new one, and when Merlin died of old age I buried his ashes there, marking the spot with a painted rock.

Aba and I developed an unspoken bond that had never existed before, the way I suppose soldiers do when they've made it through a war. He did his best, though I know it was not easy. Looking back, I think I probably took care of him during those years as much as he took care of me. When I was a senior in high school he married, with my blessing, a woman from his lab, Catherine, who has at last given him the love and stability he deserves. Still, sometimes even now I catch him with a certain distant look in his eyes, and I suspect he is not thinking of me, or of work, or of Catherine.

As for Amma, she never came back to us.

She remained at Ashoka for a few months before she decided to take that train to Trivandrum after all, and from then on she existed only in my dreams and memories. I ignored every phone call and every letter, though she persistently called and wrote up until my high school graduation, when I went east for college. Aba tried to persuade me to speak to her, but I never budged.

All these years she and Prem have lived side by side as friends and neighbors, nothing more. Although I never heard Sadhana Aunty's full revelation that last day at Ashoka, I eventually pieced together the truth. But I have kept it to myself. Krishna and Tulasi, both of whom I have been in close contact with, are mystified that they never married, nor sought comfort elsewhere. Privately, I have always wondered if it is because they cannot bear the thought of being with anyone else, or if it is just their small way of atoning for the chaos their love has wreaked.

Tulasi binds them together now. For a month after Prem took her away from the garden she was gripped by a panic, despair, and confusion so intense she could not speak. She cowered inside her bedroom at Prem's house, mute and terrified. Prem consulted one of his colleagues, a professor of psychology, who suggested that Tulasi be institutionalized, but Prem refused. He could not bear to do that to her after everything she had already been through. But she grew increasingly withdrawn, sometimes locking the door so he could not come in to see her, and opening it only to allow a servant woman to bring in food and water. At night, he heard her crying out *Teacher! Teacher!*

He persisted in trying to reach her until one day she unlocked the door and let him into her room. Though she still would not acknowledge his presence, he brought her food and water from then on instead of the servant woman, day after day, and he would sit with her as she stared at the wall, explaining things about himself, about Amma, and about the world. She would never eat or drink in his presence, but whenever he came back into the room later, her cup and plate would be clean. After weeks of this ritual, one day, she took the plate as soon as Prem brought it in, and held it in her lap while he tentatively began to talk. A few minutes later, she took a bite. Then another. Then another and another until she had finished. A week later, she spoke to him, and her first hoarse words were, *How is Rakhee?*

Since then, she has undergone years of intensive therapy and, ultimately, surgery to correct her cleft palate. She has come a long way, but I don't know that one can ever fully recover from what she has experienced. She has never been able to bring herself to see or speak to Sadhana Aunty again because, she says, it brings back too many memories of her life in the garden. These days she shuttles back and forth between Amma's and Prem's houses, and tutors schoolchildren in math, science, and English a few days a week. She remains generally shy of strangers and prefers to stay close to home, content to read, garden, and keep her parents company. Considering all she has endured, she has done remarkably well.

Although Tulasi and I have maintained our close relationship by writing to one another at least once a week and talking regularly on the phone, we have not seen each other since that summer. Tulasi does not feel comfortable leaving home, and as for me, I have not been able to find the strength to return to India because I know that it would mean seeing Amma.

Meenu and Krishna have long since left Malanad— Meenu studied dentistry at university and Krishna sociology—and both are now married. Krishna and I keep in frequent touch, and we have seen each other three times since that summer. She came to Plainfield for two weeks when we were in high school, then visited me a few years later in college, and a few years after that we met in Paris when I spent the summer there between my first and second years at Yale. Both Meenu and Krishna invited me to their weddings in Kerala, but I am ashamed to say I made excuses.

Sadhana Aunty, Vijay Uncle, and Nalini Aunty are all still at Ashoka. I am not sure if Vijay Uncle ever stopped drinking, but I know he runs the hospital now, and that my cousins regularly send money back for its upkeep. From what I hear, it is flourishing. Balu went to college in the city for a year, but ultimately dropped out, and now he, too, lives at Ashoka, where he helps his father out at the hospital. If for no other reason, I know I am a Varma by blood simply because the knowledge that the hospital is doing well and that it still belongs to our family fills me with a level of pride I have never fully understood.

And what of Sadhana Aunty? Once when I was in college Krishna sent me a family snapshot. I hardly recognized my aunt. In fact, when I first glanced at the photo I thought that the white-haired, stone-faced woman was

Hema. I wondered later how I could have made such a mistake, since they looked nothing alike, until it struck me that they both had the same hollow look in their eyes: the look of a woman who has lost the thing she loves most in this world.

This brings us to the present, with me sitting on the floor of my studio, holding the letter I just received from India in my hands:

My dear Rakhee,

I must be the last person you ever expected to hear from after all these years, and I understand if this may be an unwelcome overture, but I find I cannot keep silent any longer. In my heart, you are like a daughter, and it is with this love, and the love I have for your mother, in mind that I am penning this letter.

First, I must offer you my congratulations. It was with great joy that I heard the news of your engagement. It fills me with pride to see you doing so well, and I have been very gratified to learn of your many successes over the years. You are a credit to us all.

But I must come to my real reason for writing this letter. For years I have watched over Chitra. Her house is only a short walk from mine here in Trivandrum. It is a small but charming house, with a pond and, of course, the most exquisite garden (people come to our road just to walk by and see it). She has us for company, and there is enough money between your father and me (I am still at my teaching post at the college) to keep her comfortably. Her life here has been simple, yet peaceful. You need not worry on that account.

In spite of her constant sorrow over losing you, for years, with the help of medication, she has managed to

*keep the crippling depression that you well know she is
prone to at bay. However, as of late, ever since she heard
of your engagement, I have noticed changes in her that
worry me. At first she was thrilled to learn of your upcoming nuptials, but in the period that followed, her mood
darkened and she began to withdraw. She spent a full day
alone in her bedroom with the curtains drawn, refusing
to see anyone. We coaxed her out the next day, but she
seemed different. She was sullen and vacant. The only
thing, aside from prayer, that interests her these days is gardening. She has always been passionate about it, but her
preoccupation has become compulsive—it now borders on
obsession. I overheard her praying this morning and she
was asking God to bless your marriage. She begged God
over and over again to protect you from the fate that has
befallen her.*

*I do not tell you this to arouse your pity, but because
you should rightfully know as her daughter what is happening. I truly believe that putting an end to this long rift
will be beneficial to you both. Please know that I would
never attempt to rationalize what she did to you, but I
suppose I am hoping you can at least try to better understand her actions. For a long time she clung to a dream, a
beautiful dream, however ephemeral, that she could stitch
together the various parts of her life, old and new, and
have the family and the love she felt had been stolen from
her and had longed for ever since. All she wanted was to
fight for that dream so she could feel real happiness. She
wanted it not only for herself, but so that she could be the
best mother possible to you. She felt she was not living up to
that role, weighed down by the unhappiness of her circumstances. Some may call this naïveté, but I prefer to think of
it as purity of spirit. Purity to a fault, of course, because of*

the pain her actions caused. But I do think in some ways Chitra is like a child, and she does not always consider these complications.

Rakhee, I am writing to you now, selfishly for her, but also out of concern for you. Listening to your mother's prayer, it struck me that her fears are not unfounded. By hiding from the past rather than facing it, you are doing the same thing she once did. How can you start this new chapter of your life on the right foot if you continue to shut out your mother in this manner? She has made many mistakes, there is no question about it, but she is still your mother, and whether or not you believe it, she loves you dearly.

Come see her before you marry, I beg of you, Rakhee. I do not expect you to forget, or even to forgive, but for the sake of your own peace of mind, for the sake of your mother's emotional well-being, and for the sake of this new journey upon which you are about to embark, please face her. If I have learned one thing, it is that love is an incredible gift we are not all blessed enough to find or keep. I learned this the hard way. Do not squander it by starting your new life based on secrets. Do not repeat your mother's mistakes. I regret that the first letter I sent to your mother those many years ago came too late, and I pray now that this one reaches you in time.

It is no small feat to rise above the challenges and sorrows you have faced, many of which I acknowledge were caused by me. Please know how sorry I am for this, and that I wish nothing but joy and continued success for your future, in your academic pursuits, your marriage, and the new family you will inevitably create.

Humbly yours,

Prem Uncle

I fold up Prem's letter and sit for a long time, thinking.

This story that I am writing for you has almost come to an end, and I am still so confused.

I am not sure I have it in me to do what he asks. I am not sure I am strong enough. I am not sure I can forgive. I am not sure of so many things. It would be so much easier to crumple Prem's letter up, to throw it in the trash, to burn it, to keep running. But what would I be running toward? I close my eyes and think of you. If you were here right now, you would tell me to calm down and stop worrying about all the things I am not sure of and start concentrating on the things I do know.

I open my eyes. I do know I no longer want to hide. I do know I want to fill up that empty space I have carried inside me ever since that summer day my father and I drove away from Ashoka. I do know that I want the chance at a future with you.

I unfold Prem's letter and read it one more time.

EPILOGUE

Istep off the plane in Trivandrum, and the shock of heat makes my billowy dress stick to my limbs. As I move across the tarmac with the other bleary-eyed passengers, through customs and immigration, through baggage claim, and finally through a set of glass doors marked Exit, it occurs to me that after a series of delays in New York and London, and a long layover in New Delhi, three days have passed since I left home. Three days since I slipped out of my fiancé's sleeping arms in the dead of night. I have stayed awake most of that time, thinking about him and also about what lies ahead, but now that I am finally here, adrenaline takes hold and propels me forward toward the teeming throng of friends, relatives, and drivers holding up signs.

I scan the sea of faces, afraid at first that I will not be able to find her. But I immediately pick out the pregnant, flush-cheeked young woman standing at the front of the crowd waving her arms in the air as my cousin. Her wide, sweet smile puts me at ease right away.

"Krishna."

"Rakhee."

I find myself breaking into a run and throwing my

arms around her. We embrace, and then she pulls away and links her arm with mine, grinning.

"You didn't tell me." I nod toward her round belly.

She blushes and shrugs. "I wanted it to be a surprise. And I had a feeling you would be coming back here soon. Come, let us get out of here. The driver will take your bag."

Trivandrum is frantic. The roads are packed with people—in cars, on bikes, on motorcycles, pulling rickshaws. Horns blare, cows moo, men holler, dogs bark, but inside the car with Krishna it is peaceful. I am nervous, yet relieved. For the first time in years, there are no secrets, no façades. I can be myself.

Krishna has the driver stop and buy us lime sodas from a shop at the side of the road. We sip our cool drinks through straws and talk about married life, about school, about Meenu's new dental practice in Bangalore, and about Tulasi's students. After a while, the subject turns to Amma.

"She is really excited to see you, Rakhee," Krishna says. Over the years, Amma has been a topic we have generally avoided. "I have never seen her like this. She has been cooking nonstop ever since she found out you were coming, and she has even bought new curtains."

These details are so mundane, so normal, as if I am a child coming home to see her mother after being away at school for a few months. A lump forms in my throat.

"Do you...see her often?"

"Only once or twice a year before, but ever since Sunil and I moved here from Cochin two years ago, I visit much more often. Mostly so I can see Tulasi, who I know feels badly that I am always the one to make the trip—it takes some time, you know, since my house is on the other side of the city, and you can see the traffic for yourself—but whenever Tulasi visits me she is so timid and uncomfortable, I just hate doing that to her if I can prevent it."

"How has my mother been? Does she seem lonely?"

"I don't know, Rakhee, it's funny. In some ways, she does seem lonely. Terribly lonely, and of course that makes sense, considering her situation....She lost you and your father, and she has always been fragile. But in other ways, she seems strangely at peace and confident with the life that she leads. The people here, they talk. They do not understand why such a vibrant, attractive woman would choose to live by herself like this, like an ascetic. She has had her share of suitors, but she turns them all away, never giving anybody a chance. And Prem Uncle, too. The three of them—Chitra Aunty, Tulasi, Prem Uncle—they all keep to themselves. They are a bit of a mystery to the people here. The story going around is that Chitra Aunty and Prem Uncle were once married and that they have since divorced but remain on good terms, and while I have not corrected it I will never understand why they have remained apart all these years."

My stomach begins to churn. "But Prem, he looks after her?"

"Of course. He has been as attentive as a husband when it comes to making sure she is safe and has everything she needs. But they both seem sort of sad around each other, and I cannot quite put my finger on it."

The driver says something over his shoulder in Malayalam. Krishna turns to me. "Would you like to go straight to your mother's house, or shall we stop at my place first so you can freshen up?"

"Let's go straight there," I say automatically.

Krishna gives instructions to the driver, then leans

across the seat and touches my arm. "It will be okay, Rakhee. I will be with you."

I try to respond, but when I open my mouth nothing comes out, so we sit in silence for a while. I rest my head against her shoulder, absorbing the fact that I am not only about to see Amma but Tulasi, too. For all these years Tulasi has been a disembodied voice at the other end of the telephone or words on a page. Now for the first time since that summer, she will be a flesh-and-blood person again, my sister.

"We are getting close," Krishna says after a few minutes, and I straighten up. She smiles at me, and again I get that warm, safe sensation.

"Krishna, are you happy?"

"So happy," she says, beaming. "Sunil is wonderful. He has been very good to me, and he is so sweet about the baby. I came home the other afternoon to find that he had converted his office into a nursery. Imagine that! I do not know of a single other husband in Trivandrum who would do such a thing." She flushes and then her face darkens. "Rakhee, sometimes I feel so guilty, though, as if it is wrong for me to feel such happiness. Perhaps it is because of our family. My mother, she is such a sad woman, and she has been that way for as long as I can remember. And my sister..."

"But Meenu is doing so well—"

"Not Meenu. Gitanjali. Sometimes I think about her, about the life she should have had, and I feel guilty that I am living it instead. Sometimes I wonder if I deserve to be this happy."

Now it is my turn to touch her shoulder. "You do deserve it, Krishna. You deserve happiness more than anyone else I know."

"And what about you, Rakhee?" she says. "Are you happy?"

The lump in my throat rises, hovers, then subsides, and I smile back at her. "I will be."

~

The car turns onto the road where Amma lives, and I am suddenly short of breath. "Let me out here."

"But you will not know which house is hers," says Krishna.

"Yes, I will," I assure her.

"All right. I will meet you there later, then. Good luck."

Leaving my bag with Krishna, I make my way down the quiet road, tucked away from the jam-packed buses and graffiti-splashed walls of the city, guided by the invisible thread that connects me and Amma still, even after all these years and my desperate attempts to sever it.

I smell her garden even before I see it, and I quicken my pace to a run, stopping, breathless, at the entrance gate. I lift the latch and step inside.

Amma's touch is everywhere, in the swarms of flame-bright lilies, in the rose-dappled vines creeping along the side of the house, in the parrot-green bushes growing wild over the gate.

"Rakhee."

At first I think it is Amma, but then I realize the radiant woman with tears in her eyes coming toward me is Tulasi. I take in the long black hair and the lovely face with only a slight scar on her upper lip and a faded pink cloud on one cheek to hint at the girl she once was. I am so nervous and happy my entire body is trembling.

She must be nervous, too, because she stops in front of

me and bites her lip. We cannot stop staring at each other.

"You look so much like her," I manage to say.

"So do you," she responds, reaching out to touch my hair.

Now I have tears in my eyes, too, and I can feel my face collapsing and my shoulders beginning to shudder. Tulasi closes the space between us and puts her arms around me. We stay like that for a long time.

I separate from her only when I see a face appear at the window, and vanish just as quickly behind the curtain. My heart is racing.

How will Amma look? Will she be old? Will she be fat? Will she have white hair, like Sadhana Aunty and Hema? Will I even recognize her?

"Come, wipe your face, Rakhee," says Tulasi in a tender voice, drawing a handkerchief from her pocket. "We will have plenty of time to catch up, you and I. And she is waiting."

I pat my face dry. Tulasi extends her hand. I pause and look over my shoulder at the road, which is illuminated by the sun, caught in that fiery red moment just before it sets and everything goes dark.

This is it. My chance.

I turn back to Tulasi, take her hand in one of mine, and close the gate with the other.

"Ready?" she says, but I am no longer looking at her.

Amma has come out onto the verandah and is leaning against a pillar, watching me. Just like in my dream, she is dressed in the white cloth of a widow, but her figure is full and blooming with health, and her face, though older and tinged with sorrow, has lost none of its beauty.

"Come, Rakhee," says Tulasi.

I allow her to guide me forward through the garden

and up the verandah steps. Only when I am standing directly in front of Amma does Tulasi release my hand and move aside. Amma and I gaze at each other for a few seconds before she reaches out, grasps my shoulders, draws me forward, and presses her nose against my forehead. She takes a slow, deep breath, the way Muthashi used to do.

Then she lets go of me and reaches over to pick up a yellow plastic package and a pair of scissors from the verandah ledge.

"This just arrived for you," she says in the voice I remember. "It looks important, I think you should open it."

I cannot believe that at this moment, of all moments, Amma is concerned about something as practical as a package. I take a step back, but Amma thrusts the package and the scissors toward me, and only then do I notice the handwriting and the Connecticut postmark. Shaking, I tear it open and pull out a tiny blue velvet box. I know this box.

Tulasi nudges me. "Open it," she says, smiling.

I do as she says, and inside I find the diamond ring I left behind.

My ring.

Our ring.

"Well, aren't you going to put it on?" Amma says.

I slip the ring back on my finger, where it belongs.

"Let me see." Amma takes my hand in hers as if to examine the ring, but then she curls her fingers around mine. With her other hand she reaches for Tulasi, and soon both of our heads are buried in Amma's shoulders, and she is smoothing our hair with her hands and murmuring, "My daughters, my daughters."